MADAM PRESIDENT:
2024

LEM MOYÉ

Order this book online at www.trafford.com
or email orders@trafford.com

Most Trafford titles are also available at major online book retailers.

Print information available on the last page.

ISBN: 978-1-6987-1574-2 (sc)
ISBN: 978-1-6987-1575-9 (e)

Library of Congress Control Number: 2023921700

Trafford rev. 11/07/2023

 www.trafford.com

North America & international
toll-free: 844-688-6899 (USA & Canada)
fax: 812 355 4082

Books by Lem Moyé

- *Statistical Reasoning in Medicine: The Intuitive P–Value Primer*
- *Difference Equations with Public Health Applications* (with Asha S. Kapadia)
- *Multiple Analyses in Clinical Trials: Fundamentals for Investigators*
- *Finding Your Way in Science. How to Combine Character, Compassion, and Productivity in Your Research Career*
- *Probability and Statistical Inference: Applications, Computations, and Solutions* (with Asha S. Kapadia and Wenyaw Chan)
- *Statistical Monitoring of Clinical Trials: Fundamentals for Investigators*
- *Statistical Reasoning in Medicine: The Intuitive P–Value Primer—Second Edition*
- *Face-to-Face with Katrina's Survivors: A First Responder's Tribute*
- *Elementary Bayesian Biostatistics*
- *Saving Grace—a Novel*
- *Weighing the Evidence: Duality, Set, and Measure Theory in Clinical Research*
- *Probability and Measure in Public Health*
- *Finding Your Way in Science. How to Combine Character, Compassion, and Productivity in Your Research Career—Second Edition*
- *Catching Cold Series*
  - *Vol. 1: Breakthrough*
  - *Vol. 2: Redemption*
  - *Vol. 3: Judgment*
- *Madam President 2024*

Dedicated to all American vice presidents

Twenty-Fifth Amendment to the Constitution of the United States

Section 4: Part 1

Whenever the Vice President and a majority of either the principal officers of the executive departments or of such other body as Congress may by law provide, transmit to the President pro tempore of the Senate and the Speaker of the House of Representatives their written declaration that the President is unable to discharge the powers and duties of his office, the Vice President shall immediately assume the powers and duties of the office as Acting President.

CHARACTERS

President of the United States (POTUS)
Vice president of the United States (VP)
Vice presidential chief of staff – Nari Jeong

Joint Chiefs of Staff chairman – Gen. Kevin Caddel
Chief of staff army – Gen. Harvey Bolivar
Chief of naval operations (CNO) – Gen. Ambrose Stenton
Chief of staff air force – Gen. Johnston Hooks
Commandant of the Marine Corps – Gen. Dan Stewert
Chief of space operations – Gen. Madeleine Thompson
National Coast Guard Bureau – General Wittisen
Governor of Oregon – Cecilia Peters

Secretary of state (SecState) – Llewellyn Naser
Secretary of defense (SecDef) – Jay Ramsen
Secretary of health and human services – David Henson
National security advisor – Nicholas Serrat

President of the Russian federation – Vladimir Putin
Prime minister of Russia – Andrei Lagoshin

Leader of M1A1 tanks – Col. Jayla "Stinger" Simmons
Speaker of the House (R) – Whitney Sutton
        Senate majority leader (D) – Natalie Bousoir

When in command, command.

—Admiral William "Bull" Halsey, 1942

CONTENTS

A MEAN DAY

Saturday
September 28, 2024
10:37 a.m. (EDT)
Millbury, Ohio

The birds always noticed first.

Startled by the tremors humans couldn't feel, the sparrows burst from their nests in dark swarms, hugging the ground.

Low rumbles leaped to a roar as the two F-16Cs, Block 70/72 models, went "wet," dumping fuel from specially built injectors into their exhaust systems. The jets exploded forward, the superheated mix accelerating the aircraft to over eight hundred miles an hour. Made in Greenville, South Carolina, the planes ripped across the treetops, their sonic booms tearing through the humid atmosphere behind them.

Burning eight thousand gallons of fuel a minute, the fourth generation fighters changed their angle of ascent from zero to eighty degrees in two heartbeats, climbing at fifty thousand feet per minute. Sustaining this climb for seventeen seconds, the Falcons, armed with Sidewinder 9M air-to-air missiles, leveled off and shot southeastward toward their quarry.

With the target now in sight, the two F16Cs streaked down each side of the plane, then looped up and over, bleeding off speed. A few seconds later, they were at Angels 32, off the target's "6," behind the lumbering jet in the morning sun, creeping forward.

•

"What was that?" Pilot Chip Haley said, his converted Boeing 757 now wobbling as the fighters rocketed past. He flicked off the autopilot, taking manual control to reacquire stable flight as he peered out of the front window of the big plane.

"No warning whatsoever about this!" shouted Nicole, his new copilot. They could see out of the front of the plane as the two jets climbed in front, reversed direction, and then flew behind them.

"Can you see them?" Pilot Chip Haley said over his cockpit radio, searching for the jets now tailing his plane. He was vulnerable, and he knew it. His heart rate jumped.

"I see nothing but blue sky," she said, pulling hard against her harness, straining to look out of the right window.

The decorated pilot glanced at his emergency communication module, then looked over, straining to see out of the left window. The jets came up on them wholly unannounced and in midcourse. What—

"There." He pointed out of the left window. "Got him. One fighter. Single seater."

"I've got one coming up my side as well."

"Copilot," Haley said, turning his head left, right, then left again, struggling to keep his voice level, "we have two unannounced F-16s, one off of each wingtip. I'd guess about two hundred feet aw—"

"I see them. Getting closer now. About one hundred—Jesus," Nicole said, now shouting and turning her head to him. "They just dropped their tanks! Jesus Lord, they both dropped their fuel tanks!"

In an instant, the experienced pilot's shirt was soaked. "Stick to protocol, Copilot. One, are they declaring a safety emergency?"

She stared out of her window. "No fire or flameout that I can see. But I don't think that they're the ones in trouble, Chip."

"Have they or have they not declared an emergency, Copilot?"

"No, sir."

"Agreed. So," he said, taking a deep breath, "they want to brawl."

"With us?"

He saw her look at him, her voice up, her eyes wide.

"Well, we're over Ohio, and the Buckeyes aren't doing so well. They could be pissed about that," he said.

Nicole put her head back, adjusting switches and levers on the ceiling instrumentation. "This can't be happening. No, no, no. Something or somebody is way out of control here."

"Copilot," Haley said, looking over at her, "they can't shoot us from their current position off of our wingtips, right? They'd have to move and that gives us—"

"Sir, you must call a Mayday and get some good guys up here," she said, shaking her head. "One hit from an AMRAAM, and we're—"

"*Air Force Two, Air Force Two.*" The scratchy voice came over the cockpit radio, the static unable to disguise the southern drawl.

"Here it comes," Nicole said, her voice almost inaudible now.

Chip turned to look at her, having heard that tone from other pilots over the years—pilots who were resigning themselves to death.

He wasn't far behind.

●

"Did you get this?" the vice president of the United States, code name "Providence" said, awake and now studying her cell. She swung around, sitting in one of several leather swivel seats in the forward compartment of *Air Force Two*. "It's from Julian."

"Julian?" Nari Jeong, vice presidential chief of staff, said, sitting in the second leather chair, a soft drink in her hand. "Julian Samuels?"

The VP handed her phone over, yawning.

"You need more sleep," the COS said, putting the Diet Coke down and studying the message, the vice president watching her chief of staff's small, delicate hands scroll through the screens.

"What does he want for this ... this offer?" Nari said, looking up.

Right to the point as always. "Hopefully what we want. An answer to a vexing question. Do you see in this email that he's spoken to others?"

"Well," she said, wrinkling her nose like there was a new odor in the air, "at least it may be a different start on gun control. Does the president know?"

"He does now," the VP said, forwarding the message to the commander in chief.

"Madam Vice President, we can't get too worked up about this." She scowled.

The VP sighed, then smiled, saying, "When they take this job away from me, I shall miss your passion for paranoia very much."

Nari smiled back. "You need it. It's a warm cloak of protection shielding you from the real world," she said, holding the VP's phone out to her.

"Isn't that the truth?" The vice president took the phone back, turning it around to restudy its screen. "Maybe it's a Fomin maneuver."

Nari sighed. "The Fomin maneuver was the Russians coming to the Kennedy administration on the q.t. with a political solution to the '62 missile crisis," she said, adjusting her dark-gray jacket.

"Its contents helped to break a logjam that, left unbroken, would have killed over 150 million people," the VP explained. "I admit that the gun control issue in this country is not so catastrophic, but the knot of contention is just as tight."

"But all we have here is a simple overture from a Republican senator that will likely be a distraction. If we go down this rabbit hole," Nari said, new wrinkles appearing on her forehead, "it could be an embarrassment for you and the administration."

Of course, Nari was tough, the VP thought. *BA at Berkley, MS at MIT, MA, then a PhD at American University. Hard to avoid getting sliced up on that razor blade sharp mind.*

The VP closed her eyes. "I don't know, Nari. Maybe a little embarrassment at the beginning of a new approach to guns is not such a bad thing."

Nari nodded, picking her glass up from the vice presidential coaster. "Well, Senator Samuels is known as something of a renegade. Plus, as you saw, he's lined up two Republican senators plus five Republican house members to begin a quiet conversation with us." After a moment, she added, "Apparently."

The COS crossed her legs, shaking her head. "He's taking quite a risk sending this to you."

"Maybe not," the vice president said. "Isn't he good friends with the Senate minority leader?"

"They share an alma mater."

The VP looked out the window. "I wonder if the Senate minority leader himself is behind this, using a trusted friend to send us a message." She turned back, smiling. "Like Khrushchev used Fomin."

Nari sighed, shaking her head. "OK, what will you do?"

"I will suggest a plan to the president and see—"

The VP felt a new vibration ripple through the giant jet.

Nari shook her head. "Don't say anything about this email when we land in Chicago."

"We may not make it to Chicago," the vice president said, now staring out of the window. "It feels like something's up. Plus we have some new company."

"F-16s," Nari said, looking out of the window on the left side of the plane.

The VP saw her chief of staff turn back to her, eyes wide with questions. She nodded back but, with a new dry mouth and rapid pulse, said nothing.

•

"*Air Force Two. Air Force Two.* This is Lieutenant Colonel Buckley of *Noah's Ark*. Are you reading me?"

"We sure are, Lieutenant Colonel." His mouth raspy and dry, Chip continued. "This is Captain Haley. Did we forget to pay our speeding tickets again?"

Laughter came through the static. "That's a state police matter, Captain, and you sure don't want to mess with those folks. We're just the *friendlies* off each of your wingtips, representatives of the 112th fighter squadron, Ohio Air National Guard. Good morning."

"Good morning, sir." His mind raced. Escorts weren't standard for *Air Force Two*, certainly not starting halfway through a flight over the continental US.

He stared out of the window again. The fighters were sleek and elegant from afar, holding their positions with ease, the staple of the air force for decades. But now, up close and personal with air-to-air missiles on their wingtips, the Falcons looked damn deadly.

"Captain Haley, sorry to startle you. We were told to take our foot off the brakes to get up here. I'd come in closer to show you my ID, but I don't want any midair misunderstandings."

Haley gave a long exhale, his stomach relaxing. "Understand, Lieutenant Colonel Buckley. Pleasure to make your acquaintance. We are headed to Chicago. Care to join us?"

"Good to meet you too, Captain. Uh, given the radio chatter I picked up before coming up here on this fine fall day, I think we'd better keep this per protocol. Do you copy, sir?"

"Copy." He wanted no trouble with these General Dynamic/ Lockheed Martin performance fighters.

"*Air Force Two*, would you please switch over to two-greenstreet-three-seven-savoy-niner?"

"Will do."

"How often do we get an escort, Captain?" Nicole asked, flipping to the secure frequency. He looked her over, seeing a new patina of sweat on her forehead.

"Sometimes, when we have several dignitaries on board, they might order one up."

She looked at him. "Just seems strange, doesn't it," she said, "that our orders are coming through the air force and not the White—"

"Sir, this is Lieutenant Colonel Buckley," the static-free voice of the fighter pilot filling the cockpit. "We've been ordered to provide an escort for you. This comes from both the attorney general of the United States and the chief of staff Air Force."

"Do you have new orders for me?"

"New orders and information, sir. The president of the United States has been admitted to the hospital in critical condition. We will be returning you to Joint Base Andrews. Are you ready to change course?"

"Just need a vector."

"Coming to you now, Captain. We're going to need you to kick it up some, though. What's the maximum speed on that crate?"

Haley smiled. He knew the F-16s could attain Mach 2 and run rings around him. "We can race to JBA in fifty-three minutes, but I can always ease it back some if you need to keep up."

Buckley's chuckle came through loud and clear.

"We burned some gas getting up here, but we'll try to keep up, even if we have to glide back in. Plus, now that we're one big happy family, we'll give you some room off your wingtips."

"Much obliged."

"*Air Force Two*, you are now cleared in at Angels 29 on an initial heading of one-one-one degrees. My buddy and I will parallel. Do you copy?"

"Copy. One hundred and eleven degrees. Thank you, Lieutenant Colonel. I hope all commercial aircraft out there know of our new direction."

"Oh, I think they'll get the message, one way or the other."

"Pleasure to have your company." He knew the Falcons with their AMRAAMs plus the ability to pull 9 g would be good friends in a street fight. "Where you from, Lieutenant Colonel?"

"Living in Toledo for now but grew up in Greensboro, North Carolina."

"Winston-Salem for me."

"Piedmont Triangle. You missing home, Captain?"

"Not up here."

"It feels like a mean day, *Air Force Two*. You guys keep your heads down. We'll plow the row for you if need be. Thanks for your cooperation. *Noah's Ark* out."

He turned to Nicole. "Copilot, it's your plane. Turn us southeast and take us home. I'll inform our customers right after I change my underwear."

"I've got the airplane, Captain," Nicole said, laughing.

●

Nari stood. "Our heading has changed."

"You better sit down before somebody gets after you," the vice president said as she heard the cockpit door open, then close. *The air force didn't use F-16s to deliver good news,* she thought. She swallowed as Nari buckled in.

"Hey, Chip, how's our plane today?"

"Good as can be," the tall trim man said, all smiles. "By the way, what are we flying, Madam Vice President?"

"Why, a Boeing C-32, modified 757, operating under the Eighty-Ninth Airlift Wing."

"Ha. Great job."

They both smiled.

"Now can I take a few turns with her?" she said, straightening up in her seat.

"Not today, Madam Vice President," the pilot said. "I'm afraid that I have bad news. The president of the United States is critically ill."

"What?" Nari said, crossing her arms. "Assassination?"

"I don't know. We've been instructed to return you to Joint Base Andrews."

The VP asked, "Ordered by whom, Chip?"

7

"The attorney general and the head of the US Air Force."

"Very well. Thank you."

When the pilot returned to the cockpit, the VP and COS looked at each across the conference table.

"Well, the order didn't originate with military authorities. That's a blessing," the VP said, working to keep the tremor out of her voice. "But the attorney—"

"The AG's involvement suggests a succession issue," Nari said.

Of course, the VP thought. *Sudden illness and the attorney general's injection into the process. What else?* The vice president closed her eyes and took several deep breaths, trying to ignore the titanic gray and black storm waves of anxiety that had already started their crashing descent onto her. "Jesus. Maybe. Probably. We'll have to see."

She slid back into the leather chair. "Nari, goodness, one short conversation, and I feel like my life is changing."

"No, ma'am," COS said, already up, patting her shoulder. "It's already changed. I'll inform Chicago of our itinerary alteration without giving a reason."

The VP watched Nari walk to the rear of the plane to meet with staff.

Short and trim with close cropped hair and no trace of a Korean accent, they'd met in California four years before the 2020 election. Fierce loyalty, with discipline tight as a snare drum, her COS kept her on track.

The VP turned her head to the window, squinting in the bright autumn sun.

Be ready for everything, all at once. The Nari truism, driven into her over the years, emerged and fluttered around her mind like a bird with no place to land.

The vice president searched in vain for sleep, finding instead only dark and bottomless worry.

ROOKIE MOVES

The vice president and Nari walked as fast as they dared down *Air Force Two*'s rain-slick steps to the tarmac, then over to the waiting limousine. The VP, entering from the left, slipped, bumping her head against the GMC shell's framework getting in.

"What's our destination?" Nari called to Chester "Chess" Laso, the VP press secretary, who was sitting in a seat closer to the driver as the limo moved forward.

"Walter Reed, as you instructed."

The VP nodded, seeing the US and vice president's limousine flags fluttering on the Beast's front panels. Rubbing her head, she felt like she was swimming through molasses.

"Ma'am," Chess said, turning around from the forward seat to face them, "I have the secretary of state on the line."

The vice president leaned forward but then sat still for several moments. Sluggish, weak, and ungainly, she was disoriented. *What does Llewellyn want? He's a friend but rarely calls. If he's calling about the president's state, then what can I say? What's smart to say? Why don't I know it?* Her pulse raced, her new world spinning around her.

"Tell the secretary of state that the vice president will call him back. And let's close the back seat off for a second. That OK, Chess?"

"No problem."

The vice president stared at Nari as the shield, blocking voices from the forward row to the rest of the vehicle, slid up.

"Why did you do that?"

"Because, Madam Vice President, you are disconnected."

"From whom? What? Oh, Nari, not now," the words of anger just flying out.

"From you. You're lost."

"I'm not. I—"

"I'm not criticizing you, Madam," Nari said, placing a gentle hand on the VP's knee. "Just making an observation. Any other human being would react the same way that you are. You have just moved from holding a three-and-a-half-year sinecure to being the chief functioning civilian leader of the strongest country in the world."

Nari looked outside as the limousine departed the base, heading north. "Who takes that step without gulping?" she asked. "Only robots."

She turned back. "You're in shock, Madam."

"I feel OK."

"You don't look OK. And you're forgetting."

"OK, OK, Nari," the VP said, voice trembling with frustration. "I'm forgetting what?"

Reaching her hand out, the COS said, "Who you are."

"Nari, I—"

"Let's both be calm for a second, together." She paused for a few moments. "You're trying to take this step without understanding your unique importance in this crazy world," Nari said in low tones. "What are you bringing to the table?"

What is this? the VP thought. She was ready to rock the limo apart. Part of her thought that this was the last thing in the world she needed to hear with all the things piling up on her. She opened her mouth to speak but stopped.

What's piling up?

Nothing.

Nothing was overwhelming her. Only implications and a growing task list that she couldn't even see, less understand. It was just her reaction to the stress.

She took a deep breath. "I'm not sure that I understand, but keep talking." In a lower tone, she said, "I need to hear."

Nari smiled. "Focus on what is solely yours and won't and cannot be taken. No military leader, no political leader, no opposing political party, no voters can take that from you. It is that value that makes you substantial.

"Once you've reconnected to that, you will know again what to say. You will bring your considerable knowledge of how government works to bear. You'll again be in touch with your acumen, your experience as a prosecutor, and your sense of humor. All of that will be there for you.

"But," the chief of staff said with a smile the vice president swore warmed her own cheeks, "let's not take all day, huh? The SecState is waiting for you."

"Let me have the phone now," the vice president said as they crossed the Anacostia from Virginia into DC. "And let's put the shield down."

•

"I don't understand, Mr. Secretary," the VP said, looking out at the sheets of rain falling on Constitution Avenue. "Why are we not notifying our allies of the president's change in health?"

"Madam Vice President, my orders have come from the Joint Chiefs of Staff that we are not to notify anyone of the change."

She gripped the phone harder. "Mr. Secretary, when did you start taking orders from the Joint Chiefs?" A new edge hardened her voice. She saw Nari put her own phone down and look over.

The line was silent.

"That's what I thought. Mr. Secretary, let's you and I be clear. Your orders do not come from the military. Your orders come from the president. If he is not able to instruct you, then they come from me. And I am telling you that in the next thirty minutes, I want all of our allies notified verbally of the president's change in health status."

"Yes, ma'am."

"Sorry to be so tough, Llewellyn. I'll handle the Joint Chiefs. When you're done, meet me at the White House. Goodbye."

She looked over. "Nari, get me the chairman."

"Yes, ma'am. You'll also want to talk to the secretary of defense as well," Nari said as the vice president's entourage pushed north to the hospital.

The VP turned her attention to her COS as the rain slowed down. "I don't understand. Why is there such confusion about the communication process?"

"Because the reality of catastrophe can't be practiced," she said, shaking her head, taking another phone from Chess.

"Then we are in—"

"I have the chairman of the Joint Chiefs of Staff on the line for you."

"Ma'am?" The strong voice came through loud and clear.

"This is the vice president, General Caddel."

"Madam Vice President, how are you? It's a terrible day for this country."

"It most certainly is, General. It's your and my job to make sure that it doesn't get worse. I understand that you have asked the SecState not to contact our allies."

"I did give those orders. The chiefs and I thought it prudent to say nothing to the outside world until we understand the president's status."

Here we go. The VP took a deep breath. "General, when Pres. Woodrow Wilson was incapacitated by his stroke, not only did no one tell the vice president but also nobody told the nation for months.

"We're in a very different place now. The last thing the world needs from us is radio silence. In this paranoid time, that means trouble. Therefore, I countermanded your order. Do you understand me, sir?"

She held her breath.

"Yes, Madam Vice President, I do."

"I have ordered the secretary of state to begin contacting our allies, letting them know of the president's change in health status." Her voice was rising, and she knew it. "They have a protocol for this, and your team does not."

"I understand."

"My god, General, the doctors are going to give a press conference about the president's situation in the next few hours that will be transmitted around the world. Would you shut that down as well?"

"Ma'am, we hadn't thought about that."

"Also, General, unless you want me giving direct orders to lieutenants, midshipmen, and airmen, let's be sure that you and your team's wishes for the Department of State come through the executive branch as they always have."

"Is there anything else, ma'am?"

She gripped the phone with both hands. "I need to be sure that you understand my wishes. You can signal that by saying 'yes.'"

"Sorry, ma'am. Yes."

"Very well. I'm going to Walter Reed Hospital," she said, seeing that the rain had started again.

"Excuse me, Madam President, but I think that's a bad move. We are going to need some civilian command authority here during this time of crisis."

"I take your point, but I still want to speak to the doctors to ask my own questions." She had been tough on the chairman, she thought as a wave of regret passed through her. "Would you feel better if I asked the SecDef to join you there? He has direct access to me, as do you."

"Yes, ma'am. Jay's presence would be most welcome."

"Also, I will call in as soon as I leave the hospital and am headed back to the White House and brief you all."

"Yes, ma'am. That would also be much appreciated."

"Now, if you forgive me, I'm going to go spend a few minutes with my boss," she said, seeing that they were making good progress on Wisconsin Avenue.

"Very well, Madam Vice President."

"They're nervous," Nari said when the VP broke the connection.

"Of course they are, and I for one am glad for it. They're trained to be twitchy because the world has bad players. But we also need good, clear conduct and a clear chain of authority. Please tell the SecDef to head to the White House and meet the Joint Chiefs in the situation room Have The SecState meet them there as well.

"Well," the VP said as the limousine slid up to Walter Reed National Military Medical Center where a gaggle of reporters waited, "here we are." She took a deep breath. "I think we are all making rookie moves today."

She leaned over. "Nobody wants the president to survive more than I do."

"The universe is not your friend," Nari said, squeezing the VP's hand, "but I am."

WARD 71

"Let's, you and I, just walk in, Nari," the vice president said as the secret service agent opened the door. "I'm not going to talk to any media until I know more. Maybe I'll make a comment on the way out before the doctors' press conference. Chess?"

"Yes?" the press secretary said, hustling up.

"I need for you to let the media know that I will make a brief comment when I finish seeing the president."

"Sure thing, ma'am."

She climbed out of the car, stomach clenched in a knot, and waited for Nari while tossing an aimless hand wave to reporters.

"Is the president's death imminent?" someone yelled.

"Are you president now, ma'am?"

"Please talk to us. The American people and the world need to know."

The media knew little, and the VP knew that they were right to demand answers to new and serious questions. Outside of immediate family plus civilian and military leadership, nobody knew anything about the president's state. *Ignorance and anxiety were a powerful brew*, she thought, *and sometimes a deadly one*. Her pulse increased, and her breath caught. She began to turn back to them, her pulse throbbing. Inhaling, she opened her mouth.

Nari grabbed her arm. "Let's keep walking, Madam. We should do as you said. When we know something, we'll say it, but not now."

The VP regained her composure as the two walked through the beige entryway, surrounded by secret service, one pressing his ear, saying, "Providence in the hospital."

What you learn these next few minutes will change your life.
She faltered at the thought, stopping at the door that said "First Lady's Suite," and reached out for the handle when Nari stopped her, guiding her steps until they stopped outside the thick wooden door that said "Presidential Suite."

The vice president greeted the tall agent with black complexion and clear brown eyes. "Good morning, young man. It's a tough day."

"Yes, Madam Vice President."

"How long have you served him?"

"Since 2023."

She settled down some. "Let's hope that you serve him for years more. When it's appropriate, I'd like to speak to the head of the medical team taking care of him."

The door opened, and the agent turned. "Madam, this is her now."

"Would you be kind enough to introduce us, agent?" she said, smiling.

She saw the agents eyes widen. "I'd be honored to."

They all stepped through the doorway into the anteroom of what the VP saw as a multiroom suite.

"Madam Vice President, this is Dr. Jenneson leading the care of our president. Dr. Jenneson, meet the Vice President of the United States and her chief of staff."

"Thank you," the VP said to the agent. "Hello, Doctor."

"Any other day, this would be a pleasure," the tall thin woman said, shaking hands with the vice president. "Unfortunately, today is not that day."

"This is my chief of staff," the VP said, pointing at Nari. "What can you tell us?"

"Let's walk over here where we can all sit," the doctor said, motioning to a sofa in front a short wooden table and facing two chairs now illuminated with golden sunlight. They all sat.

"Madam Vice President," the doctor began, "the president has suffered a massive stroke. The First Lady said he never woke up at the White House this morning. He was assessed there, placed on life support at once, and brought here by helicopter."

The vice president lifted a Kleenex from her purse. *Tragic as it is, this is not so bad.* "But there is recuperative therapy, right, after you break the clot apart?" Maybe she would be acting president for just a few days, try it on for size to see if it fits. She relaxed, sighing with relief.

"Not this time," the doctor said.

The VP felt like she'd been shoved off a cliff.

Nari, wiping her eyes, asked, "Where is it?"

"Strokes are sudden acute blockages in blood vessels of the brain. Many times they occur up high," she said, running her trim left hand from the front to the back of her head just above where her auburn hair covered her ears, "up in the cerebrum, where the thought, motor, and speech centers reside. However, the president's lesion is deep in his brain stem."

The VP, stunned, tried to smile. "Dr. Jenneson, it's been a long time since I studied any neuroanatomy. Can you just break this down for me, please?"

"Of course," she said, now lowering her voice. "The brain stem controls the major functions that we need but don't control on our own. Autonomic breathing, beating heart, temperature control, and heartbeat all arise from the brain stem. It's the president's brain stem that has lost much of its nourishing blood supply. Without that, the nerves controlling these functions die. One second, please," she said as an assistant, a pale man with long fingers, handed her what looked to the VP like a data sheet.

Dr. Jenneson scanned it, then put it down. She took a deep breath. "The president's temperature is rising."

"What's the implication of that change?" Nari asked, now sitting forward.

"It means that the brain stem tissue is necrotic—dead. The immune system is moving in to digest and remove the dead nerves."

"So, that is a good thing?"

"No, ma'am. It's simply custodial and will not change the president's prognosis. The brain stem is dead and will not heal."

He's dying before our eyes, the VP thought, grinding her teeth. Swallowing hard, she asked, "Will the president recover?"

The VP watched the doctor turn to her. "I must tell you, Madam Vice President, that the chances of the president waking up are zero. He will in all likelihood die in three or four days." The doctor took a deep breath.

"I assume that you have informed the First Lady?" Nari asked.

"Yes, just before the three of us met."

The vice president stood. "Thank you very much, Doctor. I know you are busy, and we will not keep you. When are you going to have a press conference?"

Jenneson sighed. "As soon as I can assemble my medical team, who are completing their own evaluations of the president. I imagine it would be within the next hour."

So there it is. The president will be dead soon. What are you going to do? She blinked twice, pursing her lips.

Taking the doctor's hand, the vice president leaned over, whispering, "We will both find the strength that we need for today and be the better for it."

She stood back up. "Dr. Jenneson, please convey my appreciation and best thoughts to your care team."

"Thank you, Madam Vice President. If you'll excuse me."

The VP and Nari took their seats, the vice president knowing that Nari would not step on the moment with empty words.

The First Lady emerged from the kitchen. The vice president walked over opened her arms, embracing the president's wife.

"There was no time for anything this morning," the First Lady said, "not even time for a goodbye."

"As long as he is not dead, you can whisper all of the 'goodbyes' and 'I love yous' that you need," the vice president whispered. "Only he and God will hear, and each will love you for it."

"He has always been a vibrant part of our family. We are going to miss him dearly."

Gesturing to two upholstered chairs, one brown, the other blue, the vice president said, "Let's sit down. You've spoken to the doctors?"

The First Lady nodded as they both sat.

"Then you and I know the same thing. Soon, the world will know. But also know that, from now on, you are part of my family. Anything you need, any obstacle you run into, you call Nari, who will call me. I will give you all the support you need, though that pales in significance to the loss that you've sustained."

The First Lady looked at her. "I must tell you that he holds you in the highest regard."

The vice president nodded. "Well, that means so much coming from you. I'd better live up to it. Where are you staying?"

She looked around and said, "I actually don't know."

"Then stay at the White House. You just let these gentlemen know," she said, gesturing to the two secret service agents in the room, "and they'll see to it that you are taken anywhere that you want to go."

"I think I'll stay here for a bit."

"Of course."

The VP was quiet for a moment. "I wonder, may I see him?"

"Of course," the First Lady said, resting her head back on the chair, then twisting in the seat, looking for the emotional relief that the vice president knew was not yet hers.

The VP rested her hand on the First Lady's hair using soft gentle strokes to calm. "Tell him and the Almighty how you feel. They are the only ones with infinite patience and love for you."

The First Lady reached for her hand, and the VP held it until the president's wife fell asleep for a few blessed moments. Then the vice president walked in to see the president.

The president lay on one pillow, the rhythmic sound of a respirator in the background.

She shook her head at the number of IV bags pouring fluids, anti-inflammatory agents, immune suppressors, steroids, antibiotics, and pain medicines into him.

One thing that she knew: these medications would not give him life. He had done all that he could. Now he was capable of nothing. But she was still vital, still had life, still have the power to affect things. *Yes, but what will you do?* the voice hissed.

She shook her head.

A nurse came in.

"Oh. Madam Vice President, I didn't know you were here. Please don't let me get in your way."

The VP stepped back. "No, it is I who is in your way."

The nurse began her work.

"We are going to miss this man," the VP said, knowing that she would never see her president, her boss, the man who risked much to take a chance on her, alive again.

●

The nurse turned at the sound of her voice, but the vice president had already left.

•

"You ready to talk to the media?" Nari said as she, Chess, and the vice president exited Walter Reed.

"Yes, I will talk to them for a couple of seconds. Word is getting out now. They and, through them, the world need facts."

Nari leaned over to her as Chess took the lead through security. "Know what you're going to say before you say it, Madam."

The VP looked over, then, smiling, patted her chief of staff's shoulder

"Let's go."

The vice president stepped outside, noticing that in the thirty minutes that they had been in Walter Reed, the size of the attendant press had swollen from perhaps twenty to over two hundred.

She touched her press secretary's arm. "Chess, you need to make sure this is organized, and give me a mike so I can speak to everybody."

"We're all set up on the steps, ma'am."

Her head pounding, she pushed the pain aside, stepping up to the mike. On impulse, she pulled the mike off of its poll and took a step down into the audience. The media moved back.

"Good day, ladies and gentlemen of the press, my fellow citizens, and peoples of the world. It is my sad duty to inform you that our president has suffered a massive stroke."

She studied all of the anxious faces, then continued.

"Our president's situation is dire. The doctors have told me that it's going to be a very difficult fight, with little chance of recovery. All that can be done for our president is being done. The doctors and the team are heroic, but they have warned us to prepare for the worst.

"Dr. Jenneson has told me that she and her team will provide a more detailed discussion at his press conference that will be held within the hour."

"Our thoughts and prayers are with the president and the First Family. Thank you."

As she descended the steps, she saw the secret service clearing a path through the media gathering around her.

"Madam Vice President, why are you not safe in the secure facilities of the White House?"

She smiled. "I'm returning to the White House now."

"I understand that there was some confusion about contacting other countries about the president's acute illness."

Well informed, she thought. "All of our allies have been informed."

"And our adversaries?"

Reaching the Beast and seeing that Chess and Nari were now safely entering, she turned to the questioner, saying, "They no doubt already know."

"Chess," she called out over the limo, "please give Nari and me the back seat."

"Sure, Madam Vice President, although we could take the helicopter. After all, it's right here after bringing the president to the hospital."

"Good work, Chess, but the Beast is fine."

The VP, her world both crumbling and reforming at once, collapsed into the limousine next to Nari.

ROTTEN FRUIT

Vladimir Putin, president of the Russian Federation, arrived thirty seconds late. Sitting at the other end of a long ornate table, itself glowing as it reflected the gold from the ceiling, sat, small and insignificant, the political and military apparatus of the once mighty USSR.

The president smirked as the men mumbled through their insipid agenda. This fledgling federation, birthed last century from its colossal mother before she died lay groveling, sick and starving. That drunk Yeltsin breastfed her with crony capitalism, and he, Vladimir Putin, now president for twenty years, had watched with disgust as disease spread deep into the bones of the *Rodina*.

And what had he done?

Watch NATO creep east.

Poland. The historical route of all western invasions into Russia's heart was in complete NATO control. Stalin would have pushed the buttons that sent the world into oblivion. Russia gave it away with a smile.

Slovakia, Slovenia, the Czech Republic—all NATO.

Romania, Hungary, Macedonia—now managed by NATO, that bastard child of the United States.

Latvia, Estonia, Lithuania, Finland—vassal states, now in NATO's arms.

NATO was the man who came into your house, had sex with your wife, then with each of your daughters, laughing as you watched.

Two things happen: you either lose your house and soul, or kill him.

No drama. You don't have to use thallium. You don't have to sodomize him with a bayonet; that would dull a fine blade. No, a single gunshot makes the point.

Well, maybe a little drama, like Beria, security chief under Stalin, who cried at the feet of his executioner, screaming for mercy before he was shot through the forehead.

Yet, now the world laughed at modern Russia as this corrupt Ukraine dragged the beloved motherland by the nose through the stinking mud of this bitch of a war. And then what? So fat Ukraine could fuck the invader too?

Restoring the greater glory was for him to do.

Ukraine was the hors d'oeuvre; the main course lay to the west through decadent Europe and south through the Middle East with its warm water ports, full of imbecile Muslims who would serve as Russian vassals.

"We have some exciting news," an official almost shouted from the other end of the table.

"If it involves the American president, I already know this," Putin said, slouching in his huge chair.

"Yes, of course. But this is the opportunity to pursue the peace initiative that we need to get out of this Ukrainian bear trap. Do you still have the statement, sir? The proposal for cessation of hostilities in forty-eight hours, etc.—do you have it all there?"

"Yes, yes, yes," Putin said. "I have studied the fruits of your collective wisdom. So my ministers all think Russia is the mouse who said, 'Keep the cheese. Just let me out of the trap'?"

The room filled with a mix of laughter and trepidation. It reminded Putin of a condemned man joking on the way to his own hanging.

"Let's withdraw from this mess and come home, Mr. President."

"I will, gentlemen," he said, standing, signaling that the meeting was over. "It is an opportunity."

All stood and clapped enthusiastically, then gathered their things, Putin watching as they rushed out of the room as though the last one leaving would be devoured.

An opportunity, Putin thought, the first genuine smile in days crossing his face. *But not the one you think.* He walked back to his inner office, then reached for the phone.

"Get me General Slovatizov."

Putin waited. As always, the Allies will be unprepared. And now with the American president's death, NATO would dither.

And America? He snorted. Close to a third of them were on drugs. Another third were too busy playing TikTok, and the remaining third cared only about their investments. And all now led by a horse-faced, inept, mongroid woman administrator who couldn't park her bicycle straight, much less run a military action.

They were no damn good to the world.

Ukraine will fall into his hand like the rotten fruit it was. Victory, as he always knew, would be inevitable. And when Europe fell, he would have what he wanted, what all Russian autocrats from the czars onward wanted.

Power without rules.

Finally, the obsequious "Yes, sir" licked its way through the phone into his ear.

"Are forces in place for our movement south?"

"Uh, yes, Mr. President," the general answered, "but I thought that, with the American—"

"Are you a patriot, General?" Putin said, banging the phone on the table.

Putin heard the air rush out of the man's lungs. "Yes, President Putin."

"Then initiate 'Twin Hammers' at once. And, General Slovatizov, failure to bring glory to the Rodina is ... unforgivable."

Putin slammed the phone down before the general could stumble through a reply.

WILD WORLD

Thank God, the vice president thought. *I hate helicopters.*

Airplanes were fine. Bicycles were fine. Cars were fine as long as she wasn't driving. But helicopters? They were jittery and unsteady, were pushed around by the wind, and, heaven help her, were noisy. Even with headsets and mikes, you couldn't hear. People shouted, then nodded their heads like they understood what was being shouted back at them. Like loud fundraisers, helicopters were not meant for conversations.

Well, at least no helicopter today.

When the door closed, at once, the VP's palms sweated, and her head pounded so hard, she thought that it would fly off of her neck.

"Nari, how can I take this? I'm exploding, crestfallen, astonished, and frightened at once. It's like I can't rely on this brain."

She brought her left hand down on the armrest. "I can't trust myself in this state."

She said, turning right to her COS, "I see debacles coming like a surfer facing the largest waves of her life. Looking destruction in the face, I have no place to turn."

"Yours or the wave's destruction, Madam?"

The vice president stared at her. "Are you for real? There's a good chance that I will be president of the United States in a matter of hours. And God help me. I … I don't know. I've been in the 'on-deck circle' for more than three years now and am now, with little warning, told to get myself to the plate." She turned to look out the window as the drizzle started again. "I'll be thankful not to drop the bat, much less swing at a pitch."

"You did well at the hospital."

"Of course I did. That's what I spent much of the last three years doing." She sighed, stopped, and turned back, now deflated. "I wasn't that good a vice president, you know."

"You don't think you were a very good vice president?" Nari said, turning in the black leather seat to face her

The VP, looking out the window to the left, said, "No."

"Well, most people would agree with you."

The vice president turned around.

"Madam, your weakness is that you believe what idiot people say. An early survey about your popularity had your approval down to 27 percent. A bad survey with a bad analysis.

"But it didn't matter to the media. They threw it out there anyway. And people just slopped it up with a spoon. You've been a joke ever since, and people don't change their minds easily, especially when they're wrong. How can they—they don't have the heads for simple analysis and don't know what context means, much less how to apply it.

"And it's not your fault that American people don't know history. They don't know that two vice presidents were so ineffective that, when, they died in office months before the end of their terms, their president didn't bother to replace them.

"How many Americans know that Andrew Johnson, Lincoln's second VP, was so nervous that he showed up drunk at his own inauguration? He was inaugurated anyway. What would they say about you if you had to be carried to the podium snookered? Can you imagine?

"Don't forget Richard Nixon. He had to grovel before the American people explaining how he didn't take any illegal money in that ridiculous 'Checker's speech' in 1952. Yet one more low point for the office by the man who would become Eisenhower's vice president. You ever do that?

"And let's please remember Spiro Agnew, who had to be removed from the vice presidency because he was shaking down Maryland contractors in his own vice presidential office in the White House. What a disgrace. And people want to get upset with you because they don't like the way you organize your office and staff?" She shook her head.

"I screwed up immigration."

"I agree. Face it square. Did you learn lessons from it? Would you do it differently? Use another approach?"

"Sure."

"Then you learned your lesson." Her chief of staff. leaned in close, whispering, "By the way, did you kill anybody in the process?"

The vice president stared. "How could you ask me that? No, of course I didn't kill anybody. How could you possibly think—"

"Aaron Burr, as his country's third vice president, shot and killed Alexander Hamilton. Holding the office you hold, he committed murder. So I think that you're ahead of the game."

The vice president laughed in spite of herself. "Nari, you're in danger of having a stroke."

"I'm like Jim Brown. I don't get strokes—I give them."

They both laughed.

Nari exhaled. "Now, I'm not saying that there weren't very good vice presidents. There were. But your bumbles, stumbles, false starts, and hiring difficulties are nothing compared to these clowns.

"But let's speak no more of this because it no longer matters for you. You now must give yourself permission," Nari said.

The VP said nothing.

"There's not a single vice president who hasn't felt like you— scared, nervous, out of their mind with panic, and dread. Truman said that he felt like the moon, the stars, and all the planets had fallen on him when he heard FDR died.

"This job will be hard, but not too hard," Nari said, now looking straight ahead, "as long as you get out of your own way. The VP office rules no longer apply. Your VP flubs don't matter. Nobody's looking back at you as a VP anymore."

"I am."

"Then stop it, Madam, because," the COS said in a whisper, "nobody cares."

The VP looked hard at Nari, receiving only Nari's ice-water stare.

"Give yourself permission to make hard decisions.

"To take on a truculent military.

"To beat back an aggressive Congress.

"To punch through the media, the people's sycophant.

"To fight our enemies and fight them hard. And to make a mistake.

"No more holding back. No more making statements, then hiding, cringing for a rebuke. Be as tough as I know that you are.

"You have all of these qualities locked inside you, waiting your entire life to emerge. Release them. The time is here. It's now. One second." The COS pulled her cell phone, listened, then handed it over.

"Yes, General?"

"Just wanted to know your ETA, ma'am."

"Pauli," the VP called to the driver. "how long to the White House?"

"This traffic? Twenty minutes, ma'am."

"Thank you. We're looking forward to seeing you in the Situation Room."

"You're my first stop. Oh, and, General, the president suffered what looks like a fatal stroke."

"Thank you, ma'am. We didn't know.. The doctors' briefing is starting now."

She handed the phone back to Nari.

"Do you know what's coming for you in the White House Situation Room, Madam?"

"No"

"The world is wild. Be guided by your love of country, your knowledge of its laws, your morals and logic, your compassion and intellect, and let your heart change."

"What?"

"You must in your heart of hearts change. You've been wondering whether you wanted or feared being president. That time is over.

"Be the person you need to be. Be the commander and chief. Don't want to be. Don't wish to be. Don't hope to be. Open your heart and fully embrace that you are president of the United States of America. Don't fight it, don't argue and debate with it, and don't resist it. Pour the best of everything you have into it."

She listened, absorbing the message, letting the words and now her own thoughts dissolve the day's consuming tension.

"You know, you've given some great little speeches Nari, but"—the VP shook her head—"that was one of the worst."

They stared at each other, then burst out laughing.

"Can you use that phone to pull up the Twenty-Fifth Amendment, please?" the VP asked.

The two put their heads together over the small screen, studying it for the fifteen-minute remainder of the trip as new, hard rain pounded the car.

"Yes?" Nari said, putting her cell to her ear.

The VP's own phone rang. Picking it up, she heard Nari say, "Thank you. We are at the White House now."

She thanked the caller and hung up. At once, the phone rang again. She listened, answered, said "Thank you," and put it down.

"The attorney general is gathering the necessary cabinet signatures to satisfy the fourth section of the Twenty-Fifth Amendment."

"Eight votes, plus yours," Nari said.

The VP nodded, reaching for her phone. She listened. "Thank you." She looked at Nari.

"That was General Caddel. There has just been a massive chemical weapons strike on northern Ukraine."

"Well, then, Madam, good thing you're here to help."

BEDLAM

The VP, Nari, and Chess walked into the Situation Room, the long rectangular space that now overflowed with people scrambling to go from where they were to someplace else. The vice president watched some speaking in whispers. Others wrote like wildfire on pieces of paper, handing them back and forth. Fingers were pointing into chests, and hands were slamming on the table. Everyone had a cell phone plastered to their ear.

"Hit the deck, Nari," the VP ordered.

Nari at once crouched, covering her ears, as the vice president of the United States, fingers in mouth, blew a loud, long whistle over the room.

Everyone stopped and turned.

"Not another sound," she said. She turned to the chairman. "General Caddel, I believe that my chief of staff and your almost acting president need to be briefed."

She watched the chairman stare, then laugh, walking over and offering his hand. "I guess we'll need a new rule. 'No loud whistles in the Sit Room.'"

"Pity," she said, shaking his hand, smiling back. "It's such an attention getter."

She took a seat at the head of the long wooden table, strewn with devices and telephones. Nari sat to her right in an accompanying deep-brown leather seat. "Chess, I'm afraid that you need to step out," the VP said to her press secretary. "I know you'll keep your mouth shut. I'll brief you when we're done."

"How is the president doing, Madam?" the chairman said, sitting down in a chair at the center of the table as she watched Chess leave. "We missed the press conference as we dealt with these new European events. Can you tell us anything?"

She leaned forward in the chair, studying the chiefs through air thick with tension. "I will tell you what I know. The president has had a terrible stroke, affecting the part of his brain that controls essential functions such as breathing, heartbeat, temperature, and so on. It is," she said, shaking her head, "my sad duty to tell you that the doctors are not optimistic for his recovery or his survival."

She felt as much as heard the collective groan suffusing the room. At once, she was filled with grief and fatigue.

Not now, she thought, scooting her chair closer to the table.

"Madam, I don't mean to be indelicate, but we do need to have a civilian commander in chief."

"Absolutely, General Bolivar," she said to the balding chief of staff Army. "The line of succession is stipulated by the Twenty-Fifth Amendment of our Constitution, which requires that a majority of cabinet members' signatures plus mine be affixed to a letter detailing the president's inability to carry out his or her responsibilities and assigning me the role and title of 'acting president.' Once that is transmitted to the president pro tempore of the Senate and the Speaker of the House of Representatives, General, the statue's requirements are fulfilled."

She looked around the jam-packed room. "We are collecting signatures now. I'm hopeful we'll transmit before the end of business today. Ah, Llewellyn and Jay.

"You all know our secretaries of state and defense, Llewellyn Naser and Jay Ramsen. Welcome."

As the secretaries got settled into the crowded room, she remembered that part of the Twenty-Fifth Amendment has never been invoked.

It was wholly untried and unchallenged. Oh, there were circumstances when it was almost used, such as when the Reagan cabinet was concerned about the president's ability to carry out his duties in his second term. But he recovered, and the issue was dropped. The assassination attempt against Reagan led to no transfer of power to VP Bush. So while much is made about the Twenty-Fifth Amendment, she thought, the fact is that this part of it had not been tested.

Looks like that would be changing today.

"Now, what can you tell me about Ukraine?" the VP asked.

"As of 1304 (EDT)," the chairman said, tension showing on his face, "the Russians initiated a massive chemical weapons attack on Ukraine, north of Kyiv."

"Show me," she said, getting up and walking along the wood-paneled wall up to one of the large telescreens hanging in the room.

"The attacks originated in southeast Belarus and southwestern Russia where artillery hurled canisters with pinpoint accuracy on elements of the Ukrainian resistance east of Chernobyl and west of Chernhiv."

"How many casualties, General?" the VP asked.

"Maybe thirty thousand, ma'am," General Bolivar said, approaching the map.

"Making it the largest gas attack since chlorine at Ypres in World War I," the chairman added.

On tiptoes, Nari pointed first northwest, then northeast of Kyiv. "They want the roads."

"So, while the Russians have demonstrated their affinity for atrocities," the vice president said, "they haven't shown much innovation. The classic reason that one would want these roads and flat areas," she said, drawing an ellipse around the area where Belarus, Russia, and northern Ukraine, "come together is—"

"Is to use them."

She looked at the short, bald spark plug of a man addressing her.

"And you are—"

"General Stewert."

She moved to stand in front of him. "And what do you do around here, General?"

"Run the Marine Corps, ma'am."

"Then stay close."

"Madam," Llewellyn said, "it is essential that we talk to you."

She looked at the chairman. "General?"

"Of course. How about twenty minutes?"

"Thank you, General," she said as her civilian team walked out of the Situation Room.

"NO WRITTEN AUTHORITY"

"**E**veryone will feel better in that room if I am officially acting president," the VP said, walking into a large gray room with a beige sofa and brown leather chairs surrounding a wooden table.

"Thank you," she said to the officer, who smartly turned and walked out, closing the door behind her.

"Agreed, you should be certified as soon as possible," Jay said. "Where are we on the votes?"

"Let's get the attorney general on the phone," the VP said. "Llewellyn and Jay, you join us as well."

"Yes, ma'am."

"Of course."

"Mr. Attorney General," the vice president said, all of them huddled around Nari's phone on speaker.

"Hello, Madam Vice President."

"I have both the secretary of state and defense with me."

"'Good afternoon to you all. I think I know why you're calling."

"How close are we on certification, sir?" Nari asked.

"You need eight votes. You have six."

"Thank you, Mr. Attorney General," said the VP, heart pounding. "Can I ask you to please notify my chief of staff when there is any change?"

"Of course. My staff will stay in regular contact with her."

"One final question, Mr. Attorney General," the vice president said, struggling to keep the quaver out of her voice. Looking up at her cabinet members, she asked, "Does the vice president have any constitutional power to initiate military action?"

The phone was silent for a few seconds. Then the attorney general came on, his steady voice filling the room. "Very little is written about the vice president's war powers. Of course, if the vice president ascends to the presidency, then the Constitution and the War Powers Resolution govern who can declare war and engage in hostilities with prompt notification between Congress and the executive.

"However, the vice president has no written authority to initiate military action on his or her own initiative. It is possible that Congress could vote to provide the vice president such power in an exigent circumstance. But that would take quite a while and"—he paused—"induce complications."

"I may have a very difficult decision to make, Mr. Attorney General. Your information has been illuminating."

"Good luck, Madam Vice President. I am here should you need me."

Nari ended the call.

"We are close to a new major military initiative on the Ukrainian front. I don't want to think about not having the votes."

"Madam Vice President," Llewellyn said, "from what I've seen, you are playing an active role in these military discussions." He turned. "Would you agree, Jay?"

"Absolutely. And given the attorney general's clear statement about what vice presidents cannot do," the SecDef added, "I am very concerned that you are on a precipice, Madam Vice President. Have you issued any military orders?"

She thought for a minute. "No, but I'm about to."

The secretary of state pursed his lips. "Then Jay's right. You're on hazardous ground here."

She leaned forward. "The US is on hazardous ground. Our ally is on hazardous ground. Our European friends are on hazardous ground. It looks like there's enough hazardous ground for everybody tonight, including me."

The secretary of state sat straight in his chair. "We have to have good order, Madam Vice President, and that means a clear and legal chain of command. I understand what you're doing. However, we need to keep that period where you give orders to the military only as vice president small and as limited as possible in this dangerous circumstance."

"Mr. Secretary," Nari said, her face full of anguish, "I don't understand. Suppose that the Russians, rather than attack Kyiv, chose this moment to launch a massive nuclear strike against the United States and NATO. Is the vice president, rather than defend this country, to run around scrounging for cabinet member votes? I can't believe that the Twenty-Fifth Amendment opened the door to this possibility. For that matter, what if the cabinet members were assassinated and then the Russians attacked?"

"In that case, Nari, the decision would be made by another body as Congress may by law provide."

"Russian missiles take twenty minutes to reach their targets here. A submarine launch takes five. How long do you think it would take for Congress to pass a law to authorize this, quote, unquote, 'other body'?"

"It's not ideal." Jay said.

"No, it's suicide," the COS responded, looking at the VP.

"Well, tell that to the Republicans," the SecState said, leaning back in his chair. "That's what I wanted to talk with you about."

The vice president inhaled. "Go on."

"The Republicans are mounting a challenge to your succession attempt."

"What?"

"Now?"

"On what grounds?"

"No grounds, none whatsoever," the SecState replied. "They are drafting legislation that would remove the responsibility of your certification from the cabinet and place it in the hands of a new congressionally appointed select committee. They are directly engaging cabinet members, asking them not to vote on certification until they can organize their own committee."

The vice president's face burned. She could barely keep her voice down to a whisper. "Well, that's wholly consistent with the amendment. But the timing of it makes absolutely no sense. First of all, such a law's passage would take weeks. And who would sign it?"

"Well, you would not be acting president, so if it were to pass both houses, it only need sit in the White House for ten days before it becomes law."

"But it won't pass a democratically controlled Senate," Nari said.

"Also," the COS said, now walking around the room, "remember that they do not feel a moral imperative for Ukraine. If forty thousand Americans had died in the gas attack, that'd be one thing. They don't worry about forty thousand Ukrainians. In addition," she said, turning to look at the VP, "the more difficult they make the succession process, the more inept and indecisive you appear to be to the American people, crippling your chances to run successfully for the presidency in seven weeks."

"Unfortunately," the VP added, shifting in her seat, "the Speaker has chosen a time when damaging my ability to ascend to the presidency coincides with injecting exactly this kind of feckless dithering that our adversaries rely on."

"Why is the cabinet taking so long?" the SecDef asked.

"The cabinet doesn't recognize how acute the situation is, and," she said, rubbing the back of her head, "some will say that respecting and following our own laws is more important than winning a tank battle in a war that's been going on now for four years."

She put her elbows on the table, rubbing her temples with quick rough strokes. "And maybe they're right."

"But," Jay said, "allowing the Republicans to hold up certification coopts any military response against anyone, anywhere. What if the Chinese move against Taiwan? or North Korea sends a missile barrage against Japan, killing millions? Are we to sit here, ignoring our treaty obligations while we count cabinet votes at our leisure?"

"I should call the Speaker to shut this off," the vice president said.

"Our focus," Nari said, "should be getting the cabinet votes."

"Let's have the Senate majority leader call them," the VP said. Nari, can you—"

Nari approached her, lowering her voice. "I don't think—"

The phone rang.

"It's for you." Nari handed the phone to the VP.

"Madam," the attorney general said, "you now have five votes."

"I don't understand, sir. I thought we had six."

"So did I. You just lost one."

Lightning flashed through her. With no place to sit, she leaned forward, dropping her head, arms against the table supporting her.

"Thank you, Mr. Attorney General," Nari said, hanging up the phone.

"The political coup has begun," the SecState said.

"We need a moment," Nari said. "Ma'am?"

The VP stood and followed Nari outside the room, closing the door behind them.

•

The VP whirled, face flushed with anger. "Do you believe what those people are trying to do to us? They're stealing votes. There's nothing in the Twenty-Fifth Amendment—"

Nari slashed her hand out, cutting through the thick air. "There's no time for this, Madam. This is the world. And in it, despicable things happen. What did you think—that the universe would feel sorry for you and work this out nicely in the end?

"You have the skill, the drive, and the power to master this. So get out of your own way and be what you need to be to beat the hell out of it.

"This is not new, Madam. Did you know that the great Alexander Hamilton was caught trying to peel away electoral votes from John Adams simply because he didn't want Adams to appear to be strong in the Federalist Party? And that was the very first US election. Goodness."

The vice president just stared at her.

"Did you know that Louisiana, Florida, and South Carolina sent two sets of electors to Congress in 1876 because their vote-counting mechanisms broke down? To this day, nobody knows who won those states.

"And what about those malevolent, contemptible fake electors? It's only been four years, Madam. Have you forgotten? They were willing to misrepresent the voters of their states to help the Republicans cling to power."

She gripped the VP's shoulder. "Face it, ma'am. People in this country will do anything to steal your job. They will lie. They will cheat. They will say the law means one thing when it means something else. They will piss on the floor of Congress, threaten to hang vice presidents, or set the Constitution aflame, if that's what it takes for them to get the desired result.

"This has been true for hundreds of years. They simply do not care about what's right. They don't care about the rules or precedents. They are lost in the desire of their wants."

Nari shook her head, dropping her arm. "Maybe it's an anticipatable extension of politics. Maybe it's a uniquely American character defect. Maybe it's a human thing. I don't know, but I do know that it is reality. And you have to manage them, defeat them, triumph over them."

The vice president slumped against the wall, closing her eyes.

After a few moments, she felt Nari's gentle tap on her shoulder. "Now, are you ready to go back inside and give seven billion people a few more precious days of life?"

Nari stepped back. "And who picked this pant suit for you?"

"You know you love it."

"You wear that again, I'll impeach you myself."

"Well good luck because I'm not even president yet.

They laughed, smiled at each other, and walked back in.

●

As soon as the vice president and Nari returned, there was a door knock, then the thick door opened again.

"Madam Vice President," a young officer said, sweating, voice shaking, "the chairman asked me to get your team. We need you now."

The VP walked over. "What is your name?"

"Nusom, Joan Nusom, ma'am."

"Do you do your duty, Officer Nusom."

"I do, ma'am."

"Well," the VP said, smiling while resting both of her hands on the young woman's shoulders, "if you trust us all like I trust you, then we'll be OK."

WHAT WILL WE DO TO THEM?

The civilian team walked back in the situation room, and all sat except the VP, who strode up to the map.

"General Cad-0p4del," she asked, pointing, "what are those small husks on that road into Ukraine?"

"Tanks, ma'am. Hundreds of them."

She watched the chairman take a deep breath. "Russia and Belarus have amassed and are moving tanks south for a joint military operation against Ukraine."

Nari walked up. "How fast are they moving?"

The screen changed to a satellite view.

"This photo is seven minutes old," General Bolivar, chief of staff army, began. "There are two assault groups. The Belarusian group is moving southeast through Belarus toward the western sections of Kyiv. The Russian group, here"—he moved his pointer to the right—"is moving southwest through southern Russia and will strike Kyiv from the east. Kyiv will be trapped between them."

The VP steadied herself, then asked, "Do we know the strength of these two groups?"

An aide handed the general a piece of paper that he read and then looked at her. "The Belarusian group is made up of the Sixth Core. That is seventy-five T-72B tanks heading southwest through the Belarus countryside. They are highly maneuverable and pack considerable firepower. They will make good time speeding through Belarus's flatlands, although the marshes will slow them up some."

"And the Russians?" asked the COS, hands clasped behind her.

"Looks like that's the Eightieth Guards Tank Regiment of the Ninetieth Guards Tank Division, ma'am," General Bolivar said. "It is made up of only T-90 tanks."

"That's their top-of-the-line model, isn't it?" the VP noted, walking around to see southwest Russia. "How many of those do they have left?"

"The Russians have lost three thousand tanks in Ukraine," the chairman said, coughing. "They are drawing heavily from their main defensive army groups for this strike. This is the best they've got."

"So, they're moving their queen," Nari said.

General Bolivar called out. "Updated estimate of Ukrainian gas casualties: forty thousand, including noncombatants."

"Thank you, General." The VP turned to Caddel. "And you're sure that they're headed to Kyiv?"

"Well, we're sure they're headed to Ukraine, and the logical target for them is Kyiv, ma'am. They tried and failed four years ago. This is a follow-up attack, now with massive armament."

"And that explains the gas attack," the marine commandant said. The VP watched him shoulder his way into the conversation.

The vice president nodded. "They want nobody in their way? What gas did they use?"

"General Bolivar?"

"Novice V and maybe Novice VII. It's a gas that's never been used in combat and the first the world has seen of it."

The VP returned to her seat. "What effects do they have?"

"They produce a cholinergic crisis," the commandant said. "All voluntary muscles seize up and contract. All controlled movement is lost. There is no running away. No cries for help. Then breathing stops. There are arrhythmic events."

"Survivors?" the SecDef asked from his seat.

"Those that survive suffer chronic liver failure, seizures, depression, inability to concentrate," chief of staff army said. He turned to the screen. "Terrible way to live and to die."

'How long does it persist?"

"Nobody knows about the gas. The liquid may last years."

"They'd used liquid," the marine commandant said. "More potent and easier to control the circle of effect."

"We think the shells hit the strike forces' breakthrough points at the Ukrainian border," General Caddel said, pointing to the map. "We call this a classic pincer movement. The weakened defenders are forced to fight on two sides at once, increasing the likelihood that at least one side will breakthrough. They are 150 miles from their breakthrough points."

"Air power?" Nari asked as she walked to a seat.

"They have moved no air assets to positions suggesting a supportive role. Plus the thick fog and rain are not conducive to close in-combat support."

Such jargon, the VP thought, turning in her seat to face the generals.

"So, we have the largest gas attack in over one hundred years as a prelude to a blitzkrieg-like strike sans airpower against Kyiv. And this is all going public as we speak."

"That's a fair assessment, ma'am," General Caddel said.

She paused for a few seconds. "It seems to me, General, that we have one great advantage for now."

"What would that be, ma'am?"

"The Russian assumptions. First, they have attacked at the exact time when our president is near death. They expected that we would be distracted with chain of command issues and our response would be halting, tentative, and poorly reasoned.

"Second, they anticipate an easy walk through Ukraine, not expecting a punch in the face."

Everyone stared at her.

"We hit them hard. Stop them butt cold on their own territory, but"—she leaned forward—"we don't have much time."

She looked around. "Now, what are the options?"

"Ma'am, some of us wonder if this is even worth the exercise," the naval CNO said.

"Go on, Admiral."

"We've been fighting to defend Ukraine now for four years. I give the Ukrainians their due. They are tough, determined people, but the fact is that they are living next to the wrong neighbors, who will likely run over them in the future. Plus they didn't have the strongest democracy to start with. I wonder if this is the time for us to get out."

"Well, Admiral," the VP said, "we haven't even fought in Ukraine yet. We and others have provided equipment, but it's been the Ukrainians that have been doing the heavy lifting. Agreed?"

"Yes, but did it all go where it should? Let's not forget that the corruption there is real."

The vice president walked over to the chief of naval operations. "Well, yes, it is. So was the Polish government before Germany invaded them in 1939. Yet the British and French rose to their defense. It all but broke those two countries, but Europe was and is free. So was the Italian government before and during Mussolini, but that didn't stop American soldiers from fighting and dying to liberate Italy."

"Good history, Madam, but are they the best precedents?"

"We learn from history, Admiral. Tell me, should we even bother to defend France now? Many Americans don't forgive them for caving in 1940 and don't think the French are serious people.

"And what about the Brits, Admiral?" she said, walking away. "Exiting the EU the way they did, Scotland declaring independence, Ireland looking to move out. Are they worth it anymore? And how about Mexico? A corruption-infested narcoeconomy."

She turned. "Goodness, Admiral, maybe the French shouldn't have intervened on our behalf during the Revolutionary War. We were weak, losing one battle after another on our own land, our money no good, a third of the country supporting the British. Where would we be then?"

She looked up. "No, sir. If you look hard enough, you can find a reason not to fight for anybody. Admiral, when you get down to it, either everyone is worth fighting for or no one is. Do we understand each other?"

"Yes, ma'am."

"Yes, but the T-90s are formidable," General Bolivar said. "They could reduce Kyiv to rubble."

"And they have more gas."

"And when they get some sky, they can commit airpower. They will destroy the Ukrainians in detail."

The VP, heart pounding, fumed. She returned to her seat, taking several deep breaths, then, raising her voice, said, "Ladies and gentlemen, I'm being as patient as I can, but I am damn sick and tired of hearing about what this Russian-led strike force is going to do to us. From this point forward, I want to hear what we are going to do to them."

The room was still.

"For the second time, I need suggestions."

"Why? You're not the president."

YOU NEED ME

The VP kept breathing, her pulse down, her skin cool.

"And who are you?"

"Chief of space operations, Gen. Madeleine Thompson."

"Well, thank you, General Thompson." The VP stood and walked over to her. The African American woman was formidable, eyes wide open, almost blazing hot. "Stand next to me please, General."

The two stood together and, at the VP's urging, faced the room.

"General Thompson has asked a fair question, a question that is on the minds of each of you. I bear her no malice.

"I want to answer this question in the clear so that everyone understands. You each need civilian authorization to execute any military action. The proper civilian authority is comatose. You will get no answers from him. I am the vice president, the second in command, which is as far as the civilian chain of command goes for now.

"There is no question about your need for a civilian directive to authorize a strike. How you move forward depends on what I say. Now, I will be acting president in a few hours. At that point, this concern dries up, but for right now, I am your civilian boss, and I will decide which military actions go forward and which ones do not." She touched the general on the arm, and the chief of space command returned to her seat.

"Unless you all want to ignore me, go around civilian authority and begin to make military moves on your own like some third world junta, then you need me.

"Now, for the third time, can I get some options?"

"Well," the marine commandant said, sitting back in his chair, "two tactical nuclear weapons, one deployed on the Belarus force, the other one on the Russian strike unit, will solve this at once. Mission accomplished."

As the VP saw the heads nodding, she began to sweat.

"Well, Commandant," Nari asked, "over whose real estate would you drop these nukes?"

"Who cares?"

The COS shrugged. "If it were TNT, I'd agree, but now we're talking about tremendous explosive power and radiation over an unconfined area."

The chairman cleared his throat. "We could wait until the strike forces cross into Ukraine, but then what—drop tactical nuclear weapons on Ukrainian soil, killing many Ukrainian fighters and citizens?"

"Dropping a nuclear weapon on an ally to protect them from invasion will shock Ukrainians and tear NATO apart," the VP said.

"The other option is to not wait, deliver them on Belarusian and Russian territory," Jay said, taking his jacket off. "Now I grant you that Belarus is not a country whose nuclear response we'd have to contemplate, but Russia is a very different matter."

"So we obliterate the Russian column with a small nuclear weapon," the vice president said, turning to the commandant. "Sir, if you were a Russian general, what would you advocate in the face of a nuclear attack killing your tanks and massacring your soldiers?"

She thought he would explode out of his chair.

"My responsibility," he all but spat, "would be to protect my forces. I'd take out NATO nuclear-capable planes and surface rockets in Ukraine and Poland, also destroy NATO weapon stores and supplies."

"And Poland is NATO, so that's an Article 5 response, and war across the board," the SecDef added. "Or since the United States launched a nuclear response against Russian soldiers on Russian soil, why not attack the United States direct? Take out our B2s in Missouri for example."

"Our finger would be in the meat grinder, then," the VP said.

"How long do we have?" Nari asked.

"Five hours to the Ukrainian border," the chief of staff army said at once. "Two more hours to Kyiv."

The room was quiet.

"You're in a pretty bad fix, Madam President," General Hooks, air force chief of staff, said.

She turned, staring hard into his eyes. "You're in it with me."

Silence.

"Excuse me," interrupted the SecState. "We need another break."

"General Caddel," the vice president said, standing, "can we please take a brief break for a meal?"

"Of course. We all should eat. Thirty minutes."

"Thank you," she said, turning to leave. Then she stopped and turned back. "Oh, one thing: Commandant Stewert, I'm sure glad you're on our side in this fight that's coming."

"Thank you, Madam Vice President."

She walked outside the room and down the well-lit corridor with Nari and the secretaries of state and defense.

COWARD

"**I** know this is terrible news for you," the attorney general said on speakerphone. "I wanted to let you know that now it appears that vote recusals are going to be a problem."

"Cabinet members are refusing to vote at all?" She paused, hands clenched tight in front of her. "I did not consider the 'removed or recusal' contingency."

"Neither did I. Two things that you should keep in mind: First, remember the process. I collect the letters. Then when I have enough to reach a decision, I transmit them to Congress.

"The amendment is mute about the collection process itself. It doesn't specify a role for the attorney general. It doesn't say how to collect them, nor does it describe a process of letter rejection. It is mute on disallowing a vote because a cabinet member changes their mind. The vote doesn't count until my transmission of all letters to the Congress."

"I see," she said. "The Constitution stipulates nothing about cabinet members who want to change their minds or just do not vote before votes are counted by Congress."

"That's right, Madam. But if this helps, keep in mind that these votes are not about your prowess. They are supposed to be votes certifying the president's condition. If there are eight or more votes that certify his condition, then you automatically become the acting president. I fear some cabinet members are conflating a vote certifying the president's condition with a vote affirming your abilities."

"That's very helpful, Mr. Attorney General. We will talk again soon."

"I have no doubt of that. Good evening."

He hung up.

She looked at her team, stretching for the words. The complications were overwhelming.

"Anybody hungry?" the vice president said, smiling, pleased to see everyone smile with her.

"Can we get some dinner, please?" the COS asked the officer waiting outside the door.

"Nari, please call the Senate majority leader. Perhaps he can inject the AG's second point into his discussions with cabinet members."

"Yes, ma'am," she said, taking her phone out.

"If I get too comfortable, I'll go right to sleep," Llewellyn said with a tired smile.

"Let's stay up and talk through dinner. What should our response to Ukraine be?"

"Tanks."

"Do we have enough?" the SecState asked.

"That's up to the generals," Jay said, drinking a Coke, "but along with the Germans, I say yes. Ugh," he said, making a face, holding out the can, "this is old."

"Conventional response, of course," Llewellyn said, loosening his tie, "but I fear that it won't matter."

They looked at him.

"This is a terrible situation for you, Madam," the SecState continued. "We are expanding an already dangerous war with the Russians. And, in the meantime, you don't have the authority to act militarily. Whatever persuasive power you have started to slip away when you lost the cabinet member's vote."

Two calamitous problems, the VP thought, closing her eyes, *one I absolutely cannot solve, and the second I don't have the authority to solve.*

She shook her head. *I'll leave the vote to the Senate majority leader and Nari. Focus on the problem at hand.*

And the problem at hand is the Russians. It is precisely the problem for which you have no authority to act But assume that Russians know that too. They will be all the more surprised should we take decisive action.

The VP's brow narrowed. "We don't know Putin's next step," she said, "and we'll never know it. That's playing his game. We have to get control of this. And that means looking for every opportunity to get an edge and pouncing on any mistake that he makes."

The vice president leaned forward. "I think our tanks will stop them. We have the element of surprise. But we have to be ready for Putin's reaction. Oh, thank you," she said as their food arrived.

"He may want to back away from the table and call it a night, or he may want to begin some action someplace else. We have to be alert and ready to move aggressively."

"Madam Vice President, I agree, but isn't that the problem?" Jay said, digging into his salad. "How do we prepare for irrational, unthinkable options?"

"Putin is a drunk driver. You take the wheel away from him," the COS said, looking for an electrical outlet to recharge her phone.

"Look," Llewellyn said, placing a hand on the SecDef's shoulder, "an ex–US ambassador to the UN once said that when it comes to talking about nuclear weapons, which is what ultimately we're talking about here, it always pays to have a coward in the room." He looked around. "OK, I'll be that coward."

He took a deep breath. "We and our allies and adversaries have become so glib at talking about war's terror that we have numbed ourselves to what that terror means. And we start a war so ... so easily and so logically because each side wants to protect its own troops.

"So Putin responds by taking out our tanks, supplies, and personnel in Poland with a tactical nuclear weapon. As the commandant pointed out, to safeguard our own troops, we respond with aggressive protection, hitting their central and western control center. Putin responds with a tactical nuclear weapon destroying Supreme Headquarters Allied Powers Europe. We respond by taking out their central command."

"The escalation train to disaster," Nari said, sitting down.

"Yes, and then we launch the rest of our weapons while we still can against their ballistic missile silos, and they launch against ours. Both launches are too late, all missiles hit their targets, and devastation destroys society.

"In the space of ninety minutes, close to three billion people are dead in the Northern Hemisphere of the planet. There are over three hundred nuclear detonations in the United States alone."

"Three hundred?" the vice president said, dropping her knife.

"Yes," Jay said. "Every state capital from Juneau to Tallahassee will receive at least two Russian nuclear missile strikes, each in the one megaton range, because the enemy knows that it's the state capitals that govern the flow of resources during any recovery attempt.

"In addition, DC will receive five. New York City, four. Houston, with its petrochemical facilities, its major port in Galveston, plus the largest medical center in the world, will receive four or five ballistic missile attacks, Phoenix will receive four because of its distributed air force bases.

"Los Angeles, San Francisco, Atlanta will each receive two or three in this wave, with more to follow. Boston, the symbol of US independence, receives three. Kennedy Space Center will be utterly destroyed by three missile strikes. Seattle, San Diego, and Chicago will receive multiple killing attacks. Memphis, St. Louis, Tampa, Miami, Orlando, the ports of Savanna and Norfolk will be utterly demolished by multiple nuclear ground bursts. Connecticut will be demolished, the Groton and New London submarine bases completely destroyed.

"An additional hundreds of nuclear weapons will explode high in the atmosphere, wiping out all computer circuits made after 1950. All modern communication will be destroyed. All internet communication in the US will cease."

"Casualties will be, well, ghastly," Llewellyn added, removing his glasses. "A 1 megaton ground burst detonation is a city killer. We're talking about 5 to 15 percent of the population being wiped out instantly by X-ray bursts. Another 40 percent in the blast wave. Radiation's descent will kill another 30 percent. Blind and dying infants will cry themselves to death in the streets because health care is eliminated. People will emerge from their homemade bunkers into a blasted world.

"Everything that we have as a nation and that we stand for as a nation will be destroyed. The Declaration of Independence, the Constitution with its amendments, the Emancipation Proclamation, on and on will be demolished."

He looked from face to face. "Is this what we meant by 'promote the general welfare'—by 'ensuring domestic tranquility'?" The only legacy we'll have is that of a ruined nation with few living and no principle but survival."

Jay slumped into his chair. "Europe will be, well, gone, its great cities wiped out. Paris, London, Glasgow, Frankfurt, Vienna, Rome, Oslo, Budapest, Amsterdam—all eliminated. Prague, rubbed out. Continental radiation will destroy what's left of a bombed-out population subsisting in rubble.

"And, of course, Russia will convulse and die as a nation as we hurl devastating nuclear barrages against their cities and towns, killing 140 million of their people.

"People in the Southern Hemisphere will not be safe because of the drift of the radiation patterns to the south. They die in months."

"Everybody dies in a major nuclear war, ma'am," the SecState said. "Many die in the first few seconds. Many others die in the first few weeks. Everybody dies in the next few years."

"Ironically," the SecState said, "the only people who say that the world will not be rubbed out by nuclear war are the scientists who gave us these damn weapons in the first place. They are a curse on humanity.

"And a civilization that took tens of thousands of years to build and to admire dies in weeks." He rubbed his eyes, and the VP saw how old her friend looked. "What we must now ensure is that one action of a junior officer in some forgettable hovel doesn't trigger the beginning of the end of society, the massacre of humanity, the last weekend of our culture.

"But I tell you," SecState said, voice rising, "that on the last day of its broadcast, CNN, from its twisted, demolished studio, will ask, 'How did we let it come to this?' Well, folks, that's the question we face right now."

"What's the answer?" the SecDef asked, raising his arms above his hands.

"We avoid this debacle by, number one, not using nuclear weapons ourselves, and, two, not putting our opponent in a position where their only option is to use them. Then get rid of them.

"I realize how impossible that is. But what choice do we have?" All sat still.

"Ruined my dinner," Nari said, pushing her plate away.

"Llewellyn, that's some speech," the VP said in low tones, shaking her head. "It anchors us. Are we as Americans willing to accept this price for our freedom? And if we do, is there any freedom left?" She looked up at him. "Thank God you're not a proponent of using these weapons."

She sighed. "Nari, let's get Chess in here. He needs to be briefed. Then let's figure out a way for mankind to survive at least the weekend."

TAKE MY WHIPPINGS AS I GO

"**M**adam President, will you step outside with me, please?" the chairman asked as the VP reentered the situation room with the SecDef, SecState, and Nari.

The chairman turned, facing the VP as she stepped outside.

"Madam, I must inform you that the chiefs are extremely nervous about you're not yet having the cabinet votes to be our official acting president. There simply is no precedent for the US being guided in military action by a vice president."

Low tones, she thought, *he's just trying to do his job on an impossible day.*

"We're in a jam here, General. The attorney general tells me that, as we stand here, I have no real authority to initiate military action. Plus, I lost a vote."

"You lost … ?" The chairman looked up at the ceiling, then back at her. "How for the love of God does that happen?"

"I'll be frank, General. Some politicians see this as an opportunity to stop my succession. I am weighing the needs of our country against criticism I will receive for overreaching my authority."

"Yes, ma'am."

"The political debasement of the process is my concern. You and I must deal with these tanks."

She stepped closer. "General, I understand your situation. You have lost your commander in chief, and you and I are in limbo. However, if you don't accept me, you have no commander. And certainly you don't want to be in a circumstance where you have to take a military position without backing from civilian leadership."

"Why can't you and I both work through Jay?" Caddel asked. "As secretary of defense, he is the highest-ranking official at the Pentagon."

"The SecDef answers to the president. There's no precedent for his setting up shop on his own. Plus it doesn't solve your problem because, like me, he is not authorized to initiate military action. Also you'd have two different leaders." She shook her head. "That's not satisfactory at all."

She placed a hand on his arm. "I appreciate the delicacy of your situation. But right now, I am the only civilian leader that you have. And we need to work together, regardless of what happens the rest of the day, so that we can hand our country over intact to whomever the appropriate civilian leadership is. Right now, that appropriate civilian leadership *de facto* is me. Unless you want to start working with Madam Speaker of the House."

"No, ma'am," the chairman said, shaking his head. "That would not be my first choice."

"In the meantime, I commit to you that my chief of staff and I are working assiduously to procure the votes I need. I will tell you in all candor that some people are working against us. However, I am confident that we will have the eight votes we need to have today. Do you understand me?"

The chairman straightened. "Yes, ma'am."

"And if I don't and the situation remains dire, then I will order you to launch a strike. And I would like you to carry out that order. I take full responsibility for my instructions, and I have no problem telling that to your chiefs as well."

"What happens to you when this is all done?"

"Well, General," she said, looking up into his brown face, "I will have to take my whippings as I go."

They walked back into the situation room. The VP took her seat, the packed room quiet in an instant.

"I would like a strong military, non-Article 5, non-nuclear response by the United States and Germany alone," the vice president announced. "It will be a conventional attack, tank against tank. The Russians want an easy win. They will not anticipate fighting face-to-face with us. We will clip both pincer arms while giving them no rationale for a nuclear counterresponse."

"He may go nuclear anyway," chief of staff army, General Bolivar, said.

She looked at him. "That's right, General. Putin may act with a massive nuclear strike requiring our devastating counterresponse. He has talked about, but so far has not drawn from, his nuclear arsenal. But you have a point.

"General Caddel," she said, looking over at the chairman, "what is our current defense posture?"

"Fade-out, ma'am."

She thought for a moment. "Please take us to Roundhouse."

No one said a word.

"That's ... that's DEFCON 3, ma'am. Quite a step," CNO said.

"It will let him know we're watching him and are ready for anything. Plus, our priority is to protect our own people."

She stood up, seeing Nari flash a card that showed a "5" replaced with a "6"

Thank God. Just two left.

"I appreciate and understand your respect for chain of command. We are in a challenging position now because I require eight cabinet votes to be official acting president. Yet I only have six at this point, just having gained one a moment ago. I am fully confident that I will get eight soon.

"However, if we cannot wait and the situation remains critical, I will order you to initiate hostilities. I want the record to reflect that you are clearly following my order as the senior civilian leader of the United States and that you are not moving on your own initiatives.

"What happens with votes at the end of the day happens. But we cannot stand and wait while Russia or China or even Korea takes advantage of a delay in transferring command authority. The responsibility is wholly mine. Are there any questions about that?"

The room was silent.

"Very well. Should I give the order, I want those Russian and Belarusian tanks obliterated. They shouldn't be able to sell the remaining parts for scrap metal. I don't want these tanks used for another incursion anywhere in the world."

"Understood, Madam President," General Bolivar said, "but we don't have much time. We can move M1A1 Abrams and speak to the Germans about moving Leopards into the necessary positions. But those enemy tanks are only one hour thirty away from the border. We can meet them in an hour and fifteen minutes, but we must have the order now to move."

She looked at General Caddel, who nodded his head.

I didn't ask for this. It landed on me. I'm in the midst of it now. She took a deep breath.

Total command.

"I authorize the commitment of resources to this attack. General, please place your tanks. Let's move."

PREPARATIONS

The back of the vice president's mouth filled with acid and bile, and she sat up and leaned over, throwing up into the small waste can next to her seat.

She lay back on the sofa. Her pulse racing, thick sweat beads breaking out on her forehead. The small of her back was already slick with sweat.

After her order, Nari found her a room with a bed where she slept for just a few minutes.

Now she woke.

Recent events slammed home.

She was *de facto* president.

Stroke.

Joint Chiefs.

Cabinet votes?

Tanks barreling down to Ukraine.

Nuclear war imminent.

And you are running all of it.

Knock on the door.

"Madam Vice President?"

"Here I come."

She washed up, then opened the door, following the officer to the situation room.

Paper, pencils, pens, notepads, electronic pads, cell phones, all the ways people communicate in the twenty-first century, were scattered like leaves on the large table. Everyone was gathered around the telescreen.

"Thank you," the vice president said, taking, then ignoring the coffee. "What do you have for us?"

The chairman nodded. "Let's proceed." He turned to the chief of staff army.

"We have a plan that meets your specifications, ma'am," Bolivar said. His thin face with horn-rimmed glasses, pale an hour ago, now radiated a hot nucleus of fierce energy.

."We're going to break both pincer arms. We are pulling in a division of M1A1 Abrams and a regiment of German tanks.

"Our plan is to throw our US tanks head-on into the Russian tanks here on the east, stopping them just north of the Ukrainian border. The Leopard 2 tanks will be to the west, striking the Belarusian assault force there. With both pincers broken, the assault will be stillborn before Ukrainian territory is breached. We will be able to crush them in detail as you specified, not leaving a single enemy tank operational."

"Tell me about timing. How far away is the enemy?"

"Each is an hour from their Ukrainian breach points. We plan to hit them within thirty minutes."

"Seems like it's cutting it close, but I know you've thought this through," the VP said. "We need the time to get all of our teams in position. What about air support?"

"Ours or theirs?"

"Theirs first."

"Still none. We cannot identify any new Russian or Belarusian air assets moving southwest to Ukraine."

"Why?"

The chief of staff air force shrugged. "Either arrogance, shortages, or weather."

She said, "And ours?"

"Warthogs are standing by. They'll hammer the enemy tanks if needed."

The VP nodded, remembering the reputation of the ugly tank busting planes in the US arsenal.

"They are killing machines that will tear holes in any surviving Russian or Belarusian tanks. Plus Eagles and F16s to cover them. We're solid."

"Is there a need for infantry?" COS asked.

"We'll have support infantry standing by. And, of course, the Ukrainians are more than happy to support any operation."

The VP snuck a glance at Nari, who gave one headshake, then left the room for a minute.

Still stuck at six cabinet votes.

The vice president look at the chairman.

"I will need to speak to the Ukrainian president and also the prime minister of Germany."

"Also NATO must be informed," Llewellyn said. "They most know that this is not an Article 5 invocation."

"Llewellyn, can you please help us set up those calls and then inform NATO?"

"I need tech support," he said.

"Communications officers," the chairman called. Everyone looked up at the voice that filled the room.

"General Caddel, let's you and I have some more discussion while I'm having some dinner."

He had a quizzical look on his face. "Didn't you eat earlier?"

She put her hand on his sleeve. "Well, I tried."

"Let's get you another one. Pepcid?"

"Would appreciate it."

"I should have offered you one earlier." He motioned for two dinners. "We take so many around here, the Pentagon tried to grow the pills here. I'll join you, if I may."

She laughed. "Of course. And happy birthday."

He tripped. "How did you know?"

She winked. "Even *almost acting presidents* have spies. What can you tell me about this room?" she said, meandering to the back.

"The first situation room was constructed during the Kennedy administration after the Bay of Pigs," the general said, following her. "The president thought that he wasn't getting real-time information about the Cuban Beach situation and needed a room with the latest electronic equipment."

"Plus, they refurbished it after the 2001 attack on the trade centers?" she asked.

"Yes," he said, smiling. He signed off on a document delivered by an aide. "In addition, there was a critical 2006-7 upgrade."

"When the two found a corner of the room, far from the telescreen, she said, "Tell me, General Caddel, if you were in command of Russian armed forces, what would your reaction be to our strike?"

"You're scared."

The VP stared at him. "You're damn right I'm scared."

"Good," Caddel said with a smile. "We're all scared tonight."

"The only one that worries me is Putin," she said exhaling, her forehead now covered with sweat. "I don't think he's afraid at all."

"Agreed," he said, closing his eyes and sighing.

I'm not the only one exhausted, she thought.

"I'd be in a spot," the chairman continued. "I could send more tanks, but the roads are narrow, the fields boggy, and those new tanks will not be able to provide any additional support in time. The warthogs will murder us. And I would have to assume that if I sent in air assets after the warthogs, then US air assets would meet us in the air."

"How much of an escalation would air action be?" she asked, gratified that she was keeping food down.

"Well," he said, looking over the table at her, "we're already looking at Russian and American tanks engaging. That's an escalation right there. New involvement of US aircraft is a further escalation. I would take out the air bases that the US planes use. So, given all of this arithmetic, my best move would be to go nuclear."

"Where?"

"A tactical attack on the engaging tanks. The Russians are going to lose their tanks anyway. So a nuclear strike wouldn't make a difference for them but would certainly take out our hardware, stopping their advance into Russia."

"But, General," she said, working to control her voice, "the Leopard 2 and M1A1s are not going further into Russia. Their goal is to interdict the tanks coming into Ukraine. This is not a prelude to a general Russian invasion."

"Well, ma'am, you and I understand that, but we've never communicated that to Putin."

"I don't see how we could do that. What would the message be? 'We're going to destroy your tanks, which are your front line of defense for southern Russia, and then we're going to turn around and run home, forgetting about how you gassed and killed forty thousand Ukrainians just a few hours ago.' Madam, Putin has no idea what's coming. If we have done our homework, then his tanks will be destroyed before he knows what's happened. But the time he's figured out the extent of his losses, it will also be clear that our tanks are returning back into Ukraine."

"So the driving power behind escalation is—"

"Protecting your own troop and equipment."

"What if we made no response at all to Russian tactical nuclear weapon use?"

He shook his head. "That would embolden Russian generals to demand nuclear weapon release authorization."

The vice president put down her fork. "So it sounds like every step we take to avoid a nuclear war is a step right back into one." She wiped her brow. "General, some on my team argue that the only way to avoid nuclear war is to keep from backing Putin into a corner. Do you disagree?"

The general put his knife down and inhaled. "Putin was not backed into a corner before he launched the largest chemical weapon attack since World War I on nonactive combatants and civilians. Totally unprovoked."

She shook her head. "I feel like I'm playing a card game where the devil has set the rules."

"Welcome to my world."

"Thank you, General. It seems to me that this initial battle needs to be brutal, quick, and decisive. Our tanks need to be out of there as soon as the job is done."

"I like your language—sting 'em and come home quick. I hope that's right."

"Ah, Nari, welcome back."

The chairman and vice president filled her in.

The COS nodded. "This makes very good sense to me. It's wholly conventional. There is no reason for a rational person to launch nuclear weapons with this conventional blow."

"Well, that's what we think," the chairman, making room for the COS at the table. "We'll see how the Russians react."

"Nari, where are we with the votes?"

The COS looked at the general.

"I have no secrets from General Caddel on this matter," the VP said.

"Still stuck at six. It's tough to round up cabinet members. Two are overseas, and one is in the hospital."

"They may not even know of the president's condition," the general said. "I can have my signals team ferret them out."

The VP looked over at the chief of staff, who looked at her. They both nodded. "Thank you," the VP said. "We would appreciate that. If you contact somebody, can you turn them over at once to Nari?"

"Of course."

"Excuse me," she said, seeing the chief of staff army beckon her to the screen.

"One thing, Madam Vice President," General Bolivar said when they gathered, "the best position for our tanks is right here, near Nova Guta," pointing to the telescreen.

"On the wrong side of the border," the VP said.

"Yes," General Bolivar said, circling the area in red. "But we can lay the best trap there."

She saw the chairman walk over to join them as she studied the map. Tapping the screen, she said, "Border concerns are only pompous niceties now. You have my permission to set your trap there."

"That means invasion, Madam Vice President."

SHELL BREAK

She turned, staring at the chairman. "Yes, it does. By the way, what is the name of this mission?"

"Shell Crack."

She smiled. "I appreciate the lobster metaphor."

"I have President Zelensky on the phone for you, ma'am."

She and Nari hurried to the table where she was handed a phone.

"President Zelensky, this is the vice president of the United States."

"I understand. And please give the First Family my very best wishes and sincere condolences. They were true friends of the Ukrainian people."

"Mr. President, you know that there is an enemy strike force headed your way."

"I certainly do. Preceded by a terrible gas attack. The casualties are wrenching. What we humans do to each other is despicable.

"We are marshaling all of our forces that we could free up to meet them. But I must tell you, the gas attack took us by surprise. I don't know if we can withstand them, but I promise you we will die trying. Thank you for the weapons that you have provided."

"I'd be taking this battle off your hands, Mr. President."

The president's voice quavered. "I'm not sure what you mean."

"We are committing American and German forces to meet and defeat the tank brigades headed your way."

She thought she heard the president sob.

"Thank you so much. This is the kind of help that we need. Together, we can beat these beasts."

"Thank you, President Zelensky. I'll get back to you when we know more about how this is going."

"Thank you very much for informing me, Madam President."

Madam President. She hadn't heard anybody utter that before.

"Here is the German chancellor." She took the phone being handed to her.

"This is the vice president of the United States."

"A terrible time. Please convey my sympathies to the First Family."

"You are kind to do so, sir. There are several Russian and Byelorussian tank brigades bearing down on Ukraine."

"Dear God. Tell me."

She explained the situation and the plan.

"You are not invoking Article 5?"

She wasn't sure if that was a question or a criticism. "Well, Mr. Chancellor, no need. No NATO country has been invaded. I don't think we're at Article 5 yet. Besides, you and I own the best tanks in the world. I think it's time the Russians know that as well."

"Let's then teach them a lesson they will not forget. But we must move at once. You commit to this—to the end?"

"Count on it. The chain of command ends with me. When will you be ready?"

"I just signaled my generals to move into position at once. They should be in place in"—he paused—"fiftyminutes."

"I am told that your Leopards are the best in Europe."

"The world, Madam Vice President. The best in the world."

They both laughed.

"Let's stay in touch."

"Yes. I must go."

She handed the phone over.

"Madam Vice President, the Abrams are in position."

God help me. No. God help us all.

She stood up and, walking to the telescreen, said, "General Caddel, may I have the room?"

"Atten-hut."

She looked at Nari, who gave one shake of her head.

Six.

Surveying the room, she saw young women and older men called to war, all private feelings suppressed. What mattered was committing to the fight.

There was Llewellyn, an ex-army colonel, standing ramrod straight in his impeccable suit. While he was lukewarm about the plan, he was with her now.

"I am not yet acting president. But I am the senior civilian commander, sitting atop the military chain of command. An ally of ours is in peril. We will respond. I take full responsibility for this plan, its execution, and its casualties. I put my full trust in you as you have trusted me on this day."

"General Caddel."

"Yes, ma'am."

"I am ordering you, at 1930 hours, to execute Operation Shell Crack." She took a deep breath, then turned. "General Bolivar, it's up to the army now."

"The army won't let you down, Madam."

•

Walking back to her seat amid the cacophony of voices carrying out the mission, she thought, *That was my first order.*

She turned to Nari.

"It's in the military's hands now," Nari said. "Let's get some sleep. I brought some personal things to the White House for you."

"I remember a story about Lincoln," the VP said, drawing close. "As a young man, he served in the Black Hawk Wars as a junior officer. When he gave his first order in a fight, his patrol shouted back, 'Go to hell!'"

"Well," Nari said, smiling while touching her arm, "the night's still young."

TENNESSEE

Colonel Jayla "Stinger" Hawks, leader of the C Company "Crusaders," Thirty-Seventh Armor Regiment of the First Armored Division, climbed into the lead US battle tank.

"Button up," she said over the low drone of the powerful engine.

The entire tank crew, knowing what their commander expected, moved as one.

"All tanks are in place, Colonel. Even the last ten groups of three are in position. But," Phil said, lowering his voice, "you're taking a real risk with the redeployment."

Stinger just nodded, clapping her gunner on the shoulder. She took her map out. "Heads up, guys. We're at Novaya Guta, just north of the Ukrainian border right across E95 that heads south into Ukraine."

"How far out are the dollies now?" Levy, her driver, asked.

She saw him sweating. *First time for him. Me too.*

"The Russki tanks are three miles north, headed our way."

"Three miles," Levy repeated.

"We going to take these people, Colonel?"

"Command set us up beautifully, AJ," she said, wiping her wet brow. "We're sitting across the road, it's still dark, and they don't have eyes on us."

"Strange," Phil said, "very strange. Tanks moving without infantry and air support on the enemy's border."

"You'd think they'd know better, "AJ said, "after the pasting the Ukrainians gave them in '22."

"We take the lead tanks out in an M1 volley," Stinger said. "They're dead before they realize they need support."

"Damn straight they are," AJ said, looking down at the map.

63

"Check it out," Stinger said. "We're in a curved semicircle in front of them, elongated on the left into the forest. So after they get their front teeth knocked out, the dollies can either go backward, left, or right. But Jesse's group will hammer the back end of their column, so backward is not an option."

"Keep 'em in a headlock while Jesse kicks them in the butt."

"Well, Phil," she said to the gunner, smiling. "that's not textbook terminology, but it sums it up nicely enough for me. Forest and dense brush to our left with main M1A1 batteries well positioned there will block leftward movement. To the right is a short cliff with a steep decline that the dollies can't manage."

"And if they charge forward?" Levy asked.

"Then we blow them into the air until they stop. OK. Eyes on me, guys."

The tank was silent.

"Lookit. The M1A1 Abrams is the best tank hardware in the world. We've been tracking the dollies for hours. They don't know our strength or disposition. They don't even know we're here. In fifty minutes, the battle will be over, the T-90s ground to powder, and the army will sing songs about us."

Everybody laughed.

She sat straighter. "OK. Gear and weapons check, then stay at your stations. The next time you fire will be for real. Levy, I'm coming to you."

In a moment, she crouched down so only he could hear.

"You've got the willies," she said. "I get it. But your tank doesn't. This battle-tested machine is ready for this fight. It was built to kill Russians. Just get out of its way, let it do its job, and enjoy the ride."

She placed a hand on his shoulder. "If we don't stop the dollies, then they will tear Kyiv apart. Remember, the Ukrainians hate them, the world hates them, and it's on you and me to stop them. Follow your orders. Kill as many as you can. Stay focused on your mission. The team will look after you."

She rubbed his shoulder, then climbed back up to her observer position. Hearing the designated click sequence through her radio, she scoped the low silhouettes of two T-90s lumbering along the road next to each other. Arrogant and confident, the individual dolly tank commanders had their heads exposed outside of their tanks.

What was that?

She heard something.

Outside, in the night air.

Singing.

These people are singing.

Her blood, trained to be cool for years, now boiled.

"Cleared to engage," the voice over the radio spoke.

"Acknowledged."

Colonel "Stinger" Hawks, from Fairgarden, Tennessee, told by everyone all of her life that she was nothing, her future was nothing, her life was nothing, steeled her nerves.

Somebody's going to die, and it ain't us. The sweating stopped.

"All tanks. Weapons free," she said on her radio. "Tear them up."

This is how we do it in Tennessee, Putin.

HAPPY BIRTHDAY

With an ear-splitting roar, twenty M1A1 Abrams fired at once, their main guns discharging armor-piercing fin-stabilized discarding sabot (APFSDS). Traveling at one mile a second, to Stinger, they made instant contact with the T-90s. Enemy tank turrets blasted into the air, one banging her own tank hard enough to disorient her.

Shaking the blow off, she stood again as the dollies tried to withdraw. Confused and disoriented, they were unable to aim, surrounded by blazing M1A1 steel.

Some went left into the forest where well-positioned Abrams, each tank covering a small, non-overlapping sector between the trees, blew them to pieces. The T-90s were stuck, exposed tanks bursting into flames each second. The burning hulks' remaining ammo cooked off, their men sliced into burning pieces, the lucky ones abandoning their flaming tanks and disappearing into the woods.

Then she heard the roar of a tornado, followed by huge detonations down the T-90 line. *Who could that be? Not Jesse*, she thought. *Way too close.*

Then she recognized the smoke trail.

Rising high from her right up in the air, a volley of FGM-148 Javelins hit hard, demolishing the middle of the column. Ukrainians in the plain to her right firing on fixed position tanks. *Ingenious.*

Attacked by Jesse in the rear, the Javelins to the right, and Stinger in the front, the T-90 column, what was left of it, broke apart.

She saw some dollies turn to the right, lumbering over the cliff onto a forty-degree decline, doing what command said that they would not do—escaping by falling right into the waiting guns of her sixty remaining M1A1s. Their placement had been her idea.

All up and down the rough road, the T-90s struggling over the cliff had no chance. It was impossible for them to get a shot off, the angle being too steep for effective targeting. However, the angle did expose their soft turrets, and the M1A1s blasted away the top of the tanks and turned into metal fragments and burning flesh.

She saw some dollies just drive straight off the embankment, hanging in the air for a moment. But, before they fell down the cliff, the Russian tanks flew into pieces, the waiting M1A1s shooting from below, kinetic weapons piercing the T-90s' soft underbelly and blasting the tank into sizzling steel and flaming human fragments.

Others came down hard on the cliff surface before sliding to the bottom, exposing the top of the turret to Abrams direct main battery fire. She saw a shell pierce a dolly's vulnerable turret, dismembering the crew and detonating the ammunition in a huge fireball.

Black smoke climbed, swallowing the dawn up and down the long road, as one T-90 after another was dispatched. Many of them never got a shot off, unable to target effectively, and, having no appreciation of the surrounding terrain or the number of enemy, were quickly demolished by kinetic energy sabot rounds.

When a collection of twenty T-90s managed to plow through the dense woods on the left, they arrived on flat maneuvering ground. However, rather than race south to get behind Stinger's tanks, they tucked tail, turning north deeper into the Rodina. Suddenly, three volleys of Javelin streaks were seen in the air. The trajectories arched high then flat, then over the tanks turned at once into a full power descent. Several experienced Russian soldiers jumped from their dollies while the tanks were still in motion, breaking ankles and legs trying to escape the impending demolition.

The Javelins slammed into the soft turrets before exploding. The damage was lethal with new smoke plumes snaking into the sky, the few survivors falling prey to small weapons fire from Ukrainian partisans. Meanwhile, up and down the narrow road, the M1A1s shot fish in a barrel.

The Russians, in their arrogance, broke every major rule of tank fighting in committing their top-of-the-line tanks to the new Ukrainian offensive. They lumbered in narrow file down a long road with no room to maneuver on the left or right. They chose to bring no infantry support, denying themselves the eyes of soldiers who could scan for trouble. Plus, they provided no air power. Adding to that their complete ignorance of the US position turned the modern T-90s into M1A1 Abrams cannon fodder.

A wounded Russian colonel captured in the fight, when confronted with these facts, drew deeply on a filthy cigarette and shrugged, saying, "At least we remembered to bring the ammunition."

•

A half hour later, Stinger positioned her command tank to protect a listing Abrams that was leaking fuel. Two M1A1s, Seminole 1 and Seminole 2, joined her.

"Ditch the tank, just get the crew out of there!" she shouted into her radio to Seminole 2 as it arrived.

"Crusader 1, Crusader 1, this is Seminole 1. Over."

"Go ahead, Seminole 1," she said to the M1A1 two hundred yards to the east.

"I'm looking at a line of fifteen—Jesu—"

Stinger saw Seminole 1 tank blown to pieces by a T-90 hit, the turret gone, white hot flames roaring from the crew compartment.

The sun was over the horizon now. "Seminole 2, this is Crusader 1," Stinger called over the radio. "Grab the injured crew and get out of here."

"We just have to back fifty feet into that tree line."

"Agreed, I'll cover for you."

"I see the dollies. That's a lot of cover, Colonel."

"Just keep the beer cold. Now move."

She penciled off a note, then, handing it to AJ, said, "Get this to command."

The smoke of the approaching tanks was clear now. And judging by their maneuvering, she knew the dollies saw her.

•

"I just received this message," the chief of staff army said in the situation room.

The vice president noticed that the room had been especially silent since the battle started, and quieter still as casualty reports began streaming in.

"What does it say?" Nari asked, standing.

"Maybe you better read it, sir," General Bolivar said, handing the paper to General Caddel, who looked at it, closed his eyes, then, swallowing, boomed in a loud voice.

"From Crusader 1, Colonel Hawks commanding. Happy birthday, Chairman, JCS. Send us more Russians."

The room was still for a moment. Then the chief of staff air force walked over, picked up a phone and muttered, "We'll do better than that."

●

"Gunner, how many rounds do we have?"

"We've got two or three left."

"Got it." Stinger sighted carefully from her forward command position in the tank. She could stay quiet and hide, then slip away, but …

She shook her head, resolving to cover Seminole 2, giving the order to move. She could take out one or two of the tanks and give Seminole 2 a chance to escape even deeper into the woods. Plus the Russians wouldn't be looking for her in their hunt for easy Seminole 2 meat to pick.

That was the new Russian military motto: "Die first, ask questions later."

Crusader 1 moved to the north, up the T-90s' left flank. The dollies came barreling across the plain, "target fixated" adjusting their direction, searching for the Abrams tank they saw disappear into the trees. Some were firing blindly, looking for an easy hit.

She picked her target and fired, blowing the T-90 into two, the tread mechanism moving itself blindly forward until it hit a rock formation where it exploded.

The other dollies stopped, swiveling left, then right. Then her radio crackled. "Crusader 1, Crusader 1, we are the Bursting Suns. Get the hell out of there."

"All reverse," she cried.

The tank lurched backward thirty yards, then all hell broke loose.

AGM-130s fell on the T-90s like rain.

Fired from a gaggle of high-flying F15E Eagles at "stand-off" distances, the air force weapon, with its television monitor broadcasting live to the "host" aircraft, was unerringly directed to the targets. Its BLU-109 penetrator and MK-84 blast/fragmentation warheads did the rest.

Within thirty seconds, the remaining T-90s died screaming deaths.

●

After radioing in to command, Stinger and her crew climbed down from their tank, walking the dank ground in the early morning light. Fire and the combined stench of tank fuel and burning flesh filled the air.

"Prisoners, Colonel?"

She looked at her weapons officer with a smile. "You planning to surrender, AJ?"

He laughed. "No. The Russians."

Stinger heard the pop of small arms fire in the woods. "Ukrainian freedom fighters are thick around here. I think I hear them taking prisoners no—"

Turning at the explosion, she swiveled in time to see a T-90 turret fragment hurtling toward her.

SCHLACHTHOF

*O*berstleutnant Johann Baeder, placed in command of two companies of the Panzerbrigade 12, studied the map carefully with his tank company leaders.

"Herr Oberstleutnant, there is to be no CMM or Freyung for this mission?"

"We won't need telecommunication or reconnaissance today, Herr Oberst. Just our guns. Now help me solve our problem."

"The T-72s that we face are formidable and keeping good speed," one commander said, throwing his coffee on the mushy ground.

"Thank you. We expect over one hundred of them," Baeder said, standing straight and stretching. "They're nothing like the T-90s the Americans are facing but still rabble-rousers. That is not the problem. The problem is this."

He waved his pen all over the map. "Marshland. Not the best tank country. We can attack them on the main highway, but they will scatter into the damn mush and water."

"Our Leopards can swim too."

"Yes, but we are heavier," their leader said. "I don't want to wrestle in the water with them."

"How about Brahin?" one company commander said, pointing to the map.

"I like the converging highways," the Oberstleutnant said, shaking his head. "But we can't get there in time."

"Then Novi Petrivtsi it is," another commander said, pointing with a smile.

They all leaned over the map. "It's just north of the Ukrainian border, and dry," the major said. "We can strike from the west and south, driving them into the Dnipro. That is where we will engage."

"And we can see how the T-72 swims a river," a company commander laughed.

"Remember that, in a battle," the Oberstleutnant said, folding up the map, "everyone forgets our Leopards are the best in the world. It's just tank against tank. Be at your sharpest. Take the shot that looks best without hesitation and fire on the move. T-72s must stop to fire accurately. Press your advantage and hurl them into the river."

"Sir, we just learned that the Americans snapped off their eastern pincer. The Russians will certainly send air support to the west now."

"So will we, Herr Oberst. To your battalions, gentlemen."

•

Sun Yat Sen said that battles, through planning, heart strength, and determination, were won before they were fought.

By the time the Leopard 2s arrived, the T-72s were a destructive force with no direction or purpose. Having heard the news of the obliterated Russian T-90s to the east, the T-72s stopped forward progress. Like tarantulas compelled to ball into fear clumps by an approaching wasp's drone, the tank force froze, incapacitated through paralysis of leadership and indecisive action.

The Leopards pounced.

One hundred fifty Leopard 2s unleashed a volley that destroyed over seventy-five Byelorussian tanks, the Leopard 2s all but leaping off the ground by the power of their guns. Firing from the west and south, they blew what once were tons of threatening metal to pieces. The Belarusian T-72s that were not hit ran for cover, some colliding with each other.

The T-72s flailed. They could not fire on the move, forced to stay fixed as the Leopards moved, pivoted, and fired, their balance and inertial systems providing instantaneous inputs to fire command. The biggest problem for the German commander was battlefield management, as it was so easy for a Leopard 2 to fall into the field of another German's fire.

An hour later, the Leopard 2s tore through both the northern and southern flanks of the eastward retreating T-72s, the Belarus tanks proving no match for the MTU liquid-cooled, V12 twin-turbo diesel Leopard 2 engines, allowing the Germans to accelerate to 70 kph, their smooth bore cannons sweeping the field.

Baeder saw the Leopard 2 in front of him, driving forward at 50 kph, turn its gun hard right and fire without slowing, its shells demolishing three T-72s.

In three hours, all T-72s were on fire or upended in the river. Russian aircraft, unable to press home their attacks on the German tanks because of the AIM missile fusillades from the covering F-16s, fired without even aiming, then fled back north.

Later, when asked by command how the battle went, the Oberstleutnant thought, then uttered one word.

"Schlachthof."

Turkey shoot.

●

Putin could barely hear the voice on the phone over the pounding and banging on his locked door. He gave instructions to the man on the other end of the receiver, then hung up and went back to his meal, ignoring the shouts of anger and fury from his ministers.

THROWING A TREAD

"**M**adam Vice President," the chairman said, putting the phone down, "I just spoke to my counterpart in Germany. The operation was a success. The Belarusian left pincer movement has been crushed. The Leopards routed the enemy, leaving 125 smoldering T-72s burning in the marshlands or sunk in the Dnipro River.

"As you know, our M1A1s caught the right pincer by total surprise, wiping out 150 T-90s. Both pincers are broken."

"Our casualties?" Nari asked.

"Twenty M1A1s and seventy-seven crew members. We have a report of one of our M1A1s being slammed by the debris of a dead T-90. Unfortunately, it was one of our command tanks."

The vice president sighed. "I'll need names and addresses."

"Of course."

"And the Germans?" COS asked, arms crossed.

"Five Leopards, three by friendly fire. One other Leopard threw a tread. I begged Lieutenant Colonel Baeder not to court-martial the young driver."

"So this is good news," Nari said, rubbing her eye as the subdued applause died away. "But what is Putin going to try next?"

The chairman raised his head. "Patch us through to the National Military Command Center."

"NMCC, General Logan speaking."

"General," Caddel said to the Pentagon-based unit that monitors the world military situation, "you are now on speaker with all the Joint Chiefs, the vice president of the United States, and her chief of staff, plus the SecDef, and the SecState. What's the Russian military status?"

"Russian and Belarus army assets heading south into northern Ukraine were engaged and destroyed. Enemy air assets were active for one hours in southern Belarus but have now stood down. Nothing else, sir."

"Nukes?"

"Strategic watch command says they are all in bed, sir."

'Thank you. Please stay close to your station, General."

"As you wish, General Caddel."

"No activity," the chairman said, turning to the VP.

He's got to do something, the VP thought. "What's his next move?"

"Surrender," General Thompson said to some chuckles.

"Not a chance," the vice president said to the chief of staff space command. "He'll never survive capitulation. No Russian leader has survived military defeat for 150 years."

"Well, he better not go nuclear. It would put us in a terrible position."

The room was silent.

"What do you mean, General Wittisen?"

"Let me remind us all," the chief of National Guard Bureau continued, sweating, "Madam Vice President is not authorized to initiate a nuclear launch under the 'two person rule.'"

"Jesus," the chairman said, exhaling deeply, "you're right. Only the authorized chief executive can launch a nuclear attack. He or she must have a special encrypted card with a specific code sequence to authorize a launch."

"And the order to launch must be confirmed by a second authorized civilian leader." The commandant looked at the secretaries of defense and state who had come forward. "Gentlemen, I assume that you have your cards."

"Right here."

"Always."

Her heart pounded. "Can Jay initiate the strike and Llewellyn confirm?" the VP asked, a new patina of sweat on her brow.

"No, ma'am. Only the president can initiate a US nuclear response."

The VP thought, then said, "I cannot have one now, but please have one created for me and hand it over when I'm confirmed. Let's pray that I don't need it."

"I will instead pray to get you confirmed," the chairman said.

Nari's phone rang. The vice president watched her speak quietly, listen, then close the folding cell.

"You now have four votes," Nari mouthed.

Going in the wrong direction. Her stomach in knots, she surveyed the room to find the JCS chairman. Seeing Nari open her phone again, the VP motioned him over. "Chairman Caddel, can we ta—"

"The president was just given last rites," Nari called out.

●

The atmosphere was pounds heavier, everyone sighing and grunting under the weight.

"We need to prepare for the transfer of power," the VP said in low tones. "Nari, can you find a minister?"

After a moment on the phone, the COS said with a new glint in her eyes, "I found fifteen."

"What?"

"The president agreed to allow fifteen ministers a private tour of the White House this morning."

The VP's heart jumped. "Well, let's choose one and have him or her meet us in the Treaty Room."

"While I get a photographer, you should collect yourself, Madam," said the COS, walking to the door.

"Yes. General, I will not be long," she said, pushing the heavy situation room door open.

Nari's phone rung as she followed the vice president through the door. The COS stopped, listened, then turned around.

"Walter Reed. The president is dead."

"God rest his soul," the VP said. "General Caddel, thank you for your patience. We both have lost a president. It's now our job t—"

"Missile launch!" bellowed a loud voice over the speakerphone.

FIRST STRIKE

Aghast, the president rushed to the telescreen, dumbfounded as it spun and shifted from northern Ukraine to somewhere west of the United States. Others faced the speaker broadcasting from NMCC, mouths open.

Perfect silence.

Then raging pandemonium. All were talking, some shouting, some screeching orders.

"Knock it off!" Caddel yelled, the air trembling with a voice that twisted down the VP's backbone like a corkscrew. "This is not some damn baseball game. I swear to Christ that I will can anybody who speaks over General Logan's voice at the NMCC."

The room shut down at once.

Caddel leaned over the speaker. "Please proceed, General Logan. Loud and clear."

"Yes, sir."

No one breathed.

"We have visual, I say again, visual confirmation of a missile breaking the surface of the Pacific Ocean heading east-southeast to mainland US."

"Madam, come at once with me to NEACP [kneecap]."

She stared at the secret service agent. "We are five thousand miles from this missile and you want me to run for cover?"

"You have to go, ma'am," said Nari.

"No," she said, shaking her head. "If it looks like it's an East Coast destination, then sure. But why would they launch from the Pacific Ocean to attack Washington?" She crossed her arms. "No, sir. I will stay here a few minutes longer with my COS, my cabinet secretaries, and my chiefs."

"Ma'am, please follow procedures."

She stared at the agent. "I'm stickin'."

"Yes, ma'am," the agent said, stepping back.

"Then we should go to the PEOC," the chairman said, taking her arm.

●

"General Logan," Caddel said after all teams descended to the White House "bunker," "any other nuclear activity?"

"I have checked with Strategic Watch Command." the voice coming from NMCC said. "They can find none."

Caddel raised his voice, leaning over the long pine-topped table. "Is there or isn't there activity?"

"No, General. No activity."

"Launch point?" General Caddel asked.

"Five hundred miles south of Cordova, Alaska."

"Eleven minutes away from mainland US."

"Thanks to the fishing boat that eyeballed this thing and called it in," the marine commandant said.

"Not a fishing boat. The *Sacramento*. One of our attack subs."

"General," the vice president asked, "I must ask. Are we sure this is the Russians?"

The chiefs stared at her.

"Why not the Chinese or the Palestinians, who have commandeered an old boat? Or just a poorly timed mistake."

"Madam Vice President, isn't it clear?" The commandant asked. She thought his finger would break off as hard as he stabbed and jabbed it on the table. "If it walks—"

"No, it is not clear, sir. Let's not begin the day by making a staggering mistake with terrible consequences."

"We've transcribed the submarine's transmitted coded signals," the chief of naval operations said, rubbing his head, "as well as the engine plant noise. It's been identified as the "Vladimir," a Borei A class sub. It's a new model. I believe this particular boat was the first in the series."

She stared at the chief of operations navy. "The lives of millions could ride on this call, Ambrose. How sure are you?"

He took a deep breath. "It's the navy's view that this is a top-of-the-line Russian sub carrying top-of-the-line weaponry. No way that boat is populated by anything but a Russian crew taking orders through their chain of command."

"Very well, CNO, I accept your team's reasoning," the VP said, touching his shoulder. "Let's assume Russian. Looks like they saved their best equipment for us."

"Why didn't we get a digital launch detection?" CNO asked in a loud voice.

"The missile has to get some altitude before we can pick it up with our satellites," General Thompson, chief of space command, said. "It never did. Its trajectory is too low."

"Meaning?" the COS asked.

"Meaning that it's going to hit somebody in one hell of a hurry," General Hooks said, navigating behind the tables to get close to the telescreen.

The VP watched Nari take a deep breath, then say, "Target?"

"There, I've place an EPE on the screen," the chairman said.

All eyes went to the viewer. The vice president noticed a red ellipse appearing in the screen below the statement "Elliptical Probability Error" imposed over what appeared to be …

"Oregon?" she asked.

EWO

"The target looks like Portland," the commandant said, studying the map.

"But," the COS said, scratching her head, "what military assets are there?"

"None."

"Major industrial?"

"Some metal and machinery work, but the city has pivoted to high tech," said General Bolivar, studying the screen.

"Port?"

"They're on the Columbia River, but no critical import or export facilities."

"What's the population?"

'The general area holds 2.5 million people, but the population is shrinking. Many homeless and drug abusers." General Caddel shook his head.

"Not adding up for me," the vice president said.

She glanced at the young officer who had displaced Nari and was sitting next to her. A large black satchel now sat on the table in front of him with a chain stretching to his arm, which he was removing with a key.

He looked her. "I'm your EWO officer, ma'am. Your emergency war order officer."

"Well, hello," she said, placing her right hand on his left arm. "I'm glad that wasn't your name. I'm not sworn in yet," she said with a smile.

"I've been ordered to give you your card, ma'am," he said, offering her a laminated flat piece of plastic the size of a playing card. "You must keep this with you at all times."

"Let's hope you can keep your emergency war plans in your bag tonight," she said, placing the card in her shirt pocket under her dark-blue jacket. "General Caddel," she called out, facing forward, "can we take this missile out?"

"No, ma'am. It's way too low. Our missile defenses are targeted for high-altitude, rapid descent vehicles."

"Try anyway."

"Yes, ma'am." the chief of naval operations said, picking up the phone in front of him.

"General Caddel, what's that missile carri—"

"The missile is changing course," someone called out.

"And we have several new dark targets in the gulf," CNO said, covering the phone speaker with his hand.

She thought for a moment. "What's the new trajectory? Oh." She studied the map. "Nari, please get me the governor of Oregon. Ambrose, what dark targets?"

"Three subs entering the gulf."

"Russian?"

"We believe that they are."

"Are they or are they not Russian, sir?" she allowed her voice to rise, swiveling in her chair to face the CNO.

She saw the chief of naval operations stiffen, then whisper into the phone for a moment, "Yes, ma'am, they are."

"Where?

"Specifically, one 370 miles from the Houston-Galveston metroplex, one 200 miles from New Orleans, and the other standing off the coast of Sarasota. From that last position, the large nuclear detonations from her missiles will devastate southern Florida."

"So," the president said, standing and walking to the board, "they identified four regions in the United States. The least critical one they launch against, while the three remaining positions, more essential to US function, they merely threaten by their presence."

She turned. "If we respond to Portland, they will launch direct against the US gulf."

"Take have upped the ante," General Thompson, head of space command, said.

"CNO," the VP asked, hands on her hips, "what submarine depth is required for missile launch?"

"Sixty feet, ma'am. The gulf subs are well below that."

"And we know that because?"

"We have an attack submarine tracking each of these boomers." He checked his tablet. "Charlotte, Pierre, and Tucson."

"What did that Pacific sub carry?" the COS asked.

"A GRAU 3M30 Bulava. Specially built for that class of sub," General Caddel said. "It can MIRV into six 150 kiloton warheads. Each bomb is ten Hiroshimas."

"Jesus."

"That's a lot of firepower for Portland," General Thompson said, her face tightening.

The vice president stared hard at the CNO. "So, the Vladimir launched, and the other three subs are not prepared to launch." She paused. "I want you to sink those gulf submarines, plus the Vladimir that launched against us."

"Ma'am, are you giving me permiss—"

"I have Governor Peters on the line, ma'am," Nari said, holding out the phone.

The VP took the phone. Covering the speaker, she said, "Yes, Ambrose. I want to hear in thirty minutes that all four Russian subs are broken and dead on the seabed. Is that clear?"

"Perfectly."

"But," General Hooks said, "won't the Rus—"

"The Russians just launched a missile direct at the Mainland US. Right now, I don't give a damn what they think."

She turned back to the phone. "Cecilia."

"Good morning, Madam. It doesn't sound like you are having a good first day."

"I have bad news. A single Russian ballistic missile is inbound for Oregon."

"For us? By, the love of God, why?"

"I don't have a 'why.' Right now, the target looks like Portland, but it could be further north," she said, looking at the telescreen as the ellipsis shifted north toward, but not into Washington.

"How much time do—"

"Four minutes. Count on our full support starting this second."

"Thank you."

"I will get back to you. In the meantime, good luck to us all."

"Governor Ellis of Washington, ma'am."

"Good morning, Ms. Vice President." She could feel his disgust for her drip through the phone.

"I have bad news, Ken. The Russians have launched a nuclear missile whose trajectory is northern Oregon."

"What the hell do they have against Oregon?"

"Well, when the Russians get to you, Governor, then maybe you can ask to read some of their literature."

An idea hit her at once, but she held her tongue.

"The ministers are ready for the swearing in, Madam," the SecDef said.

"Tell them to continue their tour and check with me again," she said.

"Are you talking to me or what, ma'am?"

Her stomach twisted in knots by war and his small mindedness. She lowered her voice. "Now, look, Ken. I know that you and Cecilia have had differences, but you're going to have to work together to help respond to this catastrophe. FEMA is behind you 100 percent. Just tell us what you need."

"Time, Madam Vice President."

"You don't have it. The best I can say is that you have three minutes."

"Thank you for the information. But I don't know if we can spare—"

That's it.

"Ken, I'm telling you straight up. I am, at this moment, federalizing your National Guard. I'm not asking you. I'm telling you. The Department of Homeland Security will manage the transfer of authority at this point.

"Wait just a damn min—"

She hung up. "Madam President, we must be prepared to strike massively."

"Wait one, Commandant," the president said. "Nari, can you get me the director of Homeland Security?"

She now looked over at General Stewert. "Yes, sir."

"Who knows where else they've hidden their subs? And Putin is a sneaky son of a bitch," the Marine Corps general said.

She looked at General Stewert, then putting her right hand on his shoulder, called for the chairman.

"Yes, ma'am?"

"General, are we at 'Roundhouse'?"

"Yes, we are."

She thought. "Then let's go to 'Fast Pace'. Nudge the B1s into their corridors, launch the B52s, and put the Aviano B2s on their runways. But by no means is there to be Russian airspace penetration. Is that clear, General?"

"Yes, ma'am."

"Director, Homeland on the line."

"Yes, Madam Vice President?"

She explained the Washington State situation.

"I need to have papers federalizing the Washington State National Guard in here before me in the White House bunker in five minutes. Please coordinate with Nari."

"Yes, ma'am."

"Madam President," the marine commandant said, waiting for her to hang up. "Your plan gives Russian air defenses ample time to prepare."

She shook her head. "It can take our bombers hours to reach Russian targets, General. If their air defenses can't use the time they already have, a few more minutes will make no—"

The speaker scratched itself awake.

Everyone stopped to listen, but no words followed.

The VP sighed. "General Caddel, I need to be sworn in."

"Yes, but we can't have fifteen clergy down here in the bunker, for heaven's sake."

"Maybe, for heaven's sake, we should, but I understand." She turned to her chief of staff. "Nari, can you select one and have them come down here? Chairman Caddel, that would solve the chain of command issue at once. Is one minister acceptable?"

"Yes," the general said. She saw that his attention was on the telescreen.

"One minute to impact."

"This weapon is not going to MIRV," the chief of staff air force said.

"What, General Hooks?" the VP asked. "It won't disperse its weapons?"

"No, because the distance between the launch site and the target is so small that the missile can't reach altitude to deploy properly. One missile, one tremendous detonation that will be heard all the way to Idaho."

"So," the president said, "Putin is throwing away one of his best submarines to launch a top-of-the-line missile improperly that can't even deliver its entire payload as it should on an inexplicable target. Am I hearing you correctly?"

"Yes, ma'am, you are."

"General Stewert."

He stepped forward at once. "Yes, ma'am."

"Commandant, I will take all steps to defend this nation including assuming an aggressive posture. However, I am not kill millions by attacking the Russian federation."

"You can't have both, ma'am. We either are going to be passive or need to knock hell out of them."

"There are—"

"Here is the minister, and we have a Bible."

"Madam Vice President, I am Maria Cortez."

The short woman had the most intense dark eyes the vice president had ever seen.

"We need a photograph and some witnesses," Llewellyn said.

"Let's go over here to the side of the room," said Nari.

The speaker scratched to life. "NMCC here. Fifteen seconds to impact."

"… solemnly swear that I will faithfully execute the Office of President of the United States."

"And will to the best of your abilit—"

"Ten seconds."

"And will to the best of my ability …"

"Preserve, protect, and defend the Constitution of the United St—"

"Five seconds."

"—Preserve, protect, and defend the Constitution of the United States."

"So help you God."

"So help me God."

"Note the time," General Hooks called out. "Two, one … now."

"Impact."

The telescreen's thump and vibration marked the first nuclear strike upon the homeland of the United States of America.

SILVER PUCKS

Two hours later, Katie Richards, member of Portland Fire and Rescue, Department 404, exited her truck to see a white teenaged girl on fire hurled against the remnant of a concrete statue by another hot blast wave.

Katie lumbered over in her cumbersome equipment, her muscles crying that she was consuming more of the dwindling oxygen in her tank. Looking around through her smoke-stained visor, she pulled a smoldering blanket over, putting out the fire consuming the girl's limbs.

"You're better now," Katie said, holding the girl close to her, rocking her, then stopped, seeing blood flow freely from the teenager's partially decapitated head, running onto the sweltering, dirty road.

She put the body down, patting it with her thick yellow gloves.

Then standing, looking at the hell that had come calling on her beloved Portland today, Katie cried out behind her mask.

Fire roared around her as mini explosions blew concrete out from demolished buildings. The smell of burning flesh was everywhere. But there was ... something. It came through her mask, some unknown that she should know. She didn't know what radiation smelled like or even that it had a smell, but this was odd, like thick liquid that would choke you.

"Strange, very strange," she said out loud.

She walked north, over to a small park observing the same thing she'd now seen for two hours—people, naked, running, and on fire.

Seeing a young woman who lay coughing, unable to lift her head from the soaked grass, Katie ran over, lifting her to a sitting position, then tapping her back to help her cough up the toxic sludge.

After the firewoman's preliminary assessment, Katie asked, "What's your name, sweetie?"

"Jenna."

"What did you hear and see?"

"All the windows blew out. Black, stinky smoke everywhere. All you could see was fire," the twenty something young African American who looked sixty said.

Debris in her hair, shirt and pants in tatters, gray-black skin, trembling, she sat in the wet grass, running her hands through her hair again and again.

"And what is that smell?" she cried out as black pungent smoke rolled by.

It hit her. There was only one smell like this.

Rocket fuel.

But from a nuclear blast?

She looked north toward the 30B where thick smoke rose. *A missile remnant?* Above, just black sky.

This makes no sense.

Plus, Jenna had vision. In fact, Katie had encountered no blindness so far. Fire everywhere but no blinding flash.

Katie saw that Jenna had stopped coughing after Katie shared more oxygen with her.

"We have to get out of here."

Her radio squawked. "Hey, Katie?"

"Yeah," she said, trying to position Jenna so she could pick the slender woman up.

"Where are you?"

"Fernhill Park, not far from the airport."

"Our Geigers are way off the scale. You'd better get out of there."

"Evacuees?" she shouted into her crackling radio.

"Bring whom you can. Not seeing much acute radiation sickness but lots of rads. Plus particulates, PFAS, diesel exhaust. The air is poison. Go figure."

Katie picked the young girl off her feet. No huge blast wave, and nobody was blinded. Lots of fire, but the pervasive smell of rocket fuel suggested that was the accelerant. Yet radiation was critically high.

At once, she got it.

"Were we attacked?" Jenna asked.

"I don't know," Katie said, carrying her across the park with its rich sickening smell of human flesh mixed with jet fuel. She stepped over the silvery-gray twisted metal pucks back to the fire truck as it started to rain.

"But one thing I do know is that we're alive, and I'm going to keep it that way."

BRUSHBACK

"The missile detonated in North Portland," Howard Dupert, head of Homeland Security, said to the president, her staff, and Joint Chiefs on the speakerphone. "Ground assets report no, I say again, no nuclear detonation, but extensive radioactive contamination."

"Casualties?" the president asked in low tones. "I understand that it's early in the assessment."

"We estimate 125,000 Oregonians have or will die from this attack."

"Howard, please get on the phone to Governor Peters," the VP asked in low tones, "and coordinate. We may need to rely on Washington State and California resources."

"I'll do just that."

"Now," she said, accepting a cup of coffee from an aide, "can someone please tell me what happened in Portland?"

"What just happened, ma'am," the marine commandant said, standing at pointing to the telescreen, "is that Russia initiated a nuclear first strike against the United States, and we must respond instantly, brutally, and totally to save our civilization."

POTUS breathed deeply, watching several heads nod. *These guys want war*, she thought. *And I don't blame them, but ...*

"General, that's a professional opinion," she said. "In fact, it may come to that. But, first, I'd like to hear more details." She stood, up walking around the bunker's table. "It seems that we have two questions: First, why did the Russians launch against Oregon? And, second, what kind of weapon was this? Others, please."

"The Russians wouldn't start World War III by launching one missile," General Caddel said, leaning forward in his chair, hands clasped, staring at her. "They would have launched massively against our ICBM complexes in Montana, Wyoming, the Dakotas, and down through the Midwest, taking out our land-based missile capability." He sat back in his chair. "Then they would dictate terms to us before they launched against our cities."

The president began to pace. "Launching a single missile sends an incoherent message. Maybe it's a mistake."

"They haven't launched a missile at the United States as a mistake in seventy-five years." the chief of staff air force said, "Not once. I doubt they did it this time."

"Or they meant to throw us off, sowing just this kind of confusion while they prepare another strike," the commandant said

"General Logan," the COS called out, "what is the disposition of Russian naval forces? Is there any change in the Russian submarine positions off the east and west coasts of the United States?"

"No, ma'am. In fact, there is a movement away from our seaboards since the strike and our sinking of their four boomers."

"So it's reasonable to assume that the Russians are not setting us up for another strike, at least tonight," the chairman said.

The president inhaled deeply, then stepped forward at once. "It was a brushback pitch."

Everyone looked at each other.

"I ... I don't follow the sports analogy," General Thompson said.

"The single missile was a warning."

POTUS walked back to her seat.

"Let's review what happened in the last forty-eight hours. We were going through an emergency transfer of power. Putin used exactly that time to launch his initiative into the Ukraine. He expected to meet gassed and crumbling Ukrainian resistance plus a paralyzed NATO command. Instead, he runs into, for the first time, German and US forces that killed his tanks, producing a shocking defeat for him."

She tapped her finger on the table.

"I think he feared the US/German assault was a prelude to a ground invasion by NATO forces. So rather than hit NATO, a move that would trigger NATO's Article 5 and ultimately be ruinous for Russia, he launched a single nuclear weapon at the United States.

"It was a warning: 'Don't invade, or else.' And the beginning of the 'else' was the three Russian boomers that we killed in the gulf."

"That explains the target," the chairman said.

"We were asking, 'What's of national value in Portland?'" she said, shaking her head. "What else could we do? But that was the wrong question. It is precisely because there is little of national value there that he attacked them. As if to say, 'I'm not trying to hurt you but just want to mess up your hair a little.'"

"And with six nuclear warheads, I'd say that he got our attention."

"He would have, but it backfired," the chief of staff army said, coming forward, "because it wasn't delivered the way he intended."

"Yes, and instead of frightening us and confirming to the world the strength and irresistible power of the strategic rocket forces of the Russian federation," General Bolivar said, "it demonstrated yet one more Russian military infirmity."

"He's trying to use nuclear weapons as language," the president said, arms folded across her. "He should have just picked up the damn phone."

General Bolivar turned to the president. "So, the question, Madam President, is how do we respond?"

FIZZLE

"Madam President," the marine commandant said, rising from his seat, "I must say that this is fanciful thinking. We don't know what's in Putin's mind. The man is a hothead. Nobody would have predicted two days ago that he would hurl his tanks south. And let's not forget that he's in a serious predicament right now. Who knows what kind of pressure he's under in the Kremlin, or even if he's calling the shots there anymore?"

She nodded. "OK." She turned to the chairman. "So what's up with their missile?"

"Well, Madam," the chief of staff air force said, "the weapon did not detonate as planned. Essentially, it was a conventional explosion that produced the kind of devastation you'd expect in a huge forest fire. However, the uranium and plutonium that it carried have now been released over much of north central Portland, spreading east."

"Making it the first dirty bomb attack," said the commandant, sitting again.

"It was a fizzle, ma'am."

Everyone turned to the chief of space operations.

"We've been tracking Russian rocket and nuclear development for some time," General Thompson said. "They've had all kinds of difficulty with the Dulava rocket, with many explosions shortly after they were test launched from submarines."

"Yes, we tracked those as well," CNO said, putting the speaker of the phone he was using to his chest.

"They also have missile guidance issues since they never converted to GPS. Hence, the rocket's last-minute trajectory deviation today.

"But a little known problem is that the Russians have had difficulty with developing nuclear weapons."

"What do you mean?" Nari asked. "They have ten thousand of them."

The stocky African American woman stepped forward. "Well, a nuclear weapon, to work correctly, has to follow a cascade of detonations," General Thompson said. "Einstein's theory doesn't mean that you just take two pieces of plutonium, slap them together, and have a nuclear explosion. All you have there is an almost imperceptible change in mass.

"Nuclear weapons depend on the potential energy that can be released from the nuclei of atoms. The splitting apart of atoms, called fission, and joining together of atoms, called fusion, are both nuclear reactions that occur in the atom's nucleus. They occur by the quadrillions but must be controlled.

"Look," she said, leaning forward. "Think of throwing a curve ball. You just can't just rear back and release. The ball will go into the dirt or into the stands, hit the batter, the umpire, or a fan. There is a difference between a curve ball and a wild pitch. You need control.

"Same with a nuclear weapon. It, too, must be contained. But here, to control a nuclear weapons explosion, the most advanced physics, the most precise mathematics, and the need for advanced simulations are required to compute how to both release and keep control of these fissionable events to obtain the largest explosion possible from the nuclear material available.

"That's tough enough. Then you have to engineer that precision physically into the bomb."

Nuclear weapons have hundreds of physical balances that must. be carefully adjusted. It is intricate work that is not done just once, but throughout the life of the unit. Think of the old sea clocks that required balancing and calibration after each voyage. That's the kind of complexity we're dealing with here.

"Plus they degrade over time, right?" the chairman asked."

"The modernization cost hundreds of millions of dollars We finished the last phase back in 2023 and we are reinstantiating a new phase now The Russians don't do anything like that"

The president noted that General Thompson was was in complete intellectual command of the field.

"As with any complex mechanical system," General Hooks said, "nuclear weapons components degrade over time. Therefore, we have a life extension program that determines whether to reuse, refurbish, or replace key components.

"The Russians have had increasing difficulty with both the mathematics and the engineering," General Thompson continued. "Plus we know they do not do rigorous reevaluations of their weapons. The problem gets worse each year.

"It's really quite surprising," the chief of staff space said, inhaling. "After the Cuban missile crisis of 1962, the Russians became experts at stabilizing the life of uranium and plutonium in nuclear weapons. This was part of their plan to seed the United States with hidden Soviet weapons caches unbeknownst to us and then trigger them at a time of their choosing."

"What?" Jay said.

"The plan never got off the ground, Mr. Secretary," General Thompson said. "The uranium/plutonium footprint was so large that they would be easily detectable by United States surveillance systems.

"We stopped them from putting nuclear weapons in Cuba, so they tried to put them here," Caddel said. "From their point of view, I suppose it makes some sense.

"But tonight," he said, hands clasped behind his back, "what we saw was the conventional detonation of a failed Russian nuclear weapon."

"Thank God nuclear weapons are difficult to design and build," Llewellyn said, patting the SecDef on the shoulder, "or else everybody would have these things."

"We've had our problems as well," the chief of staff space continued. "Not a failure by design but by accident."

She took a long breath, then continued. "Years ago, a B-52 carrying four nuclear bombs collided with a re-fueling tanker and broke apart. The non-nuclear explosives in two of the weapons detonated upon ground impact, resulting in the contamination of a two-square-kilometer area with uranium."

"So, tonight, we experienced an intended nuclear strike but a conventional explosion?" Nari asked, looking from face to face in the room.

"We've done ourselves no favors by creating these things," the president said.

PUT THE BAG OVER US

"General Caddel," POTUS said, standing working hard to control her voice, "how did the Russians put the bag over our heads?"

"I'm sorry, ma'am?"

"They had us convinced for two generations of their fierce, unstoppable military might. For decades, we second-guessed every NATO military move in Europe, trying to factor in the Russian response, hoping not to piss them off. They threatened, over and over, the destruction of Europe.

"Yet," she said, beginning to walk, "when the Ukrainians shined a light on them two years ago, the world saw that the Russian Emperor had no clothes.

"The Russian military committed blunder after blunder. They were supposed to take the country in three weeks, so the experts said. In fact, they couldn't take Kyiv, a single city, in three years. Drones beat them back. Their soldiers fled back to Russia on foot. They used cell phones for communication for heaven's sake. They fell into one military debacle after another. They used civilian punishment and torture in a futile attempt to instill fear into fearless people.

"And when they tried to reinforce their invasion with two strike forces implementing their most modern tanks, they got hammered according to a plan that an Eagle Scout could have come up with. No offense to anybody in this room.

"And then they attack us with a top-of-the-line rocket that could barely launch, almost lost its way, and failed to explode properly. So far, they haven't gotten anything right. Who are we fighting here, the keystone cops?"

She looked around, then raised her hand. "Forgive my tirade, ladies and gentlemen."

"It's what we're all thinking, ma'am," General Hooks said.

"We should take advantage of it," she said, sitting back in her chair.

"Uh, what do you—"

"We have to react in the strongest fashion," the chief of staff army said, raising his voice, "forcefully, decisively, to protect us, to protect our country, to protect western civilization."

She looked over. "I understand that we have a strong argument to respond, General Bolivar, but I cannot see killing 90 million Russians because idiot Russian leaders used failed technology to kill 125,000 Americans. I want a response that hurts Russia without killing many innocent people. Please get to work on that."

"There are no innocent Russians," the commandant said.

"If that's true, then there are no innocent Americans," POTUS said. The president turned to walk out.

"I don't think she has the balls for the job," the marine commandant whispered.

The president whirled. She took deliberate steps until she was within five feet of Stewert, saying, "Commandant, you're right. I don't have the balls for this job, but, like they say in the movies, at least I don't have to think with them.

"Jay and Llewellyn, I'd like for you, Nari, and the CNO to join me for a few minutes."

•

"Can you believe the commandant?" the SecDef said.

The president shook her head "We have no time for that now. This is what I'm thinking."

She laid out her plan. Their heads grew closer together over the map as they considered its implications.

CSM

"Every one of your scenarios has the weakness of relying on nuclear weapons," the president said twenty minutes later under the huge telescreen that had zoomed out from Portland, now displaying the Eurasian continent.

"We were attacked with a nuclear weapon," General Hooks said.

"They attempted to attack with a nuclear weapon programed to destroy Portland and much of northern Oregon, but it exploded conventionally," COS said. "They didn't kill millions of Americans. They killed over 125,000, or will have when radiation sickness takes its toll."

"Radioactive deaths," the chief of space operations said, "require a strong response."

"You're quite right. They are radioactive," the president said, leaning forward in her chair. "However, it is nowhere near the radioactive onslaught that we would have anticipated had the bomb exploded as planned."

"By the way, General Caddel," she said, turning to the general, "what if this was a conventional attack? One conventional payload, with no nuclear footprint. Would we attack with a nuclear weapon barrage?"

"I don't know."

She paused. "They intended to attack us with a nuclear weapon. We are going to attack them and attack them hard, but we're going to do it conventionally."

The chiefs looked at each other.

"General Caddel, I think that the CNO can inform us?" Nari said, scratching her cheek.

The chief of naval operations stood. "The air force and navy have both studied the possible deployment of conventional warheads on their long-range ballistic missiles."

He looked at every person in the room while he talked. "We have developed a hypersonic glide vehicle, known as a CAV, that can carry conventional munitions on modified Peacekeeper or Trident missiles."

"What?" General Bolivar said.

"We have several ballistic nuclear submarines that carry this CSM, or conventional strike missile."

"What would be the targets?"

"I want to hit their main energy production facilities," said the president.

"Then its Novosibirsk you want."

"What? That's way east, well into Siberia," said the chief of space command.

"That's right, General Thompson. It is a major geothermal and oil energy producer. Hitting it will kill a third of the lights in Russia and most of the lights in Siberia."

"There are several more geothermal centers we could take out as well," the chief of staff army said.

"Yes, General Bolivar. But let's not turn off all the lights in Russia. This war we're waging tonight is not against the Russian people. It's against the Russian leadership. This infrastructure attack will cripple their Ukrainian war effort and bring the war home to Russia in a way that does not kill innocent civilians."

"You do this," the chief of staff air force said, eyes afire, slamming the table, "you've given Putin an open invitation to attack the major petrochemical facilities in the United States. That's the Gulf Coast, New Jersey, the Alaskan pipeline, and West Coast port facilities."

"But, General," Nari said, arms out, "they would need nuclear weapons to execute that plan, right? By our decision not to use nuclear weapons, they have no lucid rationale to go nuclear against us."

"Well, they haven't needed one so far," General Thompson said, slamming her hand down on the table.

"But I want more."

They turned to look at POTUS.

"I want to take Belarus out of the war. I'd like to go after Minsk, again with conventional weaponry. Let's give Belarusians a reason to oust their leader."

"By killing more innocent people?" Nari asked.

POTUS looked over at her COS. "Sadly, yes."

"Any discussion?" the chair asked.

"I'm not so convinced," the chief of staff air force said. "The Russians, with no nuclear provocation, launched nuclear against the US mainland. Specifically, a conventional allied response to their tank assault generated a Russian nuclear response. And we think that, by again attacking them conventionally as we did before, on their mainland as we did before, they will not go nuclear?"

"That's fine logic, General," the president said, leaning forward. "But remember that, tonight, Putin and the world learned that his great strategic missile arm is rusty and unreliable. If the Russians respond with a nuclear barrage, then we hit back, but I don't think Putin will follow one failed and condemned attack with a second and perhaps unreliable nuclear strike against mainland US that will lead to the destruction of the Russian federation."

General Caddel looked up. One at a time, the heads of the Joint Chiefs' heads nodded.

"CNO, proceed with the president's plan," the chairman commanded.

"Llewellyn," the president said, "let's you, Jay, Nari, and I inform NATO. They must know that this attack on US soil, in our view, does not prompt an Article 5 response."

ЗЕМЛЕТРЯСЕНИЕ

"**T**his is my second cruise with her," Executive Officer JJ Pettigrew on the SSBN "boomer" *New Mexico* said, leaning back in his seat. "I think Theresa's earned COB."

She'll be the service's first female 'chief of the boat.' Nobody 'outknows' her on these boats, Captain. She's earned—"

They both jumped at the high-pitched whine screaming from the phone in the captain's quarters. The captain picked up the receiver.

"Captain. Conn. We just received flash traffic. Looks like an EAM."

"Did I miss something on the displays, JJ?" Captain Rhodes said, hanging up the phone as he rushed to the command center.

"No, and neither did I," JJ called after him.

Thirty seconds later, the communications officer, JJ, and Captain Rhodes were together at steering and directional control. After confirming the emergency action message's authenticity, the communications officer disappeared as JJ and the captain read it together.

"Look at these coordinates," JJ said. "We'll have to head east-northeast at near flank speed for thirty minutes before we get there."

"Fine by me. It takes about thirty minutes to spin up the missiles. You ready?"

"As never before."

Taking the mike, the captain said, "Put me on the 1MC."

'Ready, Captain. Main circuit open."

"This is the captain to all members of the USS *New Mexico*. Battle stations missiles. I say again, battle stations missiles. This is not a drill. Spin up missiles one and twenty for strategic missile launch.

The use of ballistic missile systems has been authorized. This is the captain."

"Weps, how long?" the captain asked his weapons control officer over the phone after the XO repeated his orders, word for word, into the mike.

"Twenty-five minutes to strategic missile launch."

"COB, let's get to our destination smartly," the captain said, pointing at the map.

"Aye, Captain. Steer 081 degrees at flank speed."

"XO, you have the Conn."

"Aye, Captain."

The captain slid down the steps from control to his stateroom, where he opened a safe and extracted the two keys, one for each missile. Sweat filled his eyes as he handed the two keys to a junior officer, who then, hands shaking, carried the keys to weapons.

The young woman knew that once inserted and the final order was given, the keys would activate the missile launch tube gas generators, hurling the missiles up to the surface of the Baltic Sea and into the awakening sky of what might be the last day.

●

"Captain has the Conn," the XO announced when the captain appeared twenty-five minutes later.

"XO, are we at our destination?"

"Yes, Captain," the COB said.

"Hovering depth?"

"Yes, and we've commenced launch speed."

"Very well. Ready, XO?"

"Ready, Captain."

Captain Rhodes took out the lanyard holding the captain's key that hung around his neck at all times, pulled it over his head, and inserted it into the missile-enabling console. The two command officers held their breaths.

●

In the missile room, the launcher officer watched each of her two technicians insert their gas generator keys in silos one and twenty, signaling the weapons were "hot and ready."

•

Meanwhile, in the missile control center, Weps, from a combination lock safe near the operator console, opened then removed the firing trigger. As he did this, the FTB operator prepared to issue the final launch order to "Sherwood Forrest," the huge missile room where all nuclear weapons were housed and positioned.

"Weps," the FTB said, "the panel shows the captain's key is inserted."

"Fire one," Weps cried out, pulling the trigger. The boat rocked at the missile's ejection.

"Fire two," he called again, triggering a second time, then picked up the phone.

"Conn. Weps."

"Weps, this is the XO."

"Weapons are away, XO."

•

At 11:02 p.m. (EDT), the calm surface of the eastern Baltic ripped apart as two of the *New Mexico*'s Trident 2D5s breached.

Flash vaporized water powered the blunt-nosed missiles made by Lockheed Martin to the surface, the gas generated force providing just enough momentum to lift the 120,000-pound missile clear of the sea.

With them hanging in the rain, gravity applied its inexorable force, pulling the heavy projectiles back to the sea. Missile sensors, detecting the change in both acceleration and direction of the weapon, awakened, igniting the Tridents' main engines.

The two missiles leaped into the air, their first rocket stages roaring as they generated loud, long, and high arcs, burning for sixty-five seconds.

The first stage fire placed them over one hundred miles above sea level.

The rockets' remaining stages, controlled by onboard computers, calculated the speed of the missiles as GPS data and inertial guidance systems determined changes in acceleration. The missiles, having reached their apogees, each deployed six independent warheads that hurtled down to Belarus at fourteen thousand miles per hour.

●

Minsk, capital of Belarus, whose history dated back to the Stone Age, ended as a modern metropolis at 5:05 a.m., local time.

With a deafening roar that survivors described as *землетрясение*, or an earthquake, twelve detonations were heard throughout the city. Each was a shattering hammer blow, destroying the Council of Ministers, the National Bank, the Ministry for Taxes and Levies, and the Ministry of Finance. Blasted by two warheads each, the four buildings died into an immense cloud of gray dust.

The explosions sent huge pieces of concrete weighing hundreds of tons flying through the air at over one hundred miles an hour, toppling statues, demolishing cars, and blowing people apart.

MSQ, the Minsk airport, thirty kilometers from the Belarus capital, received two warheads, one cratering the intersection of two runways, essentially ending all flight operations. The second demolished the main terminal and control tower. A third warhead destroyed the terminal radar approach control, killing all radar operations, ripping MSQ off the international air traffic control grid.

The final warhead slammed into the Minsk transportation system, tearing apart trains, destroying track on the main transportation routes, and impairing the ability of Belarus to move troops.

It took two minutes to blow the city's infrastructure to pieces and throw Belarus out of the Ukrainian war.

●

"Casualties?" the president and chief of staff asked.

"Best estimates are now one hundred thousand out of two million."

"You may want to see this, Madam President."

The chief of staff army handed the president his cell phone, showing a man hanging by the neck from a streetlamp.

"They didn't waste any time. What does the sign around the prime minister's neck say?"

"'Traitor.'"

The president shook her head, then said, "And what about Novosibirsk?"

"Successful. We counted all thirty-two conventional detonations. All oil production equipment destroyed, per our satellites. Also, the city is off the electric grid. I'd say one-third of Russian lights went out tonight."

"How many lives were lost in Novosibirsk?" asked the COS.

General Bolivar shook his head. "My best guess is fifty thousand workers and their families. But it's way too early to offer you accurate details."

"I'm going to need that for my speech to the nation," the president said, sighing.

"NMCC," General Caddel said to the speaker hookup, "any new Russian military maneuvers?"

"This if General Logan. No, sir."

The president picked her head up from the table. "General, please excuse Nari, present cabinet members, and me. Nari, let's get Chess."

"Please stay close, Madam President," the chairman responded. "It will be a long night."

PANDORA'S BOX

The five walked back to the anteroom.

"Can we get some 'whatever the appropriate meal' is?" the president said. "By the way, what time is it?"

"It's 11:30 p.m., Sunday night."

She plopped into a chair.

"OK. Jay," she said to her secretary of defense, "you're President Putin. What do you do now?"

"Well, Putin cannot control the news media any more than we can," he said, rubbing his eyes. "By this point, his people know that his attack on Ukraine was a shambles and that you are now the president of the United States."

"The world will also know that his unprovoked attack on Portland was followed by a devastating but conventional attack on Minsk and Novosibirsk," Nari added. "And many of his people don't have electric power."

"This has been a costly war for Russia. Putin will have to deal with an unhappy populace."

"He doesn't care about his people," Llewellyn said. "Czar Peter didn't care about his subjects' complaints, and that's how Putin sees himself. He either strikes back or is destroyed." He took his tie off.

"Where does he strike?"

The SecState coughed. "He could declare war against NATO and strike aggressively west through Europe. But he knows that's going to be repelled because the US has already moved considerable assets to Europe and is ready to fight hand in glove with its allies.

"He could inaugurate a nuclear attack on the west, but as we've seen, his rocket force is unreliable. And should he try, such a step will prompt a massive US response and the death of the motherland."

"How about gas or biological weapons?" Nari asked.

Jay leaned back, rubbing his eyes.

"They are fear-generating weapons, I grant you that, but difficult to control because they depend on elements on which he cannot rely. Rain and wind drift can markedly change distribution patterns. Even now, my teams are getting reports of significant numbers of deaths among Russians from the weapons he used two days as the prevailing wind and rain push the effects north. He couldn't use these weapons effectively against a city, much less a continent."

"Plus the reprisal would be ghastly," the SecState added. "These weapons are classified as weapons of mass destruction, implying justification for the use of nuclear weapons as acceptable counterforce options."

"So a conventional attack against Ukraine has failed already, and only a madman would carry out a nuclear strike against the countries that he wants to occupy," POTUS said, rubbing her eyes.

"But," Jay said, sitting up, "Putin could poison the well for everyone."

Everyone stared at the SecDef.

"Sir?" Nari said.

"Russian attacks against Saudi Arabia and the major Arabian oil producers," Jay said, leaning forward. "It would kill Middle East oil production, plus it has its own perverse justification since his own energy production was attacked."

"Goodness," POTUS said, holding her head with her right hand. "It would paralyze oil production for the world, throwing everyone into energy chaos. But"—she paused, pointing an index finger to Jay—"he'd have to use nuclear weapons, right? His armed forces don't have the strength to heave the necessary conventional throw weight."

"Right."

"And we avoid that by taking out their tactical nukes in southern Russia and their ballistic missile systems," Nari said, sighing.

"And, again, by avoiding war, I step deeper into one," the president said. *Is this my nightmare or someone else's?*

At once, she knew but held her tongue.

"The world in general and the Muslim community in particular would rise up against Russia," said the chief of staff.

"Putin doesn't care about the Muslim community," the SecDef said. "He cares about rebuilding his Russian state on their bodies and bones, and of being the twenty-first-century czar."

"I wouldn't be too sure," Llewellyn said. "Kazakhstan had thirteen hundred nuclear weapons in the 1990s."

"But they disarmed themselves in the '90s, Llewellyn."

"Oh, sure," the SecState said. "You know, Arabs may not build these weapons, but they're not stupid either."

He stood, rubbing the back of his neck. "Does anyone think that they gave up all of their weapons willingly just because Russia and the US demanded their dismantlement twenty years ago? Living in that neck of the woods, wouldn't you keep a handful just in case?"

He twisted his neck like his very thoughts contorted him. "And Kazakhstan's population is heavily Muslim. Same for Ukraine for that matter. If Russia attacks Saudi Arabia, she might very well find herself in a short-lived nuclear war with Kazakhstan."

"That's speculative," Jay said, waving his hand.

"Oh, sure it is," the SecState nodded. "Just like it was speculative last Friday that the Russians would pour hundreds of tanks into northern Ukraine."

"We opened Pandora's box," POTUS said, head down on the table. "But," she said, sitting up, "Jay, Llewellyn, we are on a merry-go-round with the Russians. Every generation or so we come right back to the brink of total destruction with these people.

"It's gone on for so long that this dystopia existence is all that many people know. One time we'll get it wrong and we'll finally have to pay the devil."

"Madam President, what do you want to do?" Jay asked.

She turned. "End it. Finally. Definitively. Tonight."

She laid out her plans.

When done, and her team began breathing again, her chief of staff said, "I have a place and fresh things set up for you, Madam President."

The president, worn down, followed Nari out of the room.

The secretary of defense and secretary of state looked at each other across the conference room. "Well," Jay said, "good thing we know where our dual key security cards are."

DEBRIS

President Putin sat in his office after he hung the phone up. He stared at the long gray wall with its paintings of previous Russian leaders. *I will be the last*, he thought. So much the better.

He looked for his signal officer to inaugurate the mother of wars.

Where is he?

Puzzled, he walked to and opened the heavy door to the hallway.

Still didn't see him.

He looked left down the long hall. He didn't see anybody. Turning to his right, he saw a soldier lying on the floor. He opened his mouth to command him.

•

The soldier lying in the prone position didn't say a word as he squeezed the trigger once.

Putin's head exploded, the bullet lifting the president's small body into the air and throwing it backward onto the bloodstained wall. What was left of the president collapsed in a crumbled heap on the floor, his legs quivering as they tried to interpret nerve impulses from a brain sputtering to a sloppy halt.

The soldier made a phone call on his cell phone, then, taking his rifle, left.

Moments later, the Russian prime minister as well as the senior leaders of the presidium walked out from around the corner and strode to the dead body.

The prime minister, consumed with anger at the insolent dead man, looked around at all the other leaders, then, raging, he kicked the president's body hard. He kicked, then kicked again, the brutality of the blows reflecting his fury at the man who brought the Rodina to the edge of ruin. One, then another, then all joined in, shouting, cursing, kicking, and stomping the dead president until he was a liquid soup of tissue and broken bones in a filthy suit. Then they left.

In two hours, the debris was cleaned away, and a new man stepped into his office.

MIDDLE OF THINGS

"**I**'m trying to think of what I'm going to say to the nation, but I'm not really absorbed at all myself yet," the president said to Nari and Chess as they sat in the side room adjacent to the situation room after she had briefed her press secretary.

She could find no energy. She had been in the PEOC for fourteen hours, and that was after following the tank engagement in southern Russia. She had rested some, but four hours felt like four minutes.

At least for a bit.

"You have to remember that the American people will know little about this," Chess said in low tones. "So you have to explain to them in clear, simple language what the facts are. And where we stand now. I mean, we are not at the end of this thing. We're in the middle. Who knows what will happen today? Maybe it's the last day. Jesus."

"Madam President," Nari said, "I agree with Chess. This is not the speech to give explanations and motivations. It is just to say to them where we are and that America is ready for anything."

A staff officer knocked on the door and, at the president's beckoning, came in.

"Madam President, we need you."

The president stood. "Lead the way. Chess, Nari and I will brief you when we return."

"I'm not sure I want to know."

Nari turned to him placing a tired hand on his shoulder. "Today, we are stronger than we were ever meant to be."

DICTATE TERMS

The president and her chief of staff entered the PEOC. It was remarkable what a few minutes had done, POTUS thought. All the food in the bunker was gone and the table cleaned. There had been a change in staff.

I feel like I've been here all month.

She looked at General Caddel. The brown bags hung even heavier below his eyes. "Well, General, where are they striking now?"

"On the phone, Madam President," the chairman of Joint Chiefs of Staff said, holding out the black receiver to her. "Someone who says that he is the new Russian president wants to talk to you."

With no prepared remarks, the president paused. Then Saudi Arabia and the potential for future conflict welled up. Confrontation after confrontation, for seventy years now, with many believing that each morning was not the beginning of a new day but the end of humanity. Mankind could not go on this way.

Her blood boiled. *This must end, and so help me it will end today.*

"Are you all right?" Nari asked, gently tapping her arm.

"Nari, I am better now." She touched her COS on the shoulder. "You should know how much I rely on you."

"You'd better," the COS said with a smile.

She took it, ordering the Joint Chiefs, the SecState, the SecDef, and COS to pick up, and sat down, raging inside. "This is the president of the United States. To whom am I speaking?" her voice said, steady.

"You are speaking to Andre Lagoshin, the president of Russia."

She gritted her teeth. "I would have thought I'd be speaking to President Putin."

"He is not relevant anymore."

"Well, given that it was President Putin who started this debacle, I think he's quite relevant."

"Let me be clear. He is no longer in office, Madam President. I am the president now, as I said."

"What do you want?"

"I am not calling to exacerbate issues but to assuage them. Russia will not engage in any more nuclear weapon launches at the United States or its allies. I am proposing that together we build down our military alert status today, returning to our usual watchful states. Do you agree?"

The president looked at her chief of staff for a moment.

"No, I don't."

She noticed everybody was looking at her.

"I want more than that."

After a pause, "What do you have in mind, Madam President?"

"We will step down from DEFCON 3 at once," she said, nodding to General Caddel. "However, at midnight, Greenwich Meridian Time, Tuesday, I want a complete ceasefire in Ukraine. In two weeks, I want all Russian military forces out of Ukraine. In three weeks, they are to be out of Crimea."

"I also want the commitment of Russia to rebuild Ukraine with material and financial resources. All Ukrainian children are to be returned to Ukraine and all POWs exchanged under United Nations supervision."

Silence.

"Is there anything else, Madam President?"

"Yes, there is, sir. NATO forces will withdraw six hundred miles to the west, back from Russia. We will not be a threat to you."

She heard the stirring around her and swiped her hand through the air, demanding silence.

"I understand," the Russian president said. "This is acceptable. We want the restoration of peace as well."

"Good, because I'm going to ask that NATO accept Russia as a member."

Someone gasped.

She held her hand up now, demanding silence as she felt the new Russian president's relief pour through the phone. "Madam President, I have to say, that is a very generous offer. When can we join?"

She looked at Llewellyn, saying, "One week after the UN has certified that you have decommissioned all nuclear weapons and delivery systems, including ICBMs, mobile missiles, cruise missiles, and SLBMs."

Both the phone and the room were dead silent.

Finally, the Russian president said, enunciating each word carefully. "This is not a decision that I can make on my own."

She gripped the phone, a tight rein on her anger. "President Sarkov, your previous president made terrible decisions, apparently on his own. His recent ones almost pulled the world into nuclear hellfire. I suggest that you make this one and make it stick to reverse the damage he has wrought."

"Who are you to tell sovereign Russia to decommission?" the voice sputtered, mouth filled with bile. "Who are you to demand what we should do? You're the only country that has used nuclear weapons. Why aren't you being told to destroy yours?"

Straight out of the Russian can, she thought. "Because our use of nuclear weapons on Hiroshima and Nagasaki ended a war. Russia yesterday inaugurated a war with nuclear weapons. You bully countries to do as you say, threatening them with nuclear holocaust if they don't, then protest in false outrage when countries organize against you. That is not tolerable in the twenty-first century.

"Based on your actions during the past twenty-four hours, you are now a pariah among nations of the world because you cannot manage the weapons that you have produced."

"We have a right to self-defense."

"Not with nuclear weapons after that shameful attack yesterday. But that is why NATO will admit you. As you know, most members of NATO do not have nuclear weapons."

"You are asking us to disarm before the world," he said into his phone, striking the table.

"Because you do not know how to use them. In fact, you never have."

"Still, I don't know if we can do this."

"Oh, it is very easy to do. The question is if you want to."

She took a breath. "I want to be very clear with you, Mr. President. Do not agree to this peaceful decommissioning, and we will do it ourselves with prejudice. I have demonstrated tonight what our weaponry can do to Russia and to your ally."

"Are you blackmailing the Russian federation?" he said, his voice rising in rage.

"I'm saying that one way or the other, your weapons will be taken apart, never to be reassembled."

Silence.

"I do not want to take military action to destroy your weapons," POTUS said. "It should be done peacefully and with celerity under UN and NATO supervision. But it must begin at once. If my people tell me that you have slowed the decommissioning process down, then I will take the weapons in question out conventionally."

"And we will respond massively."

She let her voice rise. "Like you did in Portland? That despicable episode of yours demonstrated to the world what you cannot do. Your technology is faulty and unreliable. Our strikes, as you have seen, are right on target. Launch tonight, and I promise you that in the next twenty-four hours, Russia will suffer like she has never suffered before."

"You cannot dictate terms to us!" he shouted.

"I tell you in very clear language, sir, that the time of Russian blackmail and nuclear hegemony is over. I want a decommissioning schedule submitted to the US and UN in forty-eight hours, or we ourselves will begin to remove your weapons militarily."

"These attacks will be conventional. This is not a strike against the Russian people. It is against the Russian philosophy that you have a right to the entire world because you have nuclear weapons."

"That is not our philosophy. We are a peace-lo—"

"Mr. President, you are not talking to CNN but to American leadership. It is your *de facto* operating policy, and it is going to end. One second."

"Young man," she said to her emergency war order officer, leaving the line to the Russian leader open, "I may need your help after all, so stay close. CNO?"

"Yes, ma'am," the chief of naval operations said, standing.

"How quickly can we retarget missiles for a conventional weapons detonation on five Russian missile silos?"

"I can have them targeted in"—he looked at his watch—"thirty minutes."

"Begin the process."

"… your terms?"

"Mr. President, I did not hear you."

"Madam President, we agree to your terms."

The room was silent.

"Very well. I will have our secretary of state and secretary of defense contact your offices so we can begin this process. I am going to make a public statement to this effect to the American people and to the world."

"I will do my best to comply, Madam President."

"Don't put me to the test, President Lagoshin."

ANGLE OF ATTACK

"**M**adam President, when my heart starts beating again, I think I'll applaud you," the chairman said as the bunker exploded in relief and applause.

"So will I," General Thompson, chief of space operations, said. "But one thing I don't understand. How can you threaten a ballistic missile site with a conventional weapon explosion?"

"I'll leave the details to the CNO," the president said. "Ambrose?"

"What we learned was that one of the biggest impediments to using conventional weapons against ballistic missile sites is accuracy. It is one thing to be somewhat inaccurate with a nuclear weapon. That weapon ground detonation can be off by a few hundred feet and, through its massive detonation, can still collapse a ballistic missile site. However, the smaller yield of the conventional weapons requires that they be more accurate."

All were quiet.

"So we've done two things: one is to increase the accuracy of the missile by using GPS."

Everyone nodded.

"We also had to reduce the speed of the incoming missile and the angle of attack. This leads to a straight-down, dead-on shot of the conventional weapon on the ballistic missile site. The launch bay is cooked, the missile twisted beyond recognition, and all electronic communications with the ground fried."

"This can change everything."

"It just did," Jay said with the biggest smile she had ever seen on him.

"And you knew this, Madam President?"

"I did more than attend funerals and give bad interviews these past four years," she said, motioning for Nari to join her.

The room erupted in laughter, shaking off the hours of sweaty nervous tension in the bunker.

"Many are concerned that if we use conventional warheads on ballistic missiles that our enemies won't be sure as to what's been launched against them, conventional or nuclear. But that's not our concern tonight."

"Another issue, Madam President," the chairman said, running his hands through his hair. "We believe that the Russians have over ten thousand nuclear weapons. Over what period of time are we going to require them to drive that number to zero?"

"My tech team will drive the schedule," General Hooks, chief of staff air force, said, "but if we did three a day, it would take approximately ten years."

"Why just three? Why not thirty?" POTUS asked. "This will be a high priority for the world. It must be carried out faster than our usual expectations."

"Some of those missiles can still pack a pretty mean punch."

"That's what we've always believed. But all the information to date suggests that the Russian nuclear arsenal is in a terrible state of disrepair. It cannot be relied upon to produce a desired outcome. Once launched, some may even explode in Russian territory.

"Our missiles have demonstrated that, in fact, they can hit the target on time and deliver a weapons package that is lethal. We are going to keep that the same while we oversee their denuclearization.

"And, if the rate limiting step to decommission is personnel, then it's an easy problem to solve. But ..."

POTUS stopped for a moment, looking around the room. "I wonder if we can disconnect their missiles from central Russian command electronically."

They all looked at the chief of staff space command.

"We can't have generate EM bursts over each silo. But," General Thompson said, rubbing her forehead, "we could send an electronic signal by satellite to each missile, altering the functionality of the board. Essentially, the change would permit the board to register a 'working' response to a Russian test signal but in fact would not properly handle a validated launch order. The missile launch team would turn their keys, the board would show green, but the rocket would not fire."

"They might have spare circuit boards on site."

"That may be so," the chairman said, sipping his coffee, " but it's not the missile launch team that has the expertise to change the circuit board out. They'd have to call a repair group in to affect the change, and the strategic rocket force has over ten thousand nuclear weapons. There's no way they'd be able to respond in real time."

"Could they launch manually?"

"Sixty years ago, yes," the chief of staff air force said, tapping his foot. "But now, like us, they've gone digital."

The chief of staff army shook his head. "Certainly, the Russians would have to have some kind of guard against this electronic infiltration. We certainly do."

"But remember," General Thompson continued, scratching her forehead, "their electronics are two generations old. Their testing program is in arrears. We know they no longer upgrade."

"As old as the systems are, I'm surprised some high school student hasn't done it already," General Hooks said with a smile.

The secretary of state shook his head. "Yet one more reason to disable the system right now. The last thing we want is kids in control of nuclear weapons."

"The Russians would be furious if they discovered what happened."

"They should be angry with themselves for still relying on these decrepit systems," the chief of staff air force said.

"OK," the president, hands clasped on the table, said. "But what would they do? They couldn't launch against us, and they wouldn't dare announce it to the world because it would be yet one more huge embarrassment for them, plus an open invitation for any other country with working nuclear weapons to attack them." She leaned back in her chair. "I don't think that they would say anything."

"They could start a crash program to repair the systems."

"Of each rocket?" POTUS asked. "First, we would know it and take the miscreant missile site out conventionally. Next, they have neither the material nor human resources to carry that out. Third, they don't have the money to pay for replacements on the open market. And even if they did and we got word that another country was assembling the circuit boards they needed, we would put the kibosh on it."

"They could sub launch and, for that matter, air launch cruise missiles from their bomber fleet," CNO said, sipping coffee.

She turned to the chief of space command. "General Thompson."

"Yes, Madam President."

"These are all good questions. Please see to this with alacrity."

"Well, Madam President," General Caddel said, "it's going to be a new world."

"Count on it," POTUS said. "And about time. Please pardon me, I have a speech to review."

"One thing?" Llewellyn asked.

They all turned to the SecState.

"Why didn't the Russian president offer to go to the UN?" the secretary of state asked. "He could convert the demand that we placed on him into a plea that all nuclear weapons be decommissioned."

"Well," POTUS said, rising to stretch, "one, I think he knows that the world is just not ready to accept that proposal. It's not just the US that's involved. China, France, the UK, Israel, Pakistan, India, Iran, and North Korea would have to agree. And there is no compelling reason for them to do so. Can you imagine North Korea's reaction to a demand that they scuttle their nuclear weapons program just because the Russians launched an errant missile and got hammered for it? This is Russia's problem, and they've been told how to fix it."

"Also," she said, "the Russians never believed in the UN. Oh, the institution has been a useful tool for them when they want to play on the world's heartstrings. But they never had any real intention of following its directives. It's just who they are."

●

"Llewellyn, can you inform NATO of the result and that Russia and the US are de-escalating tonight? Oh," she said, emerging into the light, "I never thought I would miss sunlight so much. I'd love to walk to my office at the Executive Office Building."

"We can let you do that, ma'am."

She, encouraged, hurried across the street.

"Where's Chess?" POTUS asked. "We have to inform the public. Can you and SecDef work on it and get me some time at 3:00 p.m. today?"

"We need to engage congressional leadership first," Nari said, struggling to keep up. "You can freshen up and meet with them at, say, noon?"

"Why not use the White House?"

"Way too soon and intrusive."

"But you have an office there."

"Much too small."

"Even with the beginning of Russian decertification of their weapons, you can expect a hostile reaction from the Republicans," the SecState said.

"How could that possibly be?" Jay asked. "We are much closer to bringing them world peace on a platter. What are they going to say?"

"Expect anything from these people," Nari said. "But, first, get some rest."

They arrived at Executive Office Building and walked to the vice presidential suite, where the president dismissed everyone, then lay on the plush couch, planning to review the details of the last four days.

She was asleep before her head touched the pillow.

THREATS

"Welcome, Whitney," POTUS said, bending to shake the hand of the diminutive Speaker of the House. The Republican house leader, in a frumpy dress and flats, a dark lens over her right eye covering its blindness, looked like a smoker who had misplaced her cigarettes.

But the president knew she had teeth of steel that, once latched, would not let go.

"Thank you, Madam President. You must be exhausted after a demanding four days," the Speaker said with a voice so rough and husky, the president swore that she could cut wood with it.

"Nothing a ninety-minute nap couldn't fix," said POTUS, smiling, seeing that the Speaker did not. "And I'm here to tell you about all of it. Hello, Jackson," she said, greeting the Democratic minority whip and all other congressional leaders in attendance.

Over the next forty minutes, the president explained to the congressional leadership the events of her three-day presidency.

"Casualties?" the Speaker asked, looking at the blue walls, then at the desk overflowing with white paper and brown folders.

"Seventy-seven Americans died during the engagement," POTUS said, sitting back. "Those plus the unfortunate casualties in Oregon."

She's not paying attention to anything I'm saying.

"The House is going to convene an impeachment committee to hear and draw up articles of impeachment against you," the Speaker said.

•

The president leaped into lawyer mode. Perfect, absolute silence as the charge like an electric shock ran through her.

What was this? She had done all she could for her country her first days in office, and yet here she was, slapped by a house member who couldn't command children with potato guns. Her hands almost shook, but, careful not to show the surprise and hurt the comment caused, she sat still.

"Well, Whitney, I was wondering where you hid your stinger in that dress of yours. Why don't you review your specifications?"

The Speaker's eyes narrowed. "As you wish. My colleagues and I understand the complications of the transference of power with the illness and subsequent death of a sitting president, disliked as he was. There is no question that you are president now, at least for a short while.

"However, you were neither president nor acting president when you gave the order to commit US power in southern Russia, leading to the deaths of almost one hundred Americans.

"This use of US forces was beyond the level that had ever been committed before in this Democratic Party–controlled war, in fact, beyond the level that the previous president, who was a supporter of Ukraine, agreed to commit. You did what you were not authorized to do."

POTUS choked back the fact-filled response welling up inside her. *Not the time. You will not convince her. She's not the jury. Just listen.*

"I see. What else do you have?"

"You killed 125,000 US citizens."

"Oh, come now. We did not kill those citizens, Madam Speaker. Putin did."

"But if you had not inaugurated the movement against the two different tank attack groups, there would have been no need for the Russians to launch a nuclear weapon against Portland.

"A—"

Just listen. She stopped herself.

"Madam President," the Speaker said, coughing. "Can you explain to me the rationale for the US attack on Belarus?"

"Perhaps you weren't listening. I already did you the courtesy of offering that expatiation."

"Why did you use so many missiles?"

"I explained that as well. But please do go on," POTUS said, crossing her legs.

"Madam President," the House Speaker said, leaning forward. "We have enough to impeach you. It will be long, painful, and bloody, just like this Ukrainian war you've gotten us into."

"Well," the president said, sitting back in her chair, "maybe you haven't noticed, but that war is over now."

The Speaker stared at her. "However, out of respect and dignity for the office, I would like you to consider resigning. You would announce it to the nation today, and we would revert to calling you 'acting president.' You are not to announce a new vice president, who, in all likelihood, would not be confirmed.

"Also, please do not move to the White House. Just stay here at EOB, and we won't touch you." She smiled, revealing pale yellow teeth.

The president seethed. *Enough.*

Keeping her voice even, still seated, POTUS said, "Whitney, while you and your crew were concocting this impeachment fiction, I was reading about vice presidents. Upon the death of President McKinley, Vice President TR said that he felt just as much a constitutionally elected president as McKinley was."

"Well, I don't think—"

"Right, you don't think. Let me help you. The Constitution provides that in the case of death of a president, the vice president shall serve as president. That condition has been satisfied."

With a hammering pulse, fire in her heart, and ice cold eyes, she said, "I am president and shall comport myself in every word and action precisely as if I, and not the dead president, had been the candidate for whom the electors cast the vote for president."

She leaned over Whitney, fighting the temptation to pick the short woman up by the lapels as she backed her up against the wall.

"I'm the president, Madam Speaker," she said, hand on the wall just to the right on the speaker's head. POTUS put her face in close, ignoring the stale cigarette stink. "Deal with it."

POTUS saw surprise, even shock in her eye, before the traditional steel resolve returned, killing the emotion.

The majority leader of the Senate, Natalie Bousoir, stood. Stepping toward the president, the tall woman with long graying hair said, "Madam President, I think you performed phenomenally as president. I am ashamed to have had to listen to this small-minded display of ambition by the House Speaker."

"I will call before your speech," the Speaker said, pulling away and gathering her things.

The president smiled. "And, of course, I will answer."

WE DON'T GET TO CHANGE THAT

The president, Nari, and Bousoir stared at each other after the congressional leaders exited.

POTUS was stunned at the Speaker's performance, her face numb from anger.

"Can somebody tell me what just happened here?" the president finally said, holding her hands up in frustration. "I feel like a doctor who, after telling a family that their loved one is going to recover, gets punched in the face."

"Madam President," Nari said in a soft voice, "what the Republicans are telling you is that, regardless of how good a president you are, they are going to use anything they can to reduce your standing among the public so that they can take back the presidency and maybe the Senate in six or so weeks."

"I fear that your chief of staff is right, Madam President," the majority leader said, sitting back down on the couch. "Let's just think this through."

POTUS, almost shaking, sat on the sofa across from her, arms crossed.

"If the House impeaches you now, they are going to reduce your ability to function effectively as president, hoping to weaken you during the campaign, and especially during the upcoming debate. If they convince the American people that you are a fraudulent president, making decisions with little regard for loss of life, they will have accomplished their mission."

Natalie sighed. "If they get their wish and you resign, then you'll have the shortest presidency since old Tippecanoe caught pneumonia on his Inauguration Day and died. If you win the presidency, they will quicken the pace for impeachment at the beginning of your first full term, assuming that they keep the House."

The president sat back on the sofa. "Ukraine doesn't matter?"

"To many Americans, sadly, no, Madam President," the Senate majority leader said, shaking her head. "This is not unexpected."

She crossed her legs. "Forget the fables Americans like to believe about themselves. They have never been united about any war. Two-thirds of Americans either supported the British or just sat on their hands during the conflict. The main reason New Jerseyites fought for General Washington is they wanted to kill Pennsylvanians. During the civil war, approximately 30 percent of Americans let the union and confederate armies slaughter each other in their own fields and cities, doing nothing.

"It was years after hostilities broke out before the United States entered World Wars I and II. And look at Vietnam and the second Iraq war. Americans are very peculiar people when it comes to war, whether it's on their own territory or not.

"Maybe it's best that a sizable number of people should doubt what they are told about war." The senator shrugged. "I don't know."

"OK," the president said, shaking her head. "But what about the decommissioning?"

The senator leaned forward. "There's no doubt that you and your team fret about nuclear war. If it's not on your agenda every day, it's close. You have an emergency war order officer who follows you everywhere you go. You are essentially charged with saving this country if not saving the species. How could you not think about it and wonder how to avoid it?

"But, Madam, that is not the experience of most Americans. Citizens in this country don't worry about nuclear war any more than they worry about a huge hurricane striking next month when one hasn't landed near then in five years. We don't process remote events very well."

Natalie turned at once. "I think you yourself just saw this. Tell me, what was the reaction of Portland leadership when you told them they were going to be attacked by a nuclear weapon?"

"Shock," Nari responded, hand on her chin. "Not only were they not prepared, but also they had no idea how to prepare. And the fact that they only had three minutes was, well, stupefying."

"And why not?" the senator said, sitting, stretching her legs out under the table." It hadn't happened so far, so why believe that it will happen today? That's just how people are, and, try as we might, I don't think we get to change that.

"It's the same thing with decertification of the Russian nuclear weapons systems. It's going to take years to do and will not have an impact on anybody's life tomorrow. So, why should they care? What's the big deal?"

The senator stood and walked around the small office. "There's an opportunity there for you to take the high ground, I think, but you must do it fast because we only have"—the senator thought for a moment—"six weeks before the debate and another three days before the election.

"Or you could resign. With no VP, the Speaker of the House is next in line."

She sat next to POTUS, staring so hard, she thought her soul was being examined. "Well, Madam President, do you want to resign?"

"Give me thirty minutes. I may want to rework my speech to the nation." The president stood. "Please excuse me."

"I JUST GOT HERE"

The president walked into her private office, shutting the door behind her. Home to her for almost four years now, the office of the vice president seemed strange, almost alien.

She plopped down on the couch.

The speaker's performance staggered her. Nari was right. She'd fallen victim to her own expectations again, leaving the door wide open for the Republican assault.

But there was more than that. *My goodness, if the American people and I don't see eye to eye or decertification, then maybe my entire set of expectations has been off about them. I thought I understood them. But the political changes over the past eight years had so twisted—*

No. She stopped.

The disconnect was deeper than that. It's not the political expectation; it's the cultural expectation.

She had high hopes to make changes in health care, immigration, gun violence. Was she wrong in thinking that Americans really cared about those? Are they really interested in just staying in their hovels, working from home, watching reality TV, and playing TikTok?

Was Nari right? Was education in America just a joke now? Were Americans happy to be reduced to sitting on the sidelines while well-educated men and women from Taiwan, Vietnam, China, Eastern Europe, and other countries came over to give them better-tasting shrimp and faster devices?

Do we think we work hard when, in fact, we don't work anywhere near as hard as citizens in other countries? Do we think that buying a house is a right? Do we have no sense of history? Is our goal

128

to enjoy football and basketball on larger and wider TVs, getting pissed off only when we have to pay $4.19 for a gallon of gas and $2.99 to watch an Amazon Prime movie?

Who were these people? Jesus. Do I want to lead them?

POTUS breathed deeply, putting her head back on the rich leather seat.

Maybe the Speaker was right?

Not because of the ludicrous arguments that she heard just a few minutes ago but because she wasn't a good fit for America. America wanted things that she had no interest in giving.

Perhaps that's what should disqualify her from continuing as president.

So, how bad would resignation be? Her stomach rolled over at the idea, but, *well,* she thought, *let's flush it out.*

At five days, the shortest in history, her term as president would end. But, really, so what? She shrugged. She'd done a hell of a lot more than push around some furniture. She'd ended the war in Ukraine, the largest European war since World War II, on favorable terms. NATO remained strong.

Defanging the Russian nuclear threat was no joke either although the American people might just yawn. Presidents had been in office for eight years and never come close to what she done in five days.

Plus, she'd have her life back. What's wrong with that? She could leave Washington (*thank God*) of which she had had enough, return to speaking engagements, land some cushy gig at some swank foreign policy institute, and let somebody else sweat the presidential flotsam. Plus, she wouldn't have to suffer the ignominy of impeachment and maybe conviction.

When you think about it, that's not such a bad alternative.

"But, if I can do what I did in five days, think of the future?" she said to nobody out loud. Maybe only trouble. Nixon, Reagan, Clinton, and Bush 2 had all been sandbagged by disaster after winning a second term. So had LBJ after winning one outright on his own.

She shook her head. She wasn't them, and legacy just wasn't for her.

But leaving office meant opening the way for Whitney's ascension to the presidency, the first time a Speaker would be elevated directly to the White House.

Right to 1600 Pennsylvania Avenue. Don't pass go. Don't collect $200.

And Whitney would just be a placeholder for Mr. T..

Let's not forget about him.

She shifted on the couch.

If you leave, with only six weeks left before the election, the Democrats could never field a credible opponent. Mr. T.'s victory would be assured. Spewing hate and revenge, he would roar back into the White House with his bootlickers. He'd tear down much of the progress she had made plus the accomplishments of her president, allowing Russia to rearm, pouring vengeful acid on the fabric of America.

Why make yourself go through the heat? Why push yourself to your own destruction? She stirred. There had to be more.

You could save the country.

No, you can't because America doesn't need saving.

Despite the screeching of the media about the "plight" of America, the country has been through worse.

Hell, the country was born in a revolutionary war crisis. After that victory, the country couldn't figure out how to run herself, so she suffered through the Articles of Confederation and then gave birth to the Constitution.

Then transition problems. Disastrous economic embargoes. Stumbling into a war with Britain. Constitutional nullification. War with Mexico. Slavery, secession, and the civil war. Assassination, impeachment and reconstruction. Financial panics. The KKK and Nativism. Robber barons. Gangsters running cities. The depression. Pearl Harbor and WW II. The Korean War and McCarthy. Sputnik. The Cold War and the Cuban missile crisis. Assassinations, one after the other. Nam and the Movement. The oil embargos. Middle East wars. On and on.

Crises? Hell. America was always in one crisis or another. She grew through her crises. Maybe she needed her crises to grow.

But I can't deny the sense of the moment. Maybe it's just one more emergency, but America is afraid. She can survive, but she needs her groove back. Gangs and drugs. Crime. Immigration. Health care. BLM and white hate groups. Abortion and guns. Slaughter in schools and hospitals, in parades and parties, post offices and grocery stores. America didn't trust herself.

She sat up. Faith needs to be instilled.

Mr. T., with all of his disgusting behavior and childish actions, could never do that. He couldn't cure America because he doesn't want America to get better. He revels in the worst part of America, her hate, rot, and decay.

This part of America, the uniquely American sickness, has always been there. Many presidents have made noble efforts to turn the country from it and look to Lincoln's "better angels of our nature." Mr. T. likes to play in it like a disobedient child plays in the mud.

But America needs to see that these problems are dwarfed by her value, her strength, and her moral compass. She has the energy, and her wood, wet for years, is drying now. A spark of vitalism that begets new approaches could commit discipline, moral fiber, and determination to these doable tasks.

Who can rekindle that flame?

And one thing she had learned from her experience with the Joint Chiefs.

Nobody saw her ideas coming.

●

She got up and walked into her main office.

"Madam President," Nari said, holding out a cell, "the Speaker's on the phone."

POTUS took the phone. "Madam Speaker, what can I do for you?"

"Have you thought about my offer?"

"What offer was that, Whitney?"

A hard new edge slid into the Speaker's voice.

"Will you be resigning, Madam President?"

"Resign? Hell no, I just got here."

VOCALISMS

"Madam President, you'll be speaking from the Rose Garden. It's a bright afternoon. Do you need sunglasses?"

"Madam, we estimate the audience will be three billion people worldwide."

"We have received an initial copy of the agreement with Lagoshin."

"Madam, chief of staff space command, called about progress on control of individual missiles launch components. The circuits have been destroyed."

POTUS turned to her new entourage, feeling like she was being attacked by mosquitos.

"Can Nari and I have a moment, please?"

"Of course. We go live from the Rose in two minutes."

•

The two of them let the group move ahead.

"I wanted my beige suit."

"I thought black was a better look for you. How are you, Madam President?"

"Better, at last."

"Liar," COS said, smiling. "Any concerns you have vanish within seconds as you begin your talk. Remember what you know about vocalisms."

The president nodded.

"My next chief of staff will not choose my clothes."

"Shoo," Nari said, giving the president a playful push to the podium.

They both smiled.

Stepping up to the brown podium, the sun to her left, POTUS remembered whom she loved most in the world. She replaced the billions in the audience whose eyes either filled with adoring wonder or hurled hate with her beloveds, now far from here. Seeing them as her only audience, the president of the United States addressed the world as though she was talking to them.

•

"Fellow Americans, I address you for the first time as your president. While there is much to mourn with the death of our previous president and thousands of our brothers and sisters in Oregon, I must make sure that you hear and begin to understand how much our world has changed in four days.

"As I was beginning the transition of power from vice president to acting president in accordance with the Twenty-Fifth Amendment of our Constitution, President Putin of Russia used this time to launch a surprise attack against Ukraine. His forces shelled Ukrainian soldiers with nerve gas, disabling and eventually killing tens of thousands of Ukrainian soldiers and citizens. With the Ukrainian soldiers removed as a cohesive defense unit, he launched two new major tank offensives, one from Russia, the other from Byelorussia.

"This time, the attack was met not just by Ukrainian fighters but by American and German tank forces. Under my specific orders, with NATO's approval, but without general NATO military support, American M1A1 and German Leopard 2 tanks engaged Russian and Belarus invading strike forces. After one of the biggest tank battles in European history, the Russian and Belarus tank forces were destroyed. Their tanks were left in smoldering ruins. We sustained two deaths.

"Rather than end hostilities and sue for peace, President Putin attacked the United States with a submarine-launched ballistic missile carrying nuclear weapons. This attack failed. The nuclear weapon did not explode. There was no nuclear detonation on the US or Canadian mainland.

"Had that nuclear weapon gone off as Putin had planned, we would have experienced close to a million deaths. The loss of life was much smaller; 125,000 of our citizens died, a shocking and painful loss of people who were not involved in the battle but merely caring for their families and communities. We will grieve, mourn, ponder, and reflect on this tragic loss of life for years to come.

"This despicable act required an American reprisal. Again with support from NATO, the United States, under my direction, launched conventional weapons against Belarus and Russia. I say again—we did not launch nuclear weapons but only conventional weapons against Russia and Belarus.

"One weapon landed in the center of Minsk. Estimates are that ninety thousand to one hundred thousand Belarusians died. Minsk, which was the head of the Belarus Republic, is now a nonfunctioning entity, its bellicose president dead, and an interim group, seeking peace with Ukraine, is now in control.

"A second weapon landed in Novosibirsk, an energy-producing center in Western Siberia. Those conventional weapons killed approximately thirty thousand people and crippled Russia's capacity to produce petrochemical and electric energy."

She paused. "After that attack, I had a detailed conversation with the new Russian president, Pres. Andrei Lagoshin. During that conversation, I insisted on the following to which he has agreed.

"One, all hostilities in Ukraine end at midnight tonight, Greenwich Meridian time. Second, Russia must withdraw from all Ukrainian territory, including the Crimea, by October 15.

"NATO forces will withdraw all weapons that are a threat to Russia six hundred miles west, away from Russia. Russia will contribute substantial material and financial resources to the rebuilding of Ukraine.

"Finally, Russia will decommission and destroy her entire nuclear arsenal under UN supervision. This includes all ballistic nuclear weapon systems, submarine-launched nuclear weapons, tactical and air-launched nuclear weapons, and almost ten thousand Russian atomic warheads. This process commences on Monday and will continue until the task is complete. When decommissioning is complete and all Russian nuclear missiles have been destroyed, Russia will be accepted into NATO.

"We have lived under the threat of a nuclear conflagration for seventy years. It is time for that to end. An important component of that threat dies when Russia is no longer a nuclear threat to any country on this planet.

"We paid a terrible price for this victory with the loss of 125,000 American souls. They were innocent, and it weighs on my heart. Putin chose to kill them and in fact wanted to kill many more. The United States responded in a way that did not produce a large nuclear war, which we all dread, but produced a change in the government of Russia and the emergence of leadership that understands that Russia can no longer be a nuclear threat to the rest of the world.

"The secretary of state and secretary of defense will provide answers to questions that are asked by the media. But understand that I am responsible for these acts. I did not take these actions lightly. I follow the course that I believe is in the best interest of the United States. Thank you and good afternoon."

•

She walked back to the White House, and, seeing Nari sitting at the end of the hall, the president sat down.

"Anything that I can do for you, Madam President?"

She looked over to her chief of staff with eyes that felt they would melt with fatigue. "Just wondering whether all of my days in the White House will be like this."

"Oh, I'm sure most will be much more interesting," Nari said, giving her two gentle arm punches. "Be ready for everything, at all at once, and you will be fine."

OFF THE MENU

"Welcome to your new home, Madam President."

"The first polls show 75 percent of Americans support you."

"We have to schedule the debate with the Republican contender. Right now, it is Friday, November 8. Do you approve?"

"What is your vision concerning your cabinet members, Madam President? Specifically, how many will you be keeping?"

"The media is demanding a full press conference. Can I give them a date for next week?"

"Are you going to run in four weeks, or will you ask the Democratic Party to replace you?"

"The king and queen of the United Kingdom would like an invitation to visit the United States in April 2025. Can we proceed with scheduling?"

"When would you like to meet with the ex-president's widow?"

"The Joint Chiefs of Staff would like to review scenarios for future nuclear and conventional options in unexpected circumstances. They need a date by tomorrow, October 10."

"It would be unwise for you to change your schedule calls with each of the five leaders of France, Israel, Bulgaria, Australia, and South Korea today."

"Please keep your address to the UN General Assembly on the table for October 12."

"Your base needs to see more of you. Let's keep the sixteen-state campaign tour for next week on the agenda, shall we, Madam President?"

"When do you want to meet with the Progressive wing of our party? They are anxious to talk to you."

"We are in the process of making some changes to the Oval Office decorum, particularly the curtains. Can you review choices this morning?"

"The Speaker of the House of Representatives would like to schedule a meeting with you."

"Should we go ahead and schedule the traditional National Pardoning of the Presidential Turkey?"

POTUS sat for the first time behind the desk of the oval office, putting the list down, as Nari and Chess walked in.

She shared the stack of demands with them. "And that's before people know that I changed addresses. When they learn where I really live, then I'll be deluged."

"I can manage these, Madam President," Nari said, holding her delicate hand out for the list.

The president withheld them with a smile. "Some of these issues are expendable, but each of you are not. I've asked each of you to continue staying on with me. Interested?"

"It'd be my pleasure to do that," Nari said, wearing a gray suit, smiling. "To the end, however long that is."

They all laughed.

POTUS shifted in her chair. "Chess, I also want to be sure that you are comfortable staying on as my press secretary."

"I'm happy to do that, Madam President. Only one condition?"

"Oh? What's that?"

"Fewer press questions?"

The president smiled. "No promises. Seriously, how are your staffs?"

"Loyal to us and to you."

The president straightened up in the chair. "Since I've decided I'm going to stay and fight for this job, I think I'm going to need a vice president."

"I have a list for you."

The president shook her head. "I know that, Nari. You're always a step ahead of me, and I know your list is competent and professional. But is this name on it?"

They're going to hate this. POTUS wrote it down, then pushed it across the desk toward her two key aides.

She watched Chess gulp and Nari rear back.

"Madam President, you can't do that."

"Why not?"

"His choice will destroy your hold on the Progressives and your core."

"You're party will feel like you are acting more as a Republican than a Democrat," Chess added.

"And he's from red Nebraska."

"That's precisely the point," POTUS said. "When are we going to stop acting like the middle of this country is radioactive?"

"Madam President," Nari said, sitting closer, "look at all of the trouble your predecessor had in controlling the left wing of our part in the Senate on the infrastructure bill. It drove the Progressives crazy and split the party. Why double down on that?"

"We need to strengthen this party's following in that state while giving Nebraskans a palpable sense that they have a voice in this Democratic administration. It will shock Democrats to look beyond the politics."

"The pundits will kill us."

The president's eyes flashed as she placed both hands flat on the desk. "Oh. The pundits. The same pundits who said that that Enron was the business model of the future? That Ukraine would fall in two weeks back in 2022? That all Wall Street needed was deregulation? Who projected a 2023 recession? Those pundits?"

She sat down and pushed the plush brown chair away from the desk with her feet. "I'm not interested in their opinions. They are like bees without stingers, bumbling along, maybe in your way but not blocking you. Harmless."

"Oh no, you did not say that," Chess said, holding both hands up.

"Well," the president said with a smile, "at least in here I did."

They all laughed.

She took a deep breath and leaned back in the chair. "Stigs has an impeccable record. He has colleagues on both sides of the aisle who like him and push his bills forward. But let's keep this among the three of us. Nari, can you stay back, please?"

●

After Chess left, POTUS invited Nari to sit on one of the two matching couches in the Oval Office.

"Nari," she said, lying on the other, "this morning, I wondered whether this office was really mine. I know what the law says, but I doubted just the same. And then I remembered old John Tyler, who said something like 'I am now, myself, the president of these United States.' And I am better."

"OK, but he's also the only president who willfully committed an act of treason against this country."

"Yes," the president said, sitting up. "Not everybody gets it all right." She sighed. "How are you?"

She shrugged. "A little nervous today, but nothing that green tea and some quiet space can't handle."

They sat in quiet, alone, and together for a few minutes.

"Nari, I get it. In fact, you and I have spoken of VP selection many times before."

"We sure did. Gore chose Lieberman. It didn't really help with the Democratic voters, and Republicans voted against Gore anyway."

"It wasn't just Lieberman, Nari. Gore lost his own home state, for heaven's sake. But Kennedy chose LBJ—a Massachusetts blue blood choosing a good old boy from Texas. That made a good difference."

"Did it? The Kennedy-Johnson ticket got away with counting cattle in Texas and the dead in Illinois."

"But they won the election despite those rumors."

"They stole the election 'fair and square,' you mean. And LBJ seethed as vice president in the EOB after having no responsibility."

"That won't be JT's problem," POTUS said, scratching behind her ear.

"And," Nari said, putting her arms out beside her on the couch, "we had a Democratic senator as vice president, replacing you, who is now replaced by a Republican senator that the Nebraska governor chooses? That won't make Natalie happy."

"What if we ask the Republican governor to appoint a Democrat to the Senate to replace Stigs?"

She watched Nari's jaw drop.

"The only way he might do that is if you convince the Nebraska governor that Stigs will represent Republican and Nebraska interests as your vice president. And once the Progressives hear that, they will have group epilepsy."

POTUS leaned back. "Nari, your logic is inescapable." She paused for a minute. "Let's just take this one step at a time, OK? First things first. Let's see if we can get JT in here this afternoon to hear me out. You need to sit in on that."

She laid out what she had in mind for the possible Republican VP.

"Well," Nari said, "I guess we can remove the White House curtains from today's activities."

"Pity," the president said. "And, Nari, if this idea of mine crumbles, then I'll abandon the whole thing."

They both smiled.

JT

JT Stigs, senior senator from Nebraska, strode into the White House two minutes before his 4:00 p.m. appointment.

"JT, stop growing, will you?" POTUS said, looking up at the 6'4" thin, rough-hewn man, as he entered the Oval Office.

"Madam President, you do me an honor to meet with me. May I ask who else is coming?"

"Just us."

"I'm delighted. Nari?" he said with a wink. "Nice to see you again."

They all sat down. "I think that I know what this meeting is for," the senator said, "and, humbled as I am that you would meet with me, I really don't want to waste your time."

"Please, JT, "POTUS said, taking a seat on the sofa, inviting Nari and JT to join her, "do continue."

"Madam, I don't care how many Russians you killed, which I must say was good work by the way. I'm going to have a difficult time overtly supporting you as president," he said,

"JT," POTUS said, leaning forward, looking the senator square in the eye, faces not more than a foot apart, "I don't give a damn about that. I want to know whether you'll serve with me as my vice president of the United States."

She watched his countenance change from furrowed brow-fierce determination to childlike befuddlement.

"JT, you are a good friend, and I don't want to steamroll you. Let's take a break and get some refreshments. What's your pleasure?"

"How about a glass of illumination," he said, smiling.

"We all need that," Nari said. They all laughed.

"Well, I'll leave you two to the Diet Cokes," POTUS said. "I get my illumination from grape Nehi."

The big man uncrossed his legs. "I didn't know that they still made those."

"That was my first executive order. Starting today, the White House will stock grape Nehi at all times."

They laughed again.

"How do you feel your first day here?" JT asked after the drinks arrived.

The president thought for a moment, biting her lower lip. "I always thought that coming in this office, sitting in that chair behind the marvelous wooden desk, following so many great men, that it would be far more stressful than it actually was."

"But—"

"I think the first four or five days during the transition with all the angst and military maneuvers and consequences seared that out of me. I'm doing much better today than I expected, at least so far. After all, the day is still young."

"Isn't that the truth?" JT said.

●

"JT," POTUS said, leaning forward over her knees, "for four years, I have had the job that I just offered to you. It was a sinecure, and I have no interest in putting you through that."

"The way some tell it, it may only be a few weeks for me."

"Perhaps," she said, suppressing a smile, "but whatever time I had, I want to use wisely, and I need you for that."

"But, what can I do?" he said, looking forward.

"You can save the Midwest."

●

"You want me to oversee a Blue Panel Report on how to salvage that region?"

She waved her hand toward the left side of the Oval Office, stacked two feet high with blue, red, and gray binders.

"Those are reports on the destruction of the Midwest that I have digested. We both know the disease, JT. What we need is the cure, not another set of expert opinions."

"What has happened in the Midwest during our lifetime, in fact on our watch, is a travesty," the president said, now taking deep breaths.

"And a man-made one," Nari said, shaking her head. "Loss of manufacturing and jobs, lack of education, drugs, poverty, the degradation of health care."

"In countless communities and counties, these Americans bore the burdens and became the backbone of our society," POTUS said. "And now we have abandoned them. And then there is the worst."

"Despair," he said.

"I tell you, JT," POTUS said, her voice rising, "that it is a crime against nature that suicides have jumped as they have. And what is America doing? Nothing of any real impact. We should all be indicted for willful neglect."

"American meth labs are down," he said.

"Sure. And what happened? Mexican cartels have swopped in to replace them. JT," she said, "you should know that I fully intend to fight and win the war of the Midwest. I've chosen you as my general."

The Nebraska senior sat back in his chair. "Your sincerity moves me, I don't really know what to say."

"I'm doing this, JT, because inside that massive frame of yours is a heart that cares about millions of Americans you've never met. You're empathy rules you. That is how I know that I can count on you. And I'm going to equip you."

She leaned forward.

"Let me be clearer. I am going to get you half the profit of investment banks for the next five years."

JT's jaw dropped. "Madam President, that's impossible. That's got to be tens of billions of dollars."

"More than that. The people of this country gave these bankers over $700 billion after the Great Recession. Part of that money was supposed to be lent to homeowners who were being threatened with foreclosure. They didn't do that. I'd say they owe us."

"How will you get them to—"

"Remember, I'm going to war. And I have nothing to lose. And you, JT, will be the most productive VP in history."

She stood. "Hire a staff and put together a plan that focuses on recovery. Also, I want you to run it from the Midwest. I want these people to have good access to you. You'll have to coordinate with Midwest governors and mayors, who may have good ideas themselves."

"Nari," POTUS said, "can you arrange for a meeting of the top twenty banks who received TARP money, including investment bankers in two days? I also want to meet with the secretary of the treasury and the Federal Reserve chairwoman. The three of us should meet first. You be there for all of it. I want us to meet in the Federal Reserve Bank in New York."

"That's a Saturday."

"So be it," POTUS said, casting an eye over the Oval Office. She turned to face her candidate VP.

"Let me prove my sincerity by getting the funding first. If I can't get a commitment for it, then the deal's dead. But if I can, are you onboard?"

JT stood up from the blue couch. "If you do this, Madam President, then you've got yourself a committed VP."

The two friends shook hands.

"Madam President, what should I tell them the reason for the meeting is?" Nari asked.

"Tell them the president of the United States is coming to get her money back."

"I WILL NOT LIE TO YOU"

"**M**adam President, why don't you take your coat off?" the SecTreas said as she and Nari walked into the large room burnished in dark wood and leather.

"Thank you, Terry." *I don't want to be here any longer than I have to.*

The treasury secretary took her coat, and POTUS sat at the head of a table with the chiefs of the twenty major banks. Next to her sat Nari, taking notes as always. Terry Sinclair and the chairman of the Federal Reserve Board, Julia Udall, sat not at the table but in two of the tall chairs on the left side of the dark room.

The president ignored the huge paintings of banking magnates hanging high on the old wooden walls, just as she paid no attention to the rich wood walls and entryway, the plush seats, the arched ceilings, and the tiled floors.

Looks like a church, she thought, *and these people think they're gods.*

As the bank CEOs murmured in front of her, POTUS began, her voice echoing through the chambers.

"I don't hate you all personally."

The room was quiet at once.

"No, I don't. Maybe you are good people in your own hearts. Maybe you're altruistic as individuals. But I must tell you to your faces that I detest what you do. Regardless of the money that you contribute to my party, I despise the way you conduct your business."

Quiet, they sat up straight now, hands on top of the polished table.

"Almost twenty years ago, you initiated one of the largest attacks mounted on the financial stability of this country," she said, index finger pushing straight and hard on the tabletop. "Millions suffered, cities' financial instruments failed, and one country went bankrupt. That's just as background."

"We don't tell people what to do with their money," one CEO said.

POTUS stood, walked over to the CEO and, putting a hand on the top of his chair, looked down at him. "Spoken like someone who sold a starving man a poisoned fish, then, when the man died, said, 'I didn't make him eat it.' One thing that hurts your reputation as a moral person is that decrepit logic."

She picked her head up. "It doesn't matter to me that many Americans had extended beyond their ability to buy. They trusted you, and you encouraged them to spend. And then you expect them to be responsible?

"What does that mean? Is a pipe fitter or nurse's aide supposed to come home, grab some dinner, and then use difference equations to check amortization tables? Who taught them stochastic calculus? Certainly not you, but you used it to take advantage of them. They're trying to hold their lives and their families together, and you encouraged and permitted them to extend beyond their means.

"And they did, and you got rich, then greedy, and the system collapsed. So you came running to us. And we gave you money to help repair the homes and the economies of families that you destroyed. That doesn't sound like capitalism to me, but that's what we did for you. We gave you the money, and you were supposed to begin to make things right.

"You did not do that." She paused, walking away from the CEO. "Can somebody here tell me what Wall Street's public obligation is?"

She saw one banker open, then close his mouth, saying nothing. The others were quiet.

"It is, ironically, to keep America's money safe," she said in low tones. "That mission was not fulfilled.

"What you did do was pocket the money for salaries. Now I've heard the argument that you need top money to pay for the best talent. Well, let me tell you, if the best talent generates the debacle that we all lived through, and if you reflect that talent, then you should all be fired."

She noticed the new fidgeting in the room, wooden chairs scuffing across the floors.

"Then in 2023, when we had another round of failures, primarily western banks, and we all looked around, asking what happened we learned that in 2018, you undermined an important part of the post-recession regulations. You weakened the rules and subsequent banks failed.

"And, by the way," the president said, turning around to look back at the quaffed CEO, "I have no problem debating with you, but my purpose today is to give you some new truths."

She walked around the room, looking at the back of their heads, "It's the same old story. It doesn't matter how much money you have—you want more."

"That's just capitalism," someone called out, others nodding.

"Such a tepid excuse for amoral activity," she said, dismissing the comment with a wave in her hand. "Let me tell you that in a society where money is finite and social problems seem infinite, we will no longer tolerate an industry that has run amok, taking money from any source it can simply to enrich itself."

She paused. "I understand that we have no right to all $700 billion that you received, but I do want the $250 billion back for the capital purchase program."

"We don't have it," someone called out.

"Well, Madam President" another investment bank president said, "that's a worthy goal, but that money's been spent. I don't understand what you expect us to do since that money's not under our control anymore."

POTUS shook her head. "That's not true. I checked with our treasury secretary, who tells me that 10 percent of you banks are late on payments of that money back to the government.

"Here we are, sixteen years later, and many of you still haven't paid. There is no way that you would let one of your borrowers be anywhere near sixteen years in arrears keep their property. Yet the government lets you get away with this delinquency?" She shook her head. "Not anymore. That will be corrected tomorrow."

She leaned forward. "But not to waste time, I will tell you straightaway, what I want from you is your future earnings."

"That's not possible."

"Of course it is," she said, pointing. "And to make it easy for you, I'll give you a number. Fifty percent of your gross profits for the next five years to help us fund the rehabilitation of the Midwest. In addition, I want you to loan the government $150 billion with a sixteen-year term."

"What?"

"That's right. A combination of donations and 'no interest' loans. If we can get the Midwest to thrive, then paying you back in sixteen years represents no problem."

She heard a chair scrape the floor and saw a CEO rise, gathering his things.

"Where do you think you're going, Bob?" the SecTreas asked.

"I don't need to listen to this. Madam President, you're lying," he said, walking to the door.

The president, standing still, said, "Do you see that person in the blue suit?" pointing to a tall woman sitting along a dark wall of the room "That's the FDIC chairwoman. She has identified that your bank is significantly undercapitalized, Bob."

The CEO stopped in midstride as she stood, walking over to the CEO until she was in his face.

"You called me a liar. I will not lie to you. But I will announce the undercapitalization finding for your bank. I will seize your bank. I will closed it. I will put it on the market. I will sell it at pennies on the dollar. But, no, Bob, I will not lie to you."

"Talk to my lawyers."

"What lawyers?" She peered hard into his face. "By the time you get home, your bank will be scrambling so hard to raise for capital, you won't be able to pay them."

"I'll … I'll sue."

"Sure you will. And by the time the suit winds its way through the courts, you'll be bankrupt."

She pointed the way to his seat. "One of those new truths, Bob. Have a seat."

The CEO sat.

"Light up some cigars, gentlemen," POTUS said, "and I'll tell you what I'm going to do with my money."

BREAK MY PRESIDENCY

"And what about our stockholders?" a CEO asked after POTUS outlined her plan for development of the Midwest under the vice president.

"You're problem," she said, hands folded on the table, face hardening. "But I must first tell you what … cowards you are.

"When you were taking great risk with your collateralized debt obligations, tranches, and synthetic CDOs, where was your concern about the stockholders? Their money was at tremendous risk, but you didn't care. While you were taking out insurance to make sure that you didn't lose money, they suffered. You care little about stockholders then.

"But when somebody threatens to penalize you all, financially, you start whining, dragging these stockholders out, holding them up if they are some kind of shield protecting you from being damaged for your, let's call it what it is, criminal behavior."

She paused. "But you want to be sure that they continue to make money right? Here's an idea. Cut your own salaries, say, by 90 percent. You don't need the money anyway, and, over five years, you will have distributed millions to your stockholders and investors. Also, downsize your obscenely opulent homes and get the proceeds over to your investors."

"We just can't do that."

"You have convinced yourself you can't do that," she said, standing. "Let me remind you that people do this every day in this country as they try to live within their means. You need money for stockholders. This is how you can get it, so stop crying.

"Want another thought? Lose the office buildings. Nothing consumes money like expensive real estate. Move to Jersey, I don't care. This is the post-COVID era, and the rest of us are learning that new working arrangements are possible and helpful. You're not immune to that.

"Also, sell your fleets of jets. Stop the expensive, lavish recruiting parties. Reduce your bloated staffs. Fire your lobbyists."

"Lobbyists are our right!" someone shouted, now standing, banging the table.

"No, sir. Lobbying is your right. But nobody says that you can't lobby yourself. Do some real work for a change. But"—she shrugged—"in the end, stockholders are your problem. Mine is the Midwest."

"And what if we say no?"

The room was still.

"Well," POTUS said, leaning back in her seat, "that's a good question. I certainly can't take your money. But what I can do is generate real anger among millions of citizens, tired of seeing eighteen cents interest a month on a $12,000 checking account balance to demand legislation that will tax you into oblivion."

"I will increase regulation to the point where four or five more of you will wind up being considered significantly undercapitalized and be forced into bankruptcy."

"And," she said, taking out a piece of paper and a pen, "I've been looking into having the government begin to 'write paper' again."

"No."

"Never."

"That would ruin us."

"Why get so upset?" she said, arms spread wide. "The US government used to write commercial paper from the civil war into the early twentieth century."

The room was silent.

"OK," the president said, nodding. "Let's just put a pin in the fact that most major American corporations borrow hundreds of millions of dollars a day for salary and other operating costs. They borrow money every day, essentially to stay in business just for that day.

"Seems like a terrible business model, but that's what you gave us, like you gave ordinary Americans teaser rates on mortgages.

"So these corporations come to you to borrow the money each day and then pay it back over a short time. You make money on these transactions. I'd like the government to go into that business for itself."

"You can't do that."

"Nari, please show around the draft of the executive order."

Nari had one sheet of paper, walking around the table, showing it to one banker at a time. POTUS noticed some would not look.

"I'm not telling you all to get out of the business. That's not my call. I'm just saying that the US government will write these loans at a lower rate than you."

"Careful, Madam President. You are in our lane."

POTUS walked over to the contentious CEO. "Stand up."

The CEO stood, rising to a height two inches above the president.

"Say that again?"

"You are in our lane, ma'am."

"Yes, I am," she said, "and you're in my headlights."

She stood up straighter and looked around the room. "You're all money addicts, and it's time that we stop feeding your habit and start weaning you.

"But," she said, "now let's deal with the elephant in the room.

"We all know that I may not win the November election, and then you get a new president in January. Maybe this all gets reset. But keep in mind a few things.

"First, even if I lose, I am a player in the Democratic Party, and I will continue to raise holy hell about what it is you did and how you owe the government money. But before that, I will formally ask the Department of Justice to reconsider its determination not to prosecute you all civilly.

"Third, your and your lobbyists' roles in the 2018 regulatory rollback will be publically examined. We will pull back the bedsheets and deal with the scattering roaches.

"In addition, any new investment bank, seeing the bloody writing on the wall and willing to conduct themselves openly, with salary caps and real protections for investors, will be viewed favorably by the government.

"President or not, I will generate such a hue and cry across this country that you will be considered American slime—a cross between drug addicts, pimps, and pushers. Nobody would want to put money into your coffers. No one will want to do business with you. You will be metaphorically stoned.

"Gentlemen, I will break my presidency over your heads to bring your disgusting activities to heel.

"On the other hand," she said, sitting, "if you agree, then we will accept your payments. I will thank you publicly for your generous contributions to revitalizing the Midwest. We will speak no more about this other business."

She stood to leave. "Arrangements will be made for quarterly contributions to the resuscitation of the Midwest."

"Quarterly contributions? How will we know our future profits per quarter? How can we plan for this?"

She turned around. "Don't insult America. We now know of your insipid, dishonest tricks. Any company that creates CDOs, credit default swaps, and other trash can financial instruments can figure it out.

"I need an answer in twenty-four hours. And," she said, stepping back toward them, "one 'no' sinks the ship. It must be unanimous."

POTUS and Nari walked out of the den, leaving the SecTreas to work out the details.

HATED IN THE NATION

A day later, Nari received a call as they walked in from the beast to the White House.

"Who was it, Nari?" POTUS asked through a cough when they were inside, out of the driving wind.

"We've heard from the governor of Nebraska," the COS said, putting her phone away. "The Republican Senate minority leader is mad enough to chew chromium steel, but when the governor heard of your Midwest investment plan and that you now have the money, he was all in."

They walked down the hall together, POTUS keeping her long wool coat tight around her.

"So a Republican becomes my vice president, and we keep a Democratic senator in Nebraska."

"Natalie is on board as well."

The president nodded. "The Senate majority leader is smart. She knows that we all have something to gain. What are JT's preliminary plans for oversight?"

"He will report to us and Congress as you asked. But why are you insisting on Congress, ma'am? The source of money is not from Congress."

"Just trying to keep a step ahead. They would subpoena him anyway, and I want to get the jump on them by insisting on transparency."

"They'll hammer you on 'socialism.'"

She sighed. "As though capitalism has served our dying Midwest well. Let's sit down, Nari."

The two set on facing sofas in the Oval Office.

"There's only one thing that I detest about this office, and that is I don't get enough time to thank you for your devoted attention and advice to me. I know that I don't always take it, Nari, but now you need to know that I always listen. Without you, I couldn't do this job."

Nari sat back, her eyes wide open. "Madam President, I am at a loss for words."

"You don't get enough praise for what you do. I want you to get your full measure now. I need you. I want to go to Portland again. Nari, are you OK?"

"Why?" Nari asked, wiping her eyes. "You visited them after the Russian crisis."

The president shook her head. "It feels incomplete to me. I didn't say all I need to say to those people, I don't know."

She stood, now pacing in front of the desk, covered with the fall light. "Maybe it was that we were at a tail of a crisis. They were still stunned. And I … I wonder if any words can unlock the hearts of people who sustained such a recent ghastly loss. But I don't think my speech reached the mark. Therefore, I want to go back."

"What do you want to say?"

POTUS turned, explaining.

Nari listened, brushing her hand back and forth across the napkin on the table.

"Madam President," Nari said, leaning forward, "I never heard that they ever made an offer of that kind. How hard did you have to push them?"

"They came to me."

The COS took a deep breath. "You should go. I know that we are planning a campaign trip to the West before the debate. Maybe you can include it there."

"That's a good idea. I'd like it to be my last stop. When will the Progressives be here?"

"They're arriving now. This will be a tough sell, ma'am."

"You bet. They haven't controlled the House since 2022. But the previous president hadn't really helped because he tacked more to the center than to the left. And, of course, they are furious with JT's nomination," POTUS said as she stretched out on the couch.

"How did you know the banks would agree, ma'am?"

The president turned to her. "I wasn't sure. I thought I'd have to explain it all, but once I saw their expressions, I knew I wouldn't have to go all the way with them."

"All the way?"

"Tell them something that they already knew."

Nari shook her head. "What?"

POTUS stretched out her hand to her friend.

"That they are hated in the nation for what they did to this country."

Nari looked at her, then picked up her vibrating phone. "Progressives are ready, ma'am."

"Let's go," the president said, standing. *I risk everything on this meeting.*

RANCID BUTTER

We Progressives wear our hearts on our sleeves, the president thought as she and Nari worked through the packed East Room, which was nothing but frozen handshakes and frigid greetings.

"Where's the thermostat?" Nari said. "I need to bump it up."

"I almost slipped on the ice," the president said under her breath. "I don't think anybody cared when I said little Willie Lincoln's funeral was here," arriving at long last at her place in the front of the room with its ominous dark curtains.

"But remember," POTUS said, "we all want the same thing. We may push them some, but in the end, they are our friends."

The president invited everyone to sit at the numerous circular tables each with ice, soft drinks, and hors d'oeuvres. She toyed with the top of her Nehi for a moment or two, then, standing, began.

"I want to welcome the Congressional Progressive Caucus to the White House. I asked for two hours of your time to discuss our joint role in national leadership."

She watched as the over one hundred leaders, chairs, vice chairs, whips, deputy whips, chair emeriti, and house members of the Progressive Caucus looked at each other in puzzlement.

"We are here to discuss your choice of Senator Stigs as your vice presidential running mate," the chairwoman said into her portable mike, rising from her seat. "I will say this in the clear, Madam President. We are profoundly disappointed that you did not consult us on this choice. That is not a joint anything, much less joint leadership."

The president nodded. "I know that you are disappointed. It is yet one disappointment to follow the many that you have sustained since 2020. I freely acknowledge these losses. We will discuss them later today.

"But regarding your question," POTUS said, looking at the chair, "I spared you an embarrassment. If you expressed your displeasure early in the process, and I went ahead with JT's appointment for the vice presidency, you would have been more than disappointed. You would have been insulted. Agreed?"

"You shot us in the foot," someone called out.

"Noooo, I don't think I have," the president said, shaking her head. "However, I do think that you all are shooting yourselves in the foot every day."

The room was silent.

"I want this to be a cordial meeting," POTUS continued. "We are colleagues and friends, and we need to have frank discussions. I offered JT the VP position because you were not doing a critical piece of your jobs.

"I want to save rural America, yet I fear that you don't care about her because you don't own their votes."

"How is winning them back even possible?" a vice chair asked from across the room.

"Well, it's impossible if you continue to act like local leaders rather than national ones. You've diminished your roles so much that you have given up on Midwesterners when they cry out for help."

"What's the point?" someone else said, rising. "Republicans have the region locked in by either their sheer force of numbers or clever gerrymandering. And even if we swing a few votes our way, it doesn't change the electoral college arithmetic, which doesn't help you. So why bother?"

"The point is to save American lives, regardless of the party. But," she said, looking around the room, "you have an excellent point. Spoken like the classic transactional Democrats we were trained to be." She brought the black mike closer. "But, by that thinking, we will never make rural inroads because we have given up on trying.

"We stay in our cities like they are bunkers, heads down, peering out of the holes for trouble. 'Fortress Urban America,'" she said, air-quoting.

POTUS explained the plan for the Midwest in detail to the caucus.

"That will cost billions," one of the house members snorted. "Where do those funds come from?"

"Certainly not your campaign, Elliott."

She noted a light sprinkle of laughter.

"You will read about it in tomorrow's media, but I will tell you now that major banks are contributing half of their profits for the next five years."

"You mean 'investing,' don't you?"

"No. I mean 'contributing,' as in 'giving,' Devona."

"Why?"

The president walked over to the table, pulse now hammering. "Because Midwestern Americans are worth it for me to look like a fool on their behalf. That's why."

The room was silent.

"I did what desperate politicians do, Devona. I convinced people who don't like me to help me. And I was willing to look like an idiot in the process.

"That's how much I care about the Midwest. That's how much I care about Americans. And I'm challenging you today to wake up to the idea that you should be doing the same if you care."

"Yet, but they don't give the dollars to us?"

"Exactly my point, Abbie. You didn't ask for any money from them. You don't even try."

POTUS turned around. "Friends, you need to extend yourselves, and that begins with a dialogue with people that you believe don't like you. We can't act like the fat Turkish pashas of old, waiting for the entreaties and gifts of our visitors. We have to be willing to get our hands dirty."

"Well, my constituents live in the Bronx. That is whom I must listen to."

"Really, Congresswoman?" POTUS turned, staring at the young house member. "Then why are you in Congress."

"What?"

"Seriously, why aren't you some local ombudsman or district campaign leader or Bronx borough president or city councilwoman? Those are jobs whose interests are all New York City all the time. If that's what you want to do, then resign and take one of those positions. You'll do well, I'm sure.

"But," POTUS said, "you were not elected to those positions but to the US House of Representatives."

POTUS walked closer still. "That is not a neighborhood office or a borough office but a national office. And I'm challenging you.

There are national interests that you have to learn, to understand, and to help address. And you can't do that if all you want to do is study sidewalk cracks in the Bronx."

"I have been to the Midwest," the congresswoman said through clenched teeth.

"Yes, you have," POTUS said, stepping closer, "but that was only to help replace established Democrats with new Progressive left Democrats.

"I'm not talking about an intraparty scrimmage, Congresswoman. I'm speaking of doing the heavy work, of you talking to people who are not Democrats but solid Republicans about what it is you want to do for this country."

POTUS looked up, raising her voice. "Visit with these rural constituencies. Don't be so proud that you won't get your nice shoes dirty in American mud.

"Don't sell your urban programs to them. Just listen to them. They feel devalued. Give them the attention that they crave. You will hear the same pleas, see the same desperation as you see in your own constituents."

"My constituency has been craving attention for years!" someone shouted.

"And you've been providing it, Lenny. Now, for a time, pay attention to those who don't vote for you."

She patted Lenny on the back. "I get it, folks," POTUS said as she began to circumnavigate the tables. "We don't want to open ourselves up to people who don't like us. And, yes, we don't want to fail. We have political futures to build, right? My fear is that you are so afraid of jeopardizing your careers that you won't even try."

She paused. "You want to know why your initiatives on LGBTQ+ or reigning in Wall Street or expanding voting rights fail, then talk to Republicans in the Plain Truth, South Carolina, or Branson, Missouri, or Surprise Arizona, or Craig, Wyoming. They'll give you an earful.

"Start some dialogue. Get some new information into your heads. Learn what you can do to inform your legislation, and, yes, do something to help them.

"JT's a battering ram for you. He's the beachhead. And there is money available for us to solve it. He has an over $30 billion annual, repeat, annual budget to bring change to the Midwest. What we need is the innovation of new ideas and the courage to present them.

"He will need your support, your presence, your follow-through."

"Let the Republicans do that."

"They don't have the money. Now, we do. Plus the Midwest is bereft of representation because we have deserted them and Republicans have betrayed them. That must now end.

"Stop being coastal politicians. Be American representatives. Be informed by people who don't vote for you. Connect to people in states you don't usually visit by letting them do the talking. I want you to begin to be a voice for people who are unrepresented.

"Republicans have won them over by saying what a bad job we've done, promising to do better. Then they hype the culture wars while deregulating their utilities and closing their rural hospitals, saying with a shrug, 'Well, that's capitalism for you.'"

"How can we do that?"

"By giving them something of value for absolutely nothing."

"What do we say to our own constituencies?"

"Well, Skip, as often as you speak in Jersey, I'd think they'd be sick of your voice by now."

She was pleased to hear some laughter.

"Seriously, as well informed as Jerseyites are, they don't have a Midwest perspective. They are focused on local issues."

"As should we," an older man interjected.

"No, as should your state legislatures. Our national efforts commonly fail because we can't get noncoastal Americans to support them. Why should they? They don't understand the issue. And how could they possibly understand them if we don't explain how it could benefit them?

"We don't even try anymore. That, ladies and gentlemen, is an abominable failure but one that we can correct."

"This will take years."

She laughed. "And people say you have no vision, Debbie. Show them that you care beyond the transactional, beyond the short term. It's taken a long time for the Democratic Party decay to burrow deep into the Midwest. Now it's time to cut it out. That will take effort for sure. You now need a new level of commitment to the Midwest.

"I don't have time."

"What, Leon, you want my office to manage your travel schedule for you?"

Everybody laughed.

"What if we don't support what you are doing?"

She thought for a second. Then with narrowed eyes, she stood up and walked over to the congressman who asked.

"Sure," she said, looking down at the short, balding man from Maryland. "You can sit on your hands in the election in three weeks. Go ahead. Vote for the independent candidate and throw the election to the Republicans.

She pulled over a chair, sat next to the congressman, and took his mike. "How about it, Don? Are you willing to throw this country again into the hands of a fascist, mentally unstable, seditious narcissist because you don't like my suggestions? Tell me, Don, what would he do with your Progressive agenda?"

She stood. "By the time, he and his judges are done, you can forget about Progressive politics for the next fifteen years.

"If you're willing to do as I ask, fellow Democrats, then I'm willing to throw my full and absolute support behind you and what is going to be a very difficult job for this party.

"Thank you, Madam Chair," the president said, walking toward her. The chairwoman stood up, shaking her hand. POTUS shook it, pulling her close, then whispering, "I need your advice. Can we meet weekly?"

POTUS watched the chairwoman pull back, look into her eyes, absolutely puzzled. Then she broke into a smile and nodded her head with strength and vigor.

The president walked away, then turned back and picked up a mike.

"You all may think that I'm rancid butter," the president said to the caucus. "I understand. But I'm the only butter you have, and I'm on your side of the bread."

OREGONIANS

"**I**'m so glad you're back in Portland," Governor Peters said as she embraced POTUS.

"I needed to come back and finish what we started together."

"I won't lie to you, ma'am. We need a morale boost."

"Strap yourself in, Cecelia," she said, smiling, turning to the audience as the governor sat next to her on the dais.

Now facing north to the missile strike location, north to the fallout, she began.

"I was told by some people not to come here today. And I understand that some of you don't want to see me here. This is a very unique circumstance in American history, and all emotions are in play. I don't begrudge you anything.

"I am here to tell you some truths. We all know that 125,000 Oregonians died seven weeks ago. You have heard that figure numerous times. You have heard about our response against the Russians who caused this calamity multiple times. I won't repeat any of this.

"I do want to talk some about those who died. We talk about them as 'patriots.' It is one of the strongest words we have in the American culture to describe people of great valor and honor. When we think of 'patriots,' we think of people picking up guns, banding together to fight to the death and defeat an enemy that sometimes is stronger than them. It's a wonderful and vivid figure. But it's not what happened here. And that's what I want to talk to you about.

"What was experienced here was not the massacres of warriors but the destruction of peaceful citizens in a peaceful culture. They were not at war. They were not going to war. They were simply carrying out their regular activities of life. They were going to stores.

They were arranging for childcare. Teenagers were going to high school. Parents were working.

"They simply were a part of a culture that prided itself with getting through the day with understanding, courtesy, and kindness, with focused deliberate work, all to embody, embrace, and move the Oregon culture forward.

"And they were murdered for doing just that.

"This was an attack in which the Russians deliberately plotted to kill innocent people. There was no military advantage in attacking your city. You represented no threat to them.

"They killed your fellow Oregonians because of exactly the people you are not. It was up to the United States to defend you. You've heard of the steps that we have taken. But, today, I am interested in honoring your culture and, most importantly, honoring the people who were killed or injured by radiation. So this is what I want to do.

"One, I understand that Governor Peters has worked hard to put together money for a statue devoted to the 125,000 dead Oregonians. I want to add to that. I believe that she has raised almost $200,000. Can you please stand up, Governor?"

She watched as the audience clapped and cheered. Their governor, Cecilia, appearing unsure what to do, waved back and then clapped at the president.

POTUS leaned into the mike.

"I will increase that amount to a million dollars."

The governor's hands flew to her mouth as the crowd roared in delight.

"I want that statue. Oregon culture matters. The generations of work that you have put in to build up this city, injecting your thoughts and dreams and beliefs into and through it, were not in vain. Your value endures.

"Next, I will seek from Congress authorization to build a national monument in Washington DC to the Oregonians who died. Most people in this country don't know where Oregon is, sad to say, but this statue will help them to never forget. Now, once authorized, we need to raise the money. I'm ready to pitch in, but I was preempted by …"

She leaned closer to the mike. "The Hiroshima and Nagasaki Atomic Bomb Association."

Dead stillness consumed the crowd.

"Because despite their tremendous suffering, they know your pain. They stand with you, hurt with you, and they want to help you."

The crowd cried and shouted. She turned to see Governor Peters stamp her feet with pride.

"It is an international tragedy, not a state tragedy!" POTUS roared.

The crowd jumped with joy.

"Where are the T-shirts that say 'I'm an Oregonian, damn it'?" The nation should wear them."

The crowd screamed.

"The world should wear them," POTUS cried.

The crowd shouted back.

When the group quieted down, she said, "Finally, I am asking Congress to commemorate 125,000 medals, each with the name of an Oregonian who died in the attack. And those medals are to be distributed to families of the Oregonians who died. The medals can be worn by families, or they can be encased and laid to rest in their homes. But when anyone comes into a house and sees that medal, or any individual sees an Oregonian wearing the medal outside, they will know that they face relatives of people with honor—people with such value that the Russians were compelled to kill them.

She leaned closer to the mike. "And at that moment, they will know that they themselves are Oregonians too. Thank you."

●

Across the country, Mr. T. put his hamburger down, turned off the television, and grunted.

"What do you think, boss?"

"On Friday, I'm going to slaughter her."

WHO ARE YOU?

"**W**hy don't you make a presidential decision and decide not to work tonight?" Nari said, sitting on one of the chairs in the Oval Office.

"I don't know," POTUS said, smiling. "That sounds too humane."

"Your debate's tomorrow. Your campaign has been punishing with the stops in Oregon, Missouri, Nebraska, and Kansas—"

"Good crowds there," POTUS said. "It's hard to keep in mind that the Midwest initiative is about the future, not hawking votes today."

"We fly to Atlanta in the a.m.," Chess said. "You're surrounded by people all day. Let's watch TV and see what they're saying."

"Sure," the president said, smiling. "How about pizza and a few Cokes? I'll ask someone to roll a TV in here."

Chess took his cell out. "Do you call Dominoes or what?"

Nari chuckled, then laughed, then guffawed so much that they all were cracking up.

"I tried that, Chess," the president said. "Let's just go with the White House kitchen."

"You've been institutionalized, Madam President," Nari said, still chuckling as she settled into her armchair.

"Of course," POTUS said, stretching her hand out. "I always get my Nehis."

Thirty minutes later, the president sat with her chief of staff and press secretary, gorging on vegetarian pizza with pepperoni in the small room with its tall bookcases and rich carpeting, watching a moderator and a panel of experts.

"I've had enough," Chess said, burping. "Scuse me. I'm going to get my coat and head out."

The president stood. "Chess, before Christmas, I want you and Jason to come by for dinner. We'd love the company, we all need a break, and your partner is so funny."

"We'd love that. See you tomorrow."

The president and the COS turned back to the TV discussion

"Well, let's get to the debate tomorrow. Claire?"

"This was supposed to be a slam dunk for the Republicans. Here, you have an untried Democratic president, widely criticized since she came to national office as VP. Poor staff management. Flubbed answers to easy questions. On and on—"

"But look at what she's done," Robin interjected. "She has removed the Russians as an international threat. Admittedly, she had help from Putin, who did stupid things and paid for it with his life. And we don't know how she would deal with an autocrat who was less disturbed than the ex-Russian president.

"But, you know, we have to admit she did a good job. It did cost 125,000 American lives, that is true. About as many or more Russians died as well. But Russia is now removed.

"And in addition, domestically she brought in the Progressive wing of the party. And an ambitious plan with a tremendous contribution by Wall Street. That plan could change the trajectory of a declining Midwest. We'll wait and see. But this is novel, and we haven't seen this kind of focused energy in the White House for a long time.

"What do you think, Stephen?"

"Well, that is true. Who would have thought that the vice president, who was so lampooned early in her term, would, in the face of tragic circumstance, take the reins of power and begin to mobilize and move America in positive directions?

"But she's got to deal with the Republican candidate tomorrow. He's been watching all of this, no doubt. If he's not been taking notes, his people have been, and he's going to hammer her. Look at his rallies. Oregon deaths. Socialism. She was a member of a "prior corrupt administration". His usual nails. So the question is, will she be able to take the pounding?

"You know it's surprising that vice presidents are such disappointments in presidential campaigns and as presidents. This one may be an exception, I suppose, but—"

"Turn the volume down, please," Nari said.

"You have the remote."

"OK." Nari fumbled around. "Here it is. OK." The TV muted. "I don't get these media people."

"Well, maybe not, but you put your leg over the arm of that expensive chair, and I'll have you arrested."

Nari laughed, standing and stretching on the plush blue rug. "You of all people should know that the vice presidency does not prepare one to be president of the United States any more than throwing an occasional ball in the bullpen prepares you to be a starting pitcher."

"Yep."

"And the reason so many people fail as being vice president is they're engineered to fail."

"You're pizza drunk."

"What?"

"Go ahead, go ahead, 'Professor,'" POTUS said with a half smile, rooting through the pizza remnants. "No idea how this is going to help me tomorrow, but get it off your chest."

"Most of the men and one woman who became VPs were schooled, prepared, and driven not to be the VP but to be president," Nari said. "They have the intellectual energy, the horsepower, the stamina to be the president."

"Sure," the president said, swishing her Nehi in the bottle. "We have fresh ideas, cerebral power, momentum, even anger."

"But you get buttonholed into the vice presidential slot," Nari said, sitting across from POTUS. She stretched her arm out to her friend. "It's like taking a person who's six feet tall and cramming them into a five-foot, six-inch-tall cage. They can't ever stretch out. They can't do their best. They're never comfortable. And it's worse because they know that they are capable of so much more than the vice presidency demands.

"One was so beat down that he didn't even bother to show up for his second-term inauguration and tried to run for the governorship of New York while he was still VP."

The American people don't know that or don't care to know it," POTUS said, remembering the angst.

"Right. They listen to the jokes on the late night shows about vice presidents and believe the digs are true. With no knowledge to ground them otherwise, they think all VPs are bumbling knuckleheads who can't pour piss from a boot."

Nari sighed, leaning her head back on the couch. "But the fact is that the American people don't know anything about vice presidents and don't care to learn. Ask one about John Adams, and they're going to tell you that he brewed beer for heaven's sakes."

"OK," POTUS said, burping. "Americans have themselves to blame for their ignorance. Churchill said that the best argument against democracy is a conversation with the average voter. What are they missing, Nari?"

"You can't judge a vice president based on how they do as vice president, because in fact they never trained for that role and didn't want the job. Someone who trained their entire life to be a pilot is not going to do a very good job as a flight attendant. Some are real disappointments. Milliard Fillmore took over after Zachary Taylor died and really was just a sitting vice president in the White House. Chester Arthur took over after Garfield was assassinated. The one thing he did was institute civil service.

"But there are great men who become vice president, then rise to become a good president through illness or murder. Truman rose in esteem after FDR died. TR was a stupendous president after McKinley was assassinated. And look at LBJ. Weaknesses for sure, but he got Kennedy's civil rights laws through a fractious Congress.

"So, Madam President," Nari said, rooting through the sofa creases to find the remote for the TV, then shutting it off, "we come to the real question of the night. What will they say about you?"

The president, now tired, took a drink. "Dunno."

"Well, what's on your mind?"

POTUS shrugged. She felt unfocused.

"Word has it that your last debate practice was lackluster. Are you sleeping much?"

"Not really."

"OK. You go to Atlanta tomorrow acting like this, then that man will slap you into Alabama. Why don't you just come clean?"

The president shook her head, the irritation swelling like a toothache. "What do you mean? If I come clean with anybody, it's with you."

They both paused for a minute.

"I think, Madam President," Nari said, coming to sit next to her, "that you have an identity problem. You don't know who you are."

"What?" POTUS lifted her hands, then let them drop onto the couch.

"When you first became president," COS said in low tones, "remember how excited you were to debate? And why not? You were doing well, Americans were giving you a second look, but, most importantly, you had nothing to lose. There was no expectation about winning the election.

"But now you have a decent pedigree and a good performance record, It's natural to want to protect yourself and your reputation. So a part of you is saying, 'Play it safe.' But another part says, 'Rip him to shreds.'" Hence the identity crisis."

Nari looked straight ahead.

"You're not sure how to treat Mr. T. tomorrow. You can use a tempered and even-handed approach, careful to not anger his base. But by doing that, you don't excite your own. Maybe you'd squeak by the debate, maybe, but that's exactly the approach that he would use to—"

"Yeah."

"Clean up the floor with you, and you'd lose the election big time."

The president shifted on the sofa. She couldn't believe it. She was scared. *Lord, help me.*

"Another point of view says that you go out and show the world what a fraud 'Dennis the Menace' is. You eviscerate him. Now, that will excite Dems and awaken centerline Repubs and independents, but his base will go wild with anger. That could cost you as well."

"Nari, I'm afraid."

"I know, but so what?" her friend said in soft tones, resting a gentle hand on the president's shoulder. "You didn't choose this fight, Madam, but the fight is here. There are many other people who could try to debate him, but you are the one who is here.

"Without fear, you won't find courage. You knew that last September. Good that you know it again."

"Anyone of these approaches loses me his base," the president said, hanging her head. "What's the approach that wins for me?"

"Loses his base? No," Nari said, standing up. "That's not it."

"What?"

The COS leaned over her. "The hell with his base. The question is, who are you, Madam President? And who will show up in your clothes tomorrow?

•

The president slept little, pondering Nari's options for hours. Just before first light, she saw the natural choice, the one that had always been there, waiting for her commitment.

Sleep came easily and at once.

THE DEBATE

"Welcome, from Tyler Perry Studios in Atlanta, Georgia, the first and only 2024 presidential debate. This debate is sponsored by ..."

Focused on tonight's work, POTUS wasn't listening to the introduction and a lecture on the rules. Mr. T. had wanted a no mike-cutoff rule. She told her team to accede to that as long as they got the one necessary concession she needed.

She looked to her right at the ex-president. This is a man who had pulled apart expert politicians on the stage like warm bread, one after another until he became president. Incredibly, he had done it again in 2024 to the ever-shrinking Republican contender field without a real fight back. And now it was for her to stop him. Her heart pounded, but she ignored it, knowing it would slow when she spoke.

There would be five-minute question-and-answer sessions with interruptions allowed. That's the closest to a free-for-all as any presidential debate had ever been. She closed her eyes, ready.

Opening statements ended. The ex-president was asking a question.

The prosecutor in her took over.

"Before I ask you a question, I'd just like to know, Madam, why didn't you want an audience? Presidential debates so far have always had an audience. I have fans. Don't you have fans? Why can't we have an audience?"

"Because you wish it."

She watched him stare at her for a second as he stepped backward, then shrugged, looking down at his podium.

This night will be different, Mr. T..

"I was just curious," he said, taking a deep breath. "I was told that I need to be worried about you tonight because you are a 'prosecutor,'" he continued, air-quoting the word. "But the fact of the matter is you were a terrible prosecutor. You didn't do a good job in LA as a prosecutor, so you were rescued and allowed to rise and put yourself in the position where you could be on the ticket for the Democratic vice presidential nomination."

"Thanks for the history lesson, Mr. ex-President."

"No, no, I'm 'Mr. President,'" he said, shaking a hand at her.

"You are 'ex-President to me and the world."

She stared at him, his eyes now wide and wild.

"I'm not here to defend my prosecutorial record. I'm not running for that job. I'm here to defend my record as president of the United States. That's the job I'm running for. It's the job that you're running for. And I will begin my examination of you not with a question but with a statement of fact.

"You, sir, are a traitor to this great country and should be in prison."

"I am no such thing."

"When you lost in 2020—and make no mistake, you lost— you planned to overturn the election. You proclaimed evidence that never appeared. Lawyers immolated themselves for you with claims of Jewish-related, Venezuelan-related, and China-related schemes to steel the election."

"I won that election."

She watched him grip the podium hard.

"You lost. And you'd better get used to hearing that. You fomented insurrection. You wanted your own gangs to bring weapons to your January 6 rally in DC. And you encouraged them to seek out and assault the vice president when he did not do your bidding."

"I didn't encourage anything."

"Really? Well, why didn't you stop it? When you saw the crowd that you excited surge into the Capitol building; when you heard these delirious rioters shout, 'Hang Mike Pence!'; when your own advisors implored you to communicate with your followers, asking them to stop; why didn't you send messages by text, TV, and social media to say, 'Stop this. You've gone too far'?"

"I did tell the rioters to stop."

"Sure. Three hours after the carnage stopped. Surgeons don't wait three hours after bleeding starts to intervene. Air traffic controllers don't wait three hours until after they see planes are on a collision course to act. Army field officers don't wait three hours after they see signs that their troops are going to be overrun before repositioning. That's not just incompetence. That is willful neglect, and it is not upholding the Constitution.

"You wanted to and will punish anyone who stood in the way of your being president for another four years."

She turned to the cameras.

"And I will just say to Mike Pence, I probably will never vote for you, but I respect your integrity that day in standing up for our Constitution. It was an act of moral strength, political courage, and physical bravery. As a Democrat to a Republican, I say to you, 'sir, I honor you for your courage that day in resisting this man who has the gall to stand on the podium with me tonight."

She turned to face the ex-president, who she saw was purple, turning his white shirt dark with sweat.

"Sir, do you now want to ask me a question?"

He stormed from the stage.

The president took a deep breath, letting the moderator settle herself. "I'm going to ask the moderator to give us ten minutes so that the former president can regain his composure."

●

As the minutes passed, POTUS remained at her podium taking notes.

The ex-president returned.

"You are a very mean woman."

"Grow up. I am president of the United States, and I require facts to make decisions, and I insist on getting them through tough questioning. You have given us nothing new to back your false assertions."

"Did facts help you kill 125,000 Oregonians?"

"I didn't kill them. Russians killed them. I responded in a way that will not let Russians attack again."

"Those American deaths wouldn't have happened in in my administration."

She cocked her head. "Of course not. You would have let Russia roll through Ukraine. Then with your blessing, they would have invaded Bulgaria, Hungary, and Moldavia. As you have said, you would have gutted NATO, thereby blocking any coherent allied response, and Russia would now be threatening Germany again. Can you tell me what Article 5 of the NATO charter is?"

"Yes. I just know—"

"I'm going to stop you right there. When someone says, 'I just know,' they're really saying they haven't bothered marshaling and reviewing the evidence. They're just going to inflict an opinion on us. Is that what you are doing, like when you say, 'I just know I won the 2020 election'?"

"I won. That old man didn't beat me. I—"

"Would you like another break?"

He said nothing, reaching for the water on the podium to his left.

"Good, I asked you, do you know what Article 5 is?"

"Of course."

"What is it?"

"Why don't you tell us?"

Silence.

"I take that to mean that you don't know. Why did you tell this audience you knew when you didn't? Sir, why must you lie to everybody?"

He glared at her. "I don't lie to everybody."

She smiled. "You are wrong. You just lied to over a billion people watching this debate. If that's not lying to everybody, I don't know what is.

"You can stare all day, Mr. ex-President. I want an answer to my question. Why do you lie?"

He shrugged. "Everybody lies."

"No, sir. They work hard to tell the truth. Only sick people like you tell lies because it's easy, and it gets you closer to what you want."

"By the way, Article 5 is the clause in the NATO Charter that says an attack on one NATO member is an attack on all. Maybe you and your extremist folks walk away from commitments when you tire of them, but the body of America stands strong."

"I'm sorry. Your five minutes are up, sir. Madam President, you may ask a question."

"Yes." She turned to her opponent. "How would you prevent or react to the next viral epidemic?"

"Bomb China," he said with a smirk.

At once, she raised her voice and stepped toward him. "Wipe that stupid smirk off your face. We require a serious answer, not the schoolyard smart-assing of a seven-year-old."

Then she stepped back. "Almost a billion people are watching you, sir. Be serious for ninety minutes."

He stepped back from the podium, uncertain what to do, then gripped both sides of the podium with arms straight and stiff. "I need people at the FDA under my control?"

"They are scientists," she said in low tones. "Are you a scientist?"

"I knew better than they did."

"Can you describe for our audience of hundreds of millions of people what your education in science is?"

"I don't, but—"

"OK. How about your training?"

He said nothing.

"How about your experience and expertise?"

Silence.

"Well if you have no education, no training, real experience, or expertise in science, how can you control people who do?"

"They wouldn't listen to my folks."

"Oh, and by that you mean, do what they are told."

"By my group. Yes."

"They never will. They have the know-how, you don't. In fact, laws are created to protect them from domineering ignorant administrators."

"One second," the moderator said, raising her hand. "Can you answer your own question? What would you do, Madam President, to prevent or treat or react to the next pandemic?"

"Yes. I am happy to answer. First, prevention is fought, won, or lost at the community level. I would want to rely on science, but science must do two things.

"First, scientists must apologize to the American people. Scientists got a lot right with COVID-19, but they got so much wrong. It wasn't intentional, but wrong is wrong. Mask guidance and isolation guidance for starts. The messages were stubborn, inconsistent, and incoherent."

"Second, they have to repair their relations with the communities. America is not homogeneous. What works in rural Missouri doesn't work in the Hamptons, and you can't use the same explanations. We need people in public health who can build relationships, not just read from esoteric papers.

"I'd do what she said," the Republican candidate said, grinning and pointing to POTUS.

"The moderators won't tell you this, sir, but I will. There are millions of people who are watching your performance. Cut the 'Dennis the Menace' act."

"Debaters, let's take a five-minute break."

●

As she stayed at her podium, she felt two rough jabs in her shoulder.

"If I win, I'm going to destroy you."

She smiled up into his imposing seething face.

"Save your strength, sir. We have forty-five minutes to go. And, by the way, you touch me again, I'll break your fingers."

He shrugged. "Could be interesting."

●

'Sir, you may ask the president a question."

"Thank you. It's about time." He took a long sip of water, appearing to enjoy the moment. He turned to her.

"Why are you such a bleeding liberal? Some very good people I talk to say liberalism is dying."

The president turned toward him. "Who said that?"

He stood still, and she watched his eyes darting.

"Please answer the question. You said, 'Some very good people told you that liberalism is dying.' You brought this up. I'm asking who they are. You must have someone in mind. Moe, Larry, and Curly? Somebody else? Tell us all."

He said nothing.

"Then, sir, given the vapidity of your answer, I will assume this is yet one more lie you are telling the world, and we will assume that no one told you that. In any event, I will answer your question."

"First, I will announce to this nation and the world that I am, as you put it, 'a bleeding liberal.' I am proud, not ashamed. And I am a liberal because its central feature, its core principal is that everyone has the same, constant value—that God put part of himself in each of us, and that part is the best part of humanity.

"It took a while to get here, from before the Old Testament, to the Hammurabi codes, the Koran, the New Testament, the Magna Carta, the Rights of Man, the Declaration of Independence, the Constitution and its Amendments, voting rights for women, the UN Charter. It is the basis of law in the Western world.

"And the goal of liberalism is to help to ensure the same rights, same opportunities for all.

"Now, I freely admit that this principle places a great burden on us liberals and conservatives sneer at our attempts. How do we manage white people and people of color when equity has passed some or both by? How about women? LGBTQ+? the homeless? It is hard to inject these access issues into a culture that has been consistently resistant to providing these people their rights. But that's what we liberals do. It is very difficult. We fumble, and we fail, but that's our goal.

"Now, let's flip the coin and talk about conservatives. You commonly describe yourselves as relying on the solid foundations of the past. Fundamentalism. The theocracy of the affluent. On and on.

"But you have a problem. The basis of conservatism is unequal value between humans. Take two people. One is a forty-eight-year-old white engineer working at Intel who is developing a new computer chip that will provide improved flood predictions.

The second is a seventy-year-old swarthy Nicaraguan with active tuberculosis who has just come into our country illegally. A liberal will say they have the same value. A conservative will tell you, hands down, that it's the engineer that has the most value.

"The problem with that denigrating approach is that it leads to annihilation."

"For those of you in the viewing audience who have any doubt about that at all, just look up what happened to the Huguenots who were butchered by the French because they simply happen to be a different brand of Christianity. Look to see what happened to the Armenians in 1914 and in 1923—again, slaughtered for who they were, for being of less value.

"Look what happened to millions of Jews who died during Hitler's rein. Examine Year Zero in Cambodia, the Bosnian Serbs in Europe in the 1990s, and the Hutu massacre of the Tutsi tribes in Rwanda.

"And my conservative friends, you know how this all starts? It starts by describing people differently. Who are the people who are trying to get across the southern border of the United States? What do you call them? 'Illegal aliens.' I challenge you all. That is a subhuman description.

"They are people who are in a desperate situation, wanting a better future. If the situation were reversed, then you would be doing the same thing they are. To describe them as illegal aliens is to describe them as subhuman, and, therefore, if they are subhuman, then they need to be treated differently. They don't deserve to be treated like Americans deserve to be treated. That is where you are going.

"Do you know what the Hutu called the Tutsi before the abominable attacks that led to over a million Tutsi dead? Cockroaches. That, sir, occurred in Rwanda, one of the countries you described as 'shithole countries.'"

"I never said that."

"Yet one more lie to the world. Maybe your handlers will show you the videotape."

"The word *cockroaches* was all over Rwandan radio and television, in all the Hutu communities. 'These are cockroaches.' Again, descriptions of 'subhuman' people. When we humans describe someone in 'subhuman' terms, we are preparing our minds and deadening our souls to annihilate them."

"So liberalism has a terrible burden that it must meet. But conservatives, left to yourselves, are on the road to annihilation. History shows us that.

"And never forget that conservatism eats its own.

"You may take comfort in the fact that when somebody is taken away such as the illegal alien family across the street, they look different from you, and you didn't like them anyway, so, OK, take them.

"But when they come for your Catholic family or your Croatian family or your Irish family, and your rich lawyer doesn't return your call and your heart pounds, you will need help.

"Do you know who's going to come for you, who's going to defend you?

"It's the liberals. That's my answer."

She turned to the ex- president. "Did I answer you, sir?"

He looked around. "I'm not really sure."

"Well, let me give you the sixth-grade version. Liberals value people the same. Conservatives value people differently. Both belief systems have complications and challenges. But this country is at its best when liberals and conservatives work together because that's how we get to cancel out each other's weaknesses."

"Madam President, your question for the ex-president."

"You were a terrible president and a disgustingly dishonest businessman."

"I was one of the best businessmen in the nation."

"Tell that to the string of grand juries investigating you. I would ask you to take a pledge right now saying that you will follow the law in your business dealings should you be elected as the next president. But that would be unfair to you because you don't know the law, and even if you did, you wouldn't follow it. You never studied the law about business. You've always listened to other people. You've never read it or understood it yourself. You were simply interested in how to use it to get away with something. So, no, I will not ask you that."

"I hate liberals because they riot, loot, and destroy. They are bad for America," he said, raising his voice.

"I see. Unlike those 'very fine people,'" she said, raising her hand in air quotes, "who embarrassed the nation on January 6."

"Many fine people there."

"It doesn't matter if there may have been 'a few fine people there.' Too many were traitorous criminals. That there were fine people matters little if the act was so heinous, so destructive."

"Your saying that 'there were fine people there' is like defending a pitcher who gave up fifteen home runs by saying, 'Well, he threw some very fine pitches.'"

"But, look," POTUS said, raising her hands, "I'm just trying to point out to the audience, clearly, you're not changing your mind. You are sick and need help."

"What will you do as president, sir?"

"I will get the 2020 election recertified so I am declared the true winner. Then I will have the Constitution changed so I can get two more terms since I was wrongfully denied one."

"Well, that will not work, but you keep thinking that. What else?"

"When I get to be president, I will complete what I started by putting good people, my people, in charge. And we will straighten this country out, beginning with you."

POTUS laughed. "Thank you for the attention. I'm going to do you and your extremist group a more helpful service. I will tell you why you will fail."

She faced forward. "Your extremist groups will not succeed, and you won't succeed, because they are groups based solely on anger, on vengeance. I'm not saying that it wouldn't work in other countries that have no strong Democratic roots. I'm saying it will not work here."

"Movements that succeed here focus on not just its members but on the concerns of nonmembers, people on the outside. Your movement focuses only on its rights, its grievances, its pain, its suffering.

"The NAACP succeeded not because it was a great African American organization but because it excluded no one.

"The women's rights movement included men. Gay rights included heterosexuals. They put their pain aside to help others. They were compassionate, not vengeful. And it's my sad duty to inform you, sir, that your extremist groups will fail as long as they only have room in their hearts for their own pain."

"You're a socialist."

"You're going out of turn."

"She's hiding. Tell us why you are a socialist."

"I can answer," POTUS said. She looked up. "Sometimes, socialism fails. Sometimes, capitalism fails. I'm an American, and Americans want the practical. Socialism works well for health care and retirement, especially when Republicans stop trying to eviscerate them."

"Capitalism used to work well in banking and investment, but the bankers became too greedy. They caused the Great Recession with their collateral debt obligations and credit default swaps. Then when their banks fail, they cried for a socialist solution.

"What hypocrites. And we swallowed it.

"Then, when they recovered, they once again began to strip away the guardrails in 2018, during your administration, sir.

"And, once again, banks failed, especially in the west.

"But to get to your point about socialism, let me be as clear as I can about this. I, like most Americans, want plans that work. I don't care if you call it capitalism or socialism or some hybrid in between. We want plans that work, and I am perfectly willing to concede that capitalism works in some instances, but socialism works in others. We have to stop offering Hobson choices to Americans. It's not either-or."

"Final question. Madam President."

She paused, then, drawing a deep breath, said, "Sir, where is your empathy?"

"My what?"

"Your empathy. Your ability to feel someone else's pain. Your compassion."

He thought.

"I have no use for that."

"Well, thank you for your honesty. That explains why you haven't done much for rural America, why you think Americans soldiers are 'suckers' for giving their lives for their country, why in a park with choking Americans you held up a Bible to mean I don't know what."

"I don't need empathy to make me a great president."

"You need it more than ever. Nonempathy disconnects you from the world's pain. You are in a league with Hitler, Pol Pot, Milošević, Bagosora—the worst the twentieth century has to offer. You have rejected the best quality in humans and are on track to generate terrible evil.

"We can't destroy you, but we will reject you."

"I'm leaving."

He walked out.

●

She turned to the moderator.

"May I make a final statement?"

"OK. Two minutes, please. We are running late."

POTUS looked into the camera.

"I am directing my comments to the white supremacists in my own country who support the ex-president.

"You are fellow Americans, and you deserve to hear this. There is no salvation in your quest. Should the Republican candidate win, he will use you for another two years or so. Then when he has consolidated his power, he will abandon you.

"You saw tonight that he cares about nobody. If you have any doubt about your coming desertion, consider two things. Leaders like him need people like you at first to do their bidding. Your kind rampaged through the streets of Germany, maiming and killing on Hitler's behalf, murdering Jews, Catholics, priests, people of color, the impure, the mentally infirmed. Sound like fun? They thought it was.

"And what did Hitler do to them? He killed them. And he killed their leaders. Ask Ernst Röhm.

"Second, remember that many of your leaders are now in jail. And the man who encouraged you to come out in the open and rampage through the capital, to threaten his own vice president, did not pardon your colleagues from January 6.

"He said he would do it now, but why didn't he do it then? He had every opportunity to do it. He was president for over two weeks after the Capitol assault. He didn't match your loyalty to him by taking on risk and pardoning you. You were not worth his risking political power. He betrayed you. You have no friend in this man.

"You are lost. We will help you with your anger and suffering. We are Americans together. Remember, I am a liberal. Tough minded, but tenderhearted. Put your weapons down and talk to us. Save yourselves. Good night."

ONE CAR FORWARD

"Providence is on the move," the secret service said as they walked POTUS from the debate through the cold November air to the Beast.

She turned.

"Nari? Where's Nari? There you are. Why don't you sit one car forward with Chess? I need to repolarize, and you both can together talk through my performance tonight."

"Sure."

She got in, and the entourage started. *Well, the haggis is in the fire for sure now. There's no doubt that my display alienated MAGA people, but they're not voting my way anyway.* The question was, were other voters repulsed when she pulled the scabs off, releasing all the man's pus for all to see?

Red phone rang.

"Madam President, this is General Caddel."

POTUS sat up. "Tell me, General."

"Madam President, there has been a nuclear detonation in Fort Lauderdale."

CHUTZPAH

POTUS emptied her mind, taking deep breaths, struggling to keep her pulse down. "Who did this, General?"

"Initial indications are that it was not, I say again, not Russia. Our best guess is Iran."

"Not a splinter group? Not terrorists?"

"We will have our people on site shortly, but this looks like an Iranian nuclear weapon. Plus Iranian news services are bragging tonight about their attack. One second, I'm getting more information."

The president held her breath.

"Madam, Tel Aviv has just been destroyed by nuclear strike. And there are indications that there is some kind of nuclear event in New York City."

"These cities can't be random. If it's Iran, why would they—"

The gigantic blast hurled the president back in her seat. She felt her limousine rise in the air and rotate, landing on its right side, crashing back onto the concrete, the steel frame holding its shape. Her head hitting the right armrest, POTUS lost consciousness.

•

"Madam President, Madame President. Lord Jesus. Can you hear me?"

She lay still, opening her stinging eyes, letting them rove. "Yes, but my neck hurts." She squeezed her eyes tight, trying to recall something of the night. No use.

"My neck hurts," POTUS said again. She lay still.

"We are going to take you to Emory Hospital."

She felt her vision clearing. Feeling heat on her face, she turned her head to the left, where she saw flames leaping ten feet from the demolished car in front of her into the air.

She struggled to speak, coughing through the acrid smoke.

"Nari, Chess. Where are they? How are they?" She spit on the warm concrete.

"Madam President, please. I have no information. We have to get you to the hospital."

•

Thirty minutes later, POTUS sat up on a gurney. With each of her heartbeats, a new roar of sharp pain ran through her head. Lifting her right hand, she felt a bandage that, as far as she could tell, wrapped her entire head.

"Madam President, you are very lucky."

"More lucky than many Americans tonight from when I'm hearing, Dr. Dimeson." She turned to the right to see General Caddel. "General Caddel, what can you tell me?" She turned back to the physician. "Thank you, Doctor. Will you, please, excuse us?"

After the gray door closed behind the doctor, he stepped forward.

"Madam President, first, it's good to see you. How are you?"

"The mother of all headaches, nausea, plus the obligatory cuts and bruises. Other than that … filthy but OK. I'm still waiting for Nari to return from surgery. But … but they told me Chess is dead."

The urge to cry came from nowhere, but she cut if off hard. "Tell me, what's going on?"

"Madam, I will give you a brief summary, but we have to get you out of here."

"Very well. Tell me what you can. Fort Lauderdale was hit by a nuclear weapon?"

"With an Iranian signature. There was another nuclear blast in New York City. However, that blast did not occur in the city proper. It occurred in the East River, somewhere in the western Long Island sound, close to Manhattan, but no land strike. We have a note from their mayor."

"What's it say?"

"'The SOBs missed.'"

She chuckled. "He deserves the chutzpah award of the year." She paused for a second. *Something about that word. It hurts too much to think.*

"Also, as I told you, Tel Aviv has been hit. As far as I can tell, it is totally destroyed. We have fragments from the blast site. Definitely Iranian."

"Are there any other cities that have been hit with nuclear weapons tonight?"

"No, Madam. Please, we have to get you to NEACP."

"I need to see Nari first."

"We must get to NEACP. I can't stress this enough."

"I think you are right," she said, patting his hand, "but we have more time than you know."

•

The president limped through the black double doors of surgical ICU with the secret service just after Nari arrived.

"Hello, Doctor."

"I am Dr. Stevenson. I am the intensivist. Madam, I'm afraid that your chief of staff is critically ill."

"Tell me."

"She was in the car that took the brunt of the explosion tonight. She's been in surgery as you know. We just brought her here." Motioning to the hallway, she said, "Can we sit down out here, please?"

They walked into a quieter corner of the hall, so bright that the president missed her sunglasses.

"The crush injury was tremendous," the doctor continued, bringing her head closer to POTUS's ear. "We amputated both of her legs, each above the knee. We also had to amputate her right arm just below the shoulder and her left hand at the wrist. She's also lost a tremendous amount of blood and fluid. She is hemorrhaging internally. We think it's the liver. Plus we are now getting indications that she is in the early stages of kidney failure, her remaining kidney no longer fully functional."

"Remaining kidney?" the president said, looking up, puzzled.

"She only had one kidney, ma'am. Her face is, well, swollen and macerated. She will be difficult to recognize."

"But no respirator?"

"She bucked the respirator after surgery, so we extubated. Her blood gases are acceptable, so we kept the tube out." She put her hand on the president's shoulder. "I fear that your friend has very little time left."

"May I see her?"

"Of course, but she is not going to say anything."

Leaning on the doctor's arm as she stood, the president said, "She won't be doing the talking."

POTUS limped past the doctor into the bright room of her stricken COS. The IV poles were full of bottles and plastic packs, all running into her left chest.

"Nari," she said, leaning down, whispering into her right ear, "sweet Nari, I have listened to and absorbed everything you have told me. You have saved me from me more than once. Now is the time for me to find the best of myself to save this country. I miss you terribly."

She stopped, leaning her cheek on Nari's right chest, and sobbed.

"You always were a crybaby."

Stunned, POTUS turned her face to her friend's and smiled. "You're not in such hot shape yourself tonight. And how do you get to be chief of staff with just one kidney?"

"We all have our secrets. What are they saying?"

"Nothing good."

She coughed. "No heroics for me. Listen.

"The world needs you now. Do it a favor and be a good president. Be true to yourself. Face the enemy squarely. Be ready for everything. And, for heaven's sake, make sure that your next chief of staff picks your dresses. I, I, I—"

Her friend breathed her last.

"She's gone, Madam President."

"I love you too," the president said, placing the softest kiss on her chief of staff's lips.

●

The phone rang, and the Republican candidate took the call.

"What? The presidential motorcade? How bad?" He listened some more.

"Is she dead? If she died, does that mean I automatically win?"

He hung up before his attorney could answer, running his right hand over his cheek, a diabolical face with a smile plastered on it.

•

The president of the United States left her friend's side for the last time. She shook Dr. Stevenson's hand, conveyed Nari's request, thanked her for her work, and, hobbling out of surgical recovery, found the chairman of the Joint Chiefs of Staff.

"Locate my secretary of defense, please."

"He's at NEACP."

She started limping toward the exit. "Then let's not keep him waiting."

[KNEECAP]

"**I**'ve spoken to the vice president and to Llewellyn," POTUS said to Jay after stepping out of her limousine and walking to the gigantic plane at MGE airfield.

She looked up. "This plane is huge. I've not been on it before."

"This is the National Emergency Airborne Command Post," Jay said, raising his voice over the whining of the four General Electric turbofan engines. "Its friends call it 'kneecap.' It provides a safe haven for you in time of war and functions as a mobile air command operation, Madam President."

Noticing that he was now screaming over the whining engines, she pointed to the top of the steps, and they clambered up to the plane's entrance.

"Providence on NEACP," someone said.

Jay turned. "I am sorry about Chess and Nari," he said, stepping into the plane's interior.

"Chess grew into his job," the president said, following him. "Nari was born into hers. God rest their sweet souls."

"Welcome to NEACP," General Caddel said after the hatch closed behind them.

"Thank you," POTUS did her best to smile. "I would love the grand tour sometime, but the night's events press us."

"Yes, ma'am." He let them to the center of the plane. "Chief of staff air force is here tonight. The others can join us in flash conference."

"Thank you. Let's get all the Joint Chiefs, my NSA, the NMCC, Llewellyn, the vice president, and my assistant chief of staff on the line."

"We'll arrange that, Madam." He waved to a young communications officer.

•

When all joined the call, the chief of naval operations began talking on the screen.

"Madam, they came at us with a ship-based weapons system."

POTUS sat up straight. "They launched a nuclear strike against the US from the ocean?"

"You may not remember, but, four years ago, we detected an Iranian ship steaming west across the Atlantic. They're destination appeared to be either Cuba or Venezuela to deliver weapons. We sent warnings through diplomatic channels. After several days, they turned to a easterly heading back to Iranian home waters."

"They were testing their weapon systems," General Hooks said.

POTUS furrowed her brow. "And they would launch from sea because it ... of course, it cuts the range of their strike."

"Yes," CNO said. "Nobody knows if they can hit a target eight thousand miles away, but they can't miss a southern US city from the western Atlantic."

"And they hit two of three targeted cities," Jay said. "Downtown Fort Lauderdale was badly damaged by a low-yield weapon in the one-to-two-kiloton range. We're estimating the dead there at about seventy-five thousand."

"Seventy-five thousand American deaths." POTUS's eyes narrowed. "And New York?"

The SecDef inhaled. "There, we got lucky. Our Aegis Ballistic Missile Defense detected two inbound missiles. The hit-to-kill system destroyed one and altered the trajectory of the second. It fell short, landing in the sound between LaGuardia Airport and the Whitestone Bridge, east of Riker's Island. We won't know until morning, but we expect serious water damage to the airport and the bridge itself to be destroyed."

"Only water damage?"

"It was a subsurface detonation," the chief of air force said. "The explosion flash boiled a million gallons of water and produced huge waves that took out the bridge. LaGuardia sustained heavy damage on both of its runways, but they expect to be operational in one week."

"It's an ecologic and architectural catastrophe, but we don't expect nearly as many deaths as Fort Lauderdale."

She stared at the CNO on the screen. "Aegis wasn't used to protect Florida, Ambrose?"

"Yes, it was, but the flight distance and warning time were too short."

"So we missed."

"Yes, ma'am."

She thought she was the only one who noticed the plane shuddering as it took off.

"Tell me about Tel Aviv?"

"Madam President, Tel Aviv was completely destroyed," General Caddel said, sitting, hands clasped. "Iran used three nuclear missiles fired from launch pads in southern Iran that struck Tel Aviv at approximately 6:37 a.m., local time. The explosions were ground bursts, producing maximum casualties. Out of a population of 435,000, well"—he shook his head—"all but 100,000 souls are gone as well as the great record and museums of Jewish history."

Chutzpah.

She had it.

"About a quarter of a million Jews live in Broward County," she said in a low tone. She paused. "It wasn't Fort Lauderdale they were after. It was the dense Jewish community."

"The president leaned forward. "Tel Aviv, Broward County, New York City. Three centers of Jewish culture and population. This was a religious attack."

General Hooks smacked his forehead with his left hand. "Jesus, Mary, and Joseph."

"They expended their nuclear arsenal not for military gain but to exterminate a people," JT said, shaking his head. She thought the tall man was going to cry.

"Where is the prime minister?"

"We know he was not in Tel Aviv, but that's all."

"I need to speak with him."

"And," General Caddel said, "Iran was responsible for the attack on your motorcade."

She turned to him.

"Yes, let's talk about that."

"They timed it well. The missiles detonated at their targets just a few minutes before the attack on the motorcade. They hoped to distract us from a drone that took off from a low-rise building in Atlanta just after your entourage left Tyler Perry Center. It flew below the height of many of the buildings along our route, so it wasn't picked up on radar as it positioned itself over the motorcade."

He leaned closer. "Their target was you, ma'am. The motorcade ran into a delivery man who tried to cross between your car and the car in front of you. Your car stopped. The drone operator didn't see or recognize this. He assume that the last car moving forward was your car and attacked."

If you hadn't told Nari to sit in the next car, she would be alive with you now.

POTUS shook it off, getting up to walk around the tight area. "So the Iranians tried to kill me." She turned. "But there have been no sightings of me and no news alerts beyond the carnage that you just described."

She stopped. "They think that I'm dead."

"They are using the time until your successor is named to, what, gather allies?" Jay said.

She turned. "No. To rearm their launchers."

"They may have one or two nuclear warheads left," General Caddel said, breathing deeply. "So they may choose to take this time to place them on missiles and relaunch."

"How much time, General Hooks?"

"For them, they are new, so maybe six hours to retarget, hoist, check, and fuel."

She saw heads nod. "So they have three and a half hours left."

"Here is a report from a ham radio operator in Hollywood, Florida, just south of Fort Lauderdale," said a communications operator," holding out a piece of paper.

The chairman took the paper, read it, then said, "Let's hear it."

"Local reports are that heavy damage was sustained at the 811-842 intersection north of Poinciana Park and Harbordale.

"To whoever is listening, tomorrow, downtown Fort Lauderdale will look like Hiroshima. Away from the immediate blast zone, homes and other wood structures have been demolished by the nuclear blast.

"Concrete structures have survived. Further away from the blast zones, windows have been blown out, and many roofs are damaged or wholly gone.

"With prevailing weather patterns moving from northwest to southeast, South Florida is under intense fallout.

"People nearest the blast were dosed by a thousand rads or more. As of this broadcast, most of them are dead.

"Those farther away received a dose of approximately 400–500 rads and are beginning to suffer the effects: burns, loss of hair, uncontrollable nausea, and diarrhea. The death rate among these people will be about 50 percent.

"The very latest readings show Fort Lauderdale receiving between one and two hundred rads per hour. Right now, it is crucial for those in this area to stay indoors.

"Fortunately, those experiencing flash blindness from this low-yield bomb will return to at least partial vision over the next weeks.

"Deaths from radiation and fallout exposure will increase and peak probably six to eight weeks from now. Subsequently, such deaths will gradually diminish.

"Broward Health Medical Center is still standing, but its giant ER doors were blown off of their hinges. Rumors are already circulating that those patients who enter here do not leave.

"That's not true. The ER is not admitting people whom they believe are going to die. They're only admitting patients who have minor injuries because they can't do anything about everyone else.

"In the coming years, Broward County will see a significant increase in various cancers, such as leukemia. We will have a birth defect crisis many times worse than the thalidomide disaster of the 1950s. We shall also see a severe increase in the number of cataract cases."

"Thank you," General Caddel said to the communications officer. He turned to face the group. "That's it."

"Let's break for ten. Can you all, please, excuse me and my civilian team?"

"Of course, ma'am."

●

In nine minutes, the SecDef emerged

"Chairman Caddel," he said, closing the wood door behind him, "the president needs her emergency war order officer at once."

COMMAND

"Madam President," General Caddel said, now standing ramrod straight as the young EWO officer opened the thick briefcase with SIOP plans, "we await your orders."

Turning to the chief of naval operations on screen, POTUS said, "CNO, regardless of anything else, I order tonight, regardless of what is in the Systems Integrated Operational Plan, every Iranian trawler or supply ship to be treated as an enemy combatant and sunk at once. They may look like harmless container ships carrying baby food, but given the hostile actions tonight, we will take no chances. Is that clear, Ambrose?"

"Clear as a bell," the chief of naval operations answered.

"In addition, Admiral, I want the Iranian navy destroyed. All of their naval vessels, even within their territorial waters, are to be demolished.

"All submarines, frigates, and corvettes are to be destroyed. All fast-attack craft should be attacked without warning and sunk. Same with auxiliary shipping. Amphibious ships must be blown out of the water. Mining craft should be obliterated. Any naval vessels in port are to be blockaded.

"If you detect a naval vessel just weighing anchor in port, it is to be destroyed. I want no Iranian naval presence left on the planet. Coordinate with General Caddel."

Turning to the chairman, she said, "General, please coordinate with the CNO on air assets. In forty-eight hours, I want to hear that Iran has been destroyed as a naval and maritime power."

"Are we to attack conventionally or with nuclear weapons?" the CNO asked.

"Conventional weapons alone are to be used. These attacks are to commence at once, CNO."

"Yes, ma'am." He saluted and left the view of the video conference.

"General Hooks," she called out.

The chief of staff air force stood at once. "Yes, ma'am?"

"Destroy the Iranian air force in the air and on the ground."

"Yes, ma'am. Nonnuclear?"

"That is correct, General. Neither the US Navy nor Air Force is to use nuclear weapons. This mission is to be accomplished in thirty-six hours. Do you understand, General Hooks?"

"Yes, ma'am" He left the room at once.

"General Caddel," POTUS said, "we need to contact Israel to let them know our plans and to understand what their situation is.

"I also want"—she gave a piece of paper to the chairman—"to carry out this strike. I want this done as soon as possible."

"Madam President, we have an incoming call from the Florida governor and another incoming call from Israel."

"I'll take the call from Florida first."

She took the receiver handed to her. "Hello, Governor, are you OK?"

"No, ma'am. They've given me some drugs. They tell me I'll lose an arm."

"That's terrible."

"My wife died tonight."

POTUS closed her eyes. *So much personal loss. And it's not over yet.* "Governor, I have come to understand what she's meant to you. Who can my people talk to, to help Florida recover?"

He gave her the information.

"She was my world. Good night, Madam President."

"I honor you, sir, and I will come down to see you. Good night."

Another phone appeared before her. "Here's the prime minister."

She took the receiver. "Prime Minister, I understand the shocking loss that you experienced. Our indications are that this was an Iranian strike. Do you concur?"

"That is our information as well. Are you feeling well, Madam President? I understand that there was an attempt against your life."

She closed her eyes. "I'm tolerable, Prime Minister."

"Madam President, our losses today were grievous. Over three hundred thousand people killed. We must insist on the right to strike back."

"Let me tell you what I have in mind," she said, squeezing the receiver harder.

The two spoke for a minute.

"Very well, Madam President, that is acceptable to us. We are interested in going after Mashhad."

"Prime Minister, the United States has no objections. Let me ask you, though. In your intelligence service's estimation, is there any other nation that's involved in this heinous attack against you and us tonight?"

The prime minister was quiet.

"Only Iran was involved," he said. "No other countries are involved in these shattering events."

"Then it's my goal to take Iran out of the nuclear business for good."

"Even nonmilitary uses?"

"Yes."

"I understand, and I appreciate your support. Not many people stand firm with Israel these days."

She squeezed the phone hard. "You're talking to one of them who does. Let's speak again after the military operations that we have discussed are completed." She returned the black receiver.

"Speaker of the House?"

POTUS took the phone. "Why not? She's entitled."

Sitting down, she closed her eyes, keeping a grip on her emotions. "Madam Speaker, what can I do for you?"

"I just wanted to tell you that the House of Representatives is moving forward with impeachment plans against you."

"You've always been consistent, Whitney. Good night." She handed the phone back, leaving the Speaker's voice to talk to the air.

"Can I speak to Llewellyn, please?"

"We have a video link."

"Well," she said with a laugh when the SecState appeared on the screen, "you have more gray hair than I remember, Mr. Secretary."

He smiled. "I have you to thank for most of it. What can I do, Madam?"

"I want you to begin to talk to our allies, beginning with NATO, clarifying who instigated this attack and why we think they did it. Also, call Russian leadership and let them know we understand that they were not involved."

"Madam, the Russians will want you to call the president yourself."

"And I want my seventy-five thousand Floridians back. Tonight is not the night for wishes, my friend."

"Very well."

"Israel and the United States are proceeding unilaterally, bringing this aggression to a prompt conclusion."

"Can you tell me what you have in mind, Madam President?"

She gave him all the details.

He sighed. "I'm sorry it has come to this."

"In a few minutes, so will they."

"I'm hearing rumblings that the House is going to move with impeachment proceedings."

She drew closer to the screen. "It's the obvious thing for them to do. They were hurt in last night's debate, and they want to draw attention from that. Plus, they have no idea what's going on internationally at this point." She saw General Hooks approach her with the Joint Chief of Staff and SecDef and paused.

In a moment, she said, "You are one of my most trusted advisers, Llewellyn. I'm afraid that what I'm going to do tonight will disappoint you."

"And you will pay the price for that, Madam President. But I don't think you have a choice."

"Good luck, Llewellyn."

"Are we ready to proceed, Jay?" POTUS said, hanging up, staring at the SecDef.

"Yes. The Joint Chiefs are fully aligned with this plan. We are all in this together."

"Then my number is the fifth line from the bottom," POTUS said, pulling the card from her jacket pocket.

General Caddel took the card, read it, and then handed it to the EWO officer, who ran it through a decoder. One green annunciator lit.

"You are authenticated, Madam President," the chairman said. "May I have the day word, please?"

She noticed he was sweating. "The day word is Thunder."

"Code word?"

"Six-gun."

"Can you repeat that, please, ma'am?"

"Six-gun."

"Action word?"

"Spearhead."

"In accordance with the two-person rule," the general said, "I must have someone in the chain of command present who can confirm."

"I can," SecDef said, handing his card over. "My number is the third from the top."

The card was entered into the decoder, and a second green light came on.

"Do you concur?"

"I do, General."

"Then," the chairman said, "we have an authenticated and confirmed command decision using the two person rule. Execute."

The military left the two civilians alone in the conference room.

Jay slouched in his chair, running his hands through his hair. "Do you think someone can get us a bite to eat?"

She looked at him, new bags under her eyes but light within. "What, you think this plane has a chef?"

LIGHT OF THE MOON

Hansen Nace, his thirteen years of life alive and vibrating through him, leaned back on the wooden fence he and his dad repainted just two years ago. His heart pounded as he avoided staring at the fourteen-year-old next to him, an angel with red hair, the softest skin, and luscious lips.

And tonight would be the first night he would kiss them.

Oh, he had kissed other girls. He had actually gone a little further with some, but there was nobody like Stephanie. For him, there are only two lives: life without her and life with her.

And he wanted to get to the "life with" as soon as possible.

"Do you think your parents will mind that we're out so late tonight, Han?"

"I think that they are OK with it. The moon lights up the fields pretty good. We can find our way back."

"Well, maybe not right away."

His heart pounded, and he almost fainted as he put his arm around her. Nuzzling her cheek, he said in the softest of tones, "Stephanie—"

The ground shook, followed by three explosions as fire rose from the earth.

"What is that?" she said, covering her ears, burrowing her face into his chest.

He watched the birds take off from their night nests. He could hear the cows mournful mooing over at the Hazards farm, just this side of I-15 in Cascade County, Montana.

Holding her close for a moment, he stepped back, pulling her away from the fence into air now reeking of fuel. "Come on inside our house. I'm sure my parents know what's up. We can check social media and the web."

•

The thirteen-year-old knew little about either the military base or the 341st Missile Wing of the Air Force Global Strike Command. He could not know that while he brushed his lips across Stephanie's blushing cheeks, lost in a glory of nature, two soldiers received and authenticated a valid launch signal.

After certifying that their missile was "clean and green" and coordinating their action with naval command, they retrieved their keys and enabled the weapon.

The eighty-ton concrete-reinforced blast door slammed opened on receiving the "release command," the exposed hole belching out a firestorm. A Minute Man III lifted from the cauldron.

Ten seconds out of the silo, the missile completed its first roll at 1,100 fps, 8,300 feet above ground.

At forty-five seconds, the eighty-ton missile completed its second roll maneuver at 50,000 feet. Two minutes into launch, stage three separation occurred at 240,000 feet above sea level, leaving only the weapon cone in orbit.

The post-boost phase having begun, the weightless weapon receptacle flew at thousands of miles per hour to a specific point in space-time above the earth. There, it disgorged three nuclear weapons.

Three other missiles repeated these space maneuvers, and in thirty-seven seconds, twelve 335-kiloton nuclear warheads, their spin gas generators stabilizing reentry, began a timed descent into Iran.

THE BRIGHTEST LIGHT IN THE WORLD

Sixty-six hundred miles from Montana, Tehran pulsed with excitement. Social media was alive with the news of the Iranian attacks against the United States and Israel.

People danced and sang, the streets thundering with excitement, vibrating to the moves of the revelers.

"Persia's nuclear strength is here for all to see," some cried.

"No one would dare challenge her again."

"The despicable embargoes will be lifted, and Persia could rise to her full strength."

"A great nation among nations." They all repeated the joyous refrain, shouting to the world.

At 12:07 p.m., local time, everyone looked up, hearing a loud "pop" high in the sky, followed by a series of muffled booms and short crackles. Light raced through the high clouds down to the population, closer and closer. The clouds lightened until they were too bright to study, and all turned their heads away.

The crowd stopped their dancing and chanting.

Then the light dissipated, and the sky was quiet.

They looked around.

The birds still flew and sang, the dogs still chased each other, and children still laughed.

"Allah is celebrating our victory!" someone yelled.

"He has used His great power to crush the infidels."

"We are guarded day and night."

"Even our navy is fighting them. Look."

Some rushed over. "Your cell is dead, man."

The cell phone owner looked down at the black screen.

Then someone shouted, "What's wrong with my cell!"

202

"What? Mine's stopped too."

"Mine as well."

Nobody's phone worked. Nor did watches and hearing aids. People with nondemand pacemakers collapsed in the street, their hearts beating out a wild strange rhythm until they died.

Odd.

No texting, no selfies, no phone calls. People held their phones as high as they could, then brought them down again, searching for a signal, over and over, like they were making a communal offering to the sky.

But all cells were bricked.

Then someone noted that no cars were moving.

Quiet cars were strewn all along the streets. Intersections were jammed.

But horns weren't heard.

Workers were coming out of their office buildings forced to walk down many floors, the elevators having failed. The streets were crowded with people.

Meanwhile, a twelve-year-old child's MRI halted in mid examination. An obstetrician in the midst of a breech delivery on a thirty-year-old woman lost all lights. The metabolic testing on an eight-year-old with new type 1 diabetes ceased.

Dialysis units stopped all over the city in the middle of their cycles of cleansing humans of poisons. Patient portals providing lab test results to anxious patients closed.

Someone did point to the sky where it seemed that planes were bombing them.

But the aircraft weren't acting aggressively; they were simply falling.

All planes, from small, single-engine, low-altitude Cessnas up to larger private jets, were dropping out of the sky, their avionics failing, their trajectories governed by the one remaining reliable force—gravity.

The larger Boeing 767s departing from and heading to Tehran's airport seemed to be caught up in some demented dance, still powered by wild and screaming engines but having lost all electronic control of engine power, hydraulic pressure, altitude, direction, even internal atmosphere. They crashed into the airport, highways, and neighborhoods, their huge explosions sending tons of jet fuel, gas, and debris flying into the air, landing on buildings, cars, and people.

All looked at the sky again, unable to see the remnants of the single Minuteman III that had detonated all three of its warheads miles above the surface.

The simultaneous high-altitude nuclear explosions released a trillion, billion, trillion gamma radiation particles that streaked to the earth's surface at thousands of miles a second. These high-energy particles, smaller than atoms, tore through circuit boards, ripping apart semiconductors in cell phones, CT machines, tractors, clocks, audio players, televisions, cars, computers, and avionics. Any electronics built after 1950 were rendered useless for all time.

People looked at each other with wonder and, now, fear.

All still. Quiet ruled.

The next happened faster than humans could ever know.

Three W78 warheads slammed into Tehran with a terminal speed of two thousand miles an hour and a combined explosive power of over one megaton of TNT. In a thousandth of a second, the city's surface temperature increased from eighty degrees to ten million degrees, the surface temperature of the sun.

At once, the weapons discharged high-energy particles traveling close to the speed of light.

It was the brightest light the planet had known in billions of years. Those who saw it paid with their eyesight, retinas burned off forever. A fraction of a second later, the person vaporized, obliterated by intense X-ray bursts.

Unable to stand the X-rays and temperature, for the first time in earth's history, life disappeared in an instant. It vanished.

Living skin, tissues, organs, blood, and bone instantly turned into nothing.

Couples playing with babies, young people crying in jubilation for the earlier Iranian attack, men standing in front of cars with open hoods disappeared. Students released from school, children chasing each other, and old men sitting in parks all disappeared in a flash. Any outdoor ceremonies from funerals to graduations, to the opening of art museums and new holy places were at once devoid of any people.

Grass, plants, and flowers were gone. Mosquitos, beetles, mice, dogs, and cats were vaporized. Camels, elephants, lions, monkeys, and gorillas in the zoo disappeared in an instant. There was no noise or feces, no stink of sweat or smell of burnt flesh. They were just gone.

Radiation jumped from well less than a rad an hour to thousands of rads per second. For hundreds of thousands of people who were not vaporized, death from hyperacute radiation poisoning exploded through them. They had no chance to be sick before they died.

This was followed by the loudest sound in history.

A shock wave of unimaginable power traveling faster than sound slammed through Tehran, tearing buildings apart, sending hundreds of thousands of tons of rebar, concrete, and steel through the air, the glass already having melted.

Flying debris shredded the surviving population. Citizens unable to avoid collisions with tons of bricks, rebar, concrete, and cars were demolished. No living thing had a chance. The city was a killing field of radiation, stone, and steel.

No one survived within a five-mile radius of the blast. Of the 8.7 million Tehran residents, 7 million perished in the first three minutes. It was a city stunned into oblivion.

The mushroom clouds generated by the three weapons twisted and wound their way around each other as they rose to nine thousand feet, visible from Azerbaijan to the northwest, and northeast to Turkmenistan. No one heard the explosions coming from the east as the Israeli nuclear strike forces destroyed Mashhad.

Raging fires consumed anything that was left. Five hundred thousand people, now blinded, stumbled over hot asphalt through burning streets. Where they were going no one knew because, for millions, there was no home anymore.

Anyone surviving within seven miles of the blast had their skin denuded with large third-degree burns. The tissue damage was extensive. With no water and shredded immune systems, the combination of hypovolemia, shock, renal failure, and infection set in, and victims suffered in agony in the streets for hours until death mercifully arrived.

Twenty minutes after detonation, Tehran was a windy, burning ghost town. Radiation was the last thing on any survivor's mine, but it came anyway. And with all communication down, Tehran vanished from the electronic grid.

No one in Tehran knew that there were other Minutemen missiles ranging over southern Iran, dropping their payloads over missile launch sites, testing grounds, and nuclear reactor locations across the country. In each locale, stupefaction, death, and destruction ruled as Iran descended through darkness into nonexistence as a nation-state.

SOIL OUR LAND

"**A**nd with that, I conclude my prepared remarks," POTUS said to the media audience that packed the James S. Brady Press Briefing Room, Monday, the day preceding Election Day.

"But"—she shook her head—"this is a day without equal in the history of the world, and, therefore, this press briefing takes place in unprecedented circumstances. So I am going to stay here and answer as many questions as you have for me. This will continue to be televised and on the record.

"I was able to sleep last night," she said, stepping back from the podium, "so I think that I can keep up with you," she said, smiling. "However, I am going to move away from the podium and sit down as I answer your questions."

She shielded her eyes. "Can I also ask that the light intensity up front here be reduced or focused on something else?"

"Yes. Thank you," she said as the brightness was reduced.

She turned to her left. "Can we bring a chair out for me? Thank you. Who's first?" she said, accepting the portable microphone.

"Madame President, in the space of thirty-six hours, you have authorized the death of more people than there were American soldiers killed in all US wars since our country's existence. How do you react as a person to that?"

The president put the microphone in her lap, turned, and sobbed for a moment as the intensity of what she had done drove deeper into her heart. Then she picked up the mike and, facing forward again, said, "I can't know yet the depth of the grief that I feel. I know neither where it starts nor ends. It surrounds me, and I am lost in it. Probably for all of my time.

"It is also true that in this slaughterhouse of a world, good people must do terrible things. So President Truman learned when he authorized the use of nuclear weapons in 1945.

"Friday night, as you already know, hundreds of thousands of innocent Israeli and US citizens were killed by a regime waging an undeclared nuclear holy war against the Jewish religion. We anticipated that there would be another wave of missiles against other Jewish population centers killing hundreds of thousands more. We were obligated to stop the war with a profound retaliation.

"I responded in accordance with my presidential oath. But now," she said, leaning forward, "please keep in mind that my oath doesn't say that I won't kill people."

She paused as the audience murmured. "There's nothing about killing people embedded in the oath of office to become president of the United States. The oath says I will preserve, protect, and defend the Constitution. I use every tool in my means to do that, including death. The United States and one of our principal allies weren't just threatened. We were attacked. We responded in a way that removed the attacker from the equation. Am I sick about it? Yes. Did I do the right thing? Yes."

"So, ma'am, you're saying that your hand was forced and that you had to do this?"

"No. Friday night, we had many options going forward, spanning the range from doing nothing to responding with cataclysmic resolve, destroying several countries in the region. We chose an intermediate option that removed the aggressor from the table."

"What do you say to the dead?"

She paused, looking up into the darkness. "I say to them, 'The best part of war is its ending.' And I did everything in my power to end this war as quickly as possible. I'm sorry that they are dead, but I'm also relieved that millions more did not die."

"Were their coordination efforts between Israel and the United States defense commands?"

"Yes, there were," she said, scratching her forehead. "We had our first conversation early Saturday morning, before dawn. The prime minister and the United States both proceeded on independent courses of action, which combined to produce concordant results."

"Are you aware that Mashhad, the city that the Israeli's destroyed, is, or was, a holy Islamic community?"

"Yes. I appreciate the notion of holy communities. But I must say that a person is not of less value because they happen to live on secular ground. Why should Mashhad be off-limits because it holds the Imam Resa holy shrine, when Iranian missiles essentially roamed our eastern seaboard looking for targets? People in Savannah, Raleigh-Durham, Norfolk, Boston were all at risk, as were those in Haifa, Beersheba, and Nazareth.

"So in the US/Israeli joint response, all Iranians were at risk, just as all Jewish people were at risk from their attacks. Just because an individual lives in a holy community does not confer a special right to survive.

"But the real question is, how do we punish brutal warlord-style leaders and not their innocent people?" Her voice softened, and she dropped her head. "I fully concede that there are people in Tehran and Mashhad who wished no ill will against Israel or the United States, who wanted to be healthy, who wanted to raise their children, who wanted to have a family of some prosperity and contentment. That's all they were looking for from life. And they are now dead. We need to find a way to avoid their deaths.

"I am not sure that the international community is mature enough to generate an answer to that question. But it's an answer that we need to seek if we want to survive in peace and in freedom."

"Was there any dispute or controversy over the course of action? Whose initial idea was it to use nuclear weapons against Iran?"

"I'm not sure I can remember everything in the exact sequence that it occurred. Once we had the facts of the attack, I pulled together my secretaries of state and defense and my vice president to talk and develop options, so it was a matter decided by civilian leadership. We then presented that to the Joint Chiefs of Staff, who worked through details. And they produced an attack plan that was wholly consistent with what we as civilian leadership had produced.

"In the end, it was a consensus among all senior civilian and military parties that this was the best tack to take.

"Madam President, the American people have already started to vote and will continue to vote through this Tuesday. Do you think that your actions have helped or destroyed your presidential campaign?"

She shook her head. "I don't know. I do know that both my opponent and I will miss the thousands of people in Fort Lauderdale who are dead or so badly injured that they can't vote. I'm told that in New York, early voting continued through the weekend, and the pollsters are projecting a heavy turnout in New York City tomorrow. But that's all I know."

"Madam President, was there ever a point in the terrible events of this weekend when you did not want to be president?"

POTUS leaned forward in the chair. "There were several points where I did not want to make a decision that I knew would kill millions of people. But I believed I could make a correct choice, that I could successfully integrate all of the moral concerns, the military concerns, and the cultural and societal concerns together into one answer.

"I did not like the solution. In fact, I despised it. But I was confident that that solution was correct. And let me be clear: I take full responsibility for actions of the United States in the past forty-eight hours."

"We have not heard much from Iranian leadership, but they rely heavily on their ability to move foodstuffs and textiles by sea. Sinking their transport ships makes that impossible. You shut them off from humanitarian aid."

"No, sir. They shut themselves off when they decided to surreptitiously hide a weapon inside an otherwise innocent tanker."

"So for the time being, Madam President, how do you expect that humanitarian aid to get to Iran?"

"They can work it out. But I did not prohibit air traffic."

"At that rate—"

The president put her hand up. "Actions have consequences. The Iranians would not have this new panoply of problems in they hadn't killed almost a half million people, Friday night. We all reap what we sow."

"Madam President, why did you also conduct an electromagnetic attack on Iran? Our reports are that over 70 percent of the population have no electric power and most people cannot connect to the web. Wasn't the one-megaton bomb ground burst enough?"

"No. I wanted to totally disarm Iran, and that meant electronically as well as physically. EM, or electromagnetic, pulses don't end electricity forever. They don't stop electrons from moving. What they do is destroy all the electronic components that we rely on. Thus, the Iranians will have to spend a good deal of time rebuilding their electronic infrastructure. I'm not prohibiting that;, I am just taking them out of the international equation for the foreseeable future."

"We understand and grieve with you over the loss of your press secretary and also the loss of your chief of staff. I understand that you saw Nari before she died. What was that like?"

She paused. "Chess, over the years, had become a solid, reliable press secretary. He enjoyed his job, and he never stopped liking you all. It was just this year that you discovered when his birthday was and sang to him 'Happy Birthday.' What you don't know is after that press conference, he called me. He said nothing, but I heard him crying into my cell. He never cried about anything. I can't say that he was easily moved, but you each touched him."

She took out a Kleenex and, taking a deep breath, said, "Nari was my good friend and trusted advisor. She was a part of me that ... that you never saw. Lying there in the hospital, suffering through multiple amputations, IV tubing everywhere, knowing that her kidney was failing, I ... I felt some of the light leave my life. I will never be the same after that."

She shifted in her seat. "It's not just her advice but it was her companionship. She was able to always show me my weaknesses that I didn't know existed in me while pointing out strengths that I wasn't using. Maybe I will find somebody who can do that for me. I don't know, but I will tell you all honestly today, I feel like her death took a part of me."

"Was the vice president involved in these discussions you had before you decided to attack Iran?"

"Absolutely. We had a conference call where I discussed the facts as they came in. It included my major cabinet members, as well as the Joint Chiefs, some of whom were present, some not. The vice president was a full participant in that call. We then had a subsequent call with just civilian leadership, where the vice president was on the phone, and we talked about potential responses to Iranian aggression."

"Do you think Iraq is now going to take advantage of the situation by attacking Iran?"

"Iraq is in no position to attack anyone, and the radiation footprint in Northern Iran is so intense that no one would dare cross that dangerous territory.

"You know, the Middle East is a chess game where all the moves seem bad. It may be a knot that Western civilization cannot unravel. But let me remind you, Iran got herself into this mess, and she's going to have to get out of it, hopefully with more enlightened leadership."

"Your Republican contender said this morning that Iran would never have attacked the US and Israel if he was in office."

She studied the questioner for a second. "He is as much to blame for the Iranian crisis as every other previous president. And as for the rest, he … No. I'll just ignore it."

"What do you tell the Jewish community in this country who suffered this horrendous attack?"

She stood. "This is the largest attack on Jewish people in this country. But it's not the only attack. We have seen since 2015 an increasing number of attacks against Jewish people simply because they are Jewish.

"A problem we have in this country is that we get inured to these assaults. We begin to accept them into the state of our normal affairs when we should revile them. Extirpate them, rather than weave them into the fabric of normal American behavior.

"I will, therefore, ask Congress to create a national holiday to celebrate Jewish people. It announces as a nation our respect and love for Jewish people while giving us as individuals an opportunity to learn more about them and what they have suffered.

"What Iran did was heinous. But every day of their sad lives, the American haters of the Jewish communities want to destroy these people.

"I can't stop people from saying ridiculous, bloodthirsty, and despicable things on the internet. That's protected speech.

"But should that cross the line into action, the federal government will come down with both feet. And if found guilty, these people will be punished to the full extent of the law. An ethnic or religious crime is an attack not on a people but on America.

"I did not vote for Ronald Reagan, but I do agree with that ex-president when he said that freedom is something you have to fight for every day. He was absolutely right. And it's truer now. And I am fully engaged in that fight against a clear and present danger to us. You soil our land at your own risk."

"Madam President, thank you for talking with us and the world. I must ask you, though, why would you want to continue to be president now? If you look at the past four months, you have initiated military conflict with Russia that have led to attacks on Portland. You have been threatened with impeachment. You have destroyed Iran as an international presence and maybe as a cohesive nation. Why do you want to be re-elected for four more years of … of this?"

"Well, if last September, God had placed His arm around me, showing me the debacles that I would face, I would have recoiled. And as we all sit here now, who knows what's coming for us in 2025?"

"The universe is not a friendly place. It destroys, transforms, generates challenges that we can't turn from and offers no *quid pro quos*. But we have a choice. Running away from your problems is running toward death. Facing them regenerates the vitality of your life.

"For adults, there is never an excuse to stop growing up. We always face a challenge we didn't anticipate, and that we don't deserve."

"The presidency is just growing up on steroids."

"Madam President, what mistakes have you made in your presidency?"

She dropped her head, and her breaths came fast and hard for a moment as the emotion broke through the floodgates.

"Only one. In the last motorcade, I asked Nari not to sit with me but to sit in the car in front of me. It was that car that received the brunt of the blast. I desperately want that moment back. For anything else, well, you'll have to ask my Republican opponent. No doubt he's got some ideas."

"Thank you Madam President."

ELECTION DAY

"**W**e were afraid that weather would divert you from Joint Base Andrews," Jeff Fields, her new press secretary, said over his cell.

"We made it. Good to hear your voice," the president said, walking through the White House doors after an Indianapolis Election Day campaign stop, the last of the season. "Who's here?" She was just able to catch the familiar "Providence is in the house" from her secret service detail as she walked down the hall.

How much longer will those announcements last? she wondered, stomach clenching.

"All senior campaign staff and cabinet members, except—no, here's the vice president now. Everyone is here, ma'am. We're set up in the Oval office, plus the Roosevelt and Cabinet rooms. TVs are everywhere."

"Be there in a few … a few minutes."

POTUS walked up to the private residence, nausea welling up. She held ruthless control over herself, greeting and thanking her personal staff for their best wishes as she passed them on the steps.

It wasn't until she hurried down the hall toward the master bedroom that her pulse hammered, and her shaking right hand barely permitted her to twist the doorknob.

Just able to close the bedroom door behind her, the president's breath coming in uneven gasps, she took three steps, then collapsed onto the bed.

The emotional pain now physical, she could only lie there, rolling onto her stomach, then back, then stomach again.

You are a murderer. You killed Nari. You massacred millions. Is this really you?

The self-destructive thoughts piled on, speeding up, like dirty water circling a drain, swirling faster and tighter.

Her heart, too long denied, exploded.

The agony ripped through her in deep, ragged gasps, and she cried out. Stomach tightening, her mouth full of a metallic taste, she leaned over the bed's edge, vomiting into the trashcan.

POTUS lay back down, wiping her mouth, then sat up at once, throwing up again.

After a few minutes, her stomach relaxed and her heartbeat slowed, breaths now coming quiet and steady. She closed her eyes, sleep upon her at once.

Waking a few minutes later, the president opened herself to the past weekend's tragedy. The terrible thing, the monumental violation, the crime of humanity waited for her. The UN, world leaders, her own party, even the Republicans said her actions were justifiable, supportable, and defensible.

Yet they were also horrid and compassionless acts. *Where was my overall consideration for the millions of dead? Could I feel no pain for them? Where was my empathy?*

And, could you do it again?

She jumped at the thought, unwilling to absorb it, then sighed.

Seeing that it was almost 6:00 p.m., she groomed and changed. Then, wishing she was anywhere else than at her own election party, the president of the United States left her bedroom, walking downstairs to join the revelry.

RETURNS

"**D**oesn't anybody have to work tonight?" the president said five minutes later to smiles and applause as she joined everyone in the crowded Oval Office. "I love it that you and your families are here. That's blessing enough, regardless of the election's outcome.

"But before we take part in the buffet," she said, pointing to the man just down the row from her, "I first want to introduce Jeffrey Fields, our new press secretary. He's intelligent, articulate, and knowledgeable. Plus," she said with a grin, "he loves interacting with the press. But, don't worry, we'll cure him of that. On the serious side, though," POTUS said, now clapping, "we're lucky to have him. Welcome, Jeff."

Everyone applauded as he nodded, running his hands through his red hair.

"Now, what do we know?" POTUS asked, pointing to the televisions now in the Oval Office.

"Well, Madam," Llewellyn said, dressed as always in a suit, "early voting complicates the process, since many states can't count early ballots until the polls close, and nobody knows how many will vote today —"

"So we're in the dark, ma'am," Jeff said, laughing.

They all joined in.

"The fact that people are voting at all today is a statement of confidence in you."

She turned around to see a tall African American man with short cropped black hair facing her. "Madam President, I am Kevin Wells. I was asked to be here."

She shook his hand. "Thank you. I know. Let's talk in a few. But for right now, let's see what they're saying."

Someone turned the TV up.

●

"It's 7:00 p.m. Many voting locales are just closing on the eastern seaboard.

"I must say that we are stunned by the Election Day turnout. In red states and in blue, urban communities and rural, turnout has been off the charts according to local reports. Now, that's usually good for the Republicans, but this is not a usual election season.

"Also, at least so far, there have been no reports of voter intimidation in the face of a record turnout. Whatever else happens tonight, that's good news for America.

"So here we go. Out first results are from Vermont, whose voter turnout is tremendous. And we can tentatively call that state for the president. South Carolina, we can say, is leaning ever so slightly for the Republican. In Florida, at this point, the president has a slim lead, but it's too early for us to call. Georgia, a slight lean to the president, also too early to call. In Virginia, the president has taken a sizable lead there, but again way too early to be definitive."

●

Jay turned the television down. "The rest is just conversation until 8:00 p.m."

Watching her SecDef go over to the buffet table, wheeling his wife in front of him, POTUS said, "Kevin, can you, please, join me in my private office?"

●

"Thank you for coming tonight," the president said, taking a seat in the small room just off of the Oval Office.

"It's my pleasure," Kevin said. "I have to say, though, that I don't know why I'm here."

"Have you been to the White House before?" she asked, offering him the plush blue chair.

"Yes," he said, sitting, "when I was eight."

They both laughed.

She leaned back in the leather seat behind the desk and crossed her legs. "What did you think of my press conference yesterday?"

The president watched him purse his lips for five, then ten seconds, studying the beige walls. She shifted in the chair. *Something about this, man. Maybe he didn't—*

"It was a masterful read of the world's population."

She cocked her head. "Why?"

"People are used to the horror of death and pain of war. They have seen it for generations. But this time"—he shook his head—"no one has ever experienced so many humans beings dying so fast. Every one out of a thousand people on this planet died during your two months in office, and most of them in one day."

"One out of a thousand," she repeated, her voice trailing off.

"That's never happened in history. And, without a precedent, people need both time and context to absorb these titanic events. They need to know that their world still makes sense, even in the face of this horror."

He sat back in the chair. "You gave them both. You spoke to the world's population in an open, comforting way, answering all questions. Not everybody agrees with you, but they at least had the opportunity to see your situation and why you did what you did.

"I also must tell you that I was very sad to hear about Nari." Kevin lowered her voice. "How are you doing without her?"

POTUS looked at the ceiling. "I am beginning to make peace with Nari's death. I've gone over it a thousand times. There is no way I could have known what was going to happen to their car."

"It's only been three days since her death," he said, moving his chair closer to her. "The released emotions are powerful forces, and they don't respect your personal boundaries. They aim to make a mess of your life."

"Why?"

'So that you can start the long walk to recovery." He dropped his head. "Have you broken down yet?"

"What do you mean?" She grimaced.

He looked at her.

"Yes," she said, sighing, pushing back from the wooden desk, "once, today in fact."

"You hide it well. Expect more of them until you do what you need to do."

She looked up. "And what would that be exactly?"

She watched Kevin lean forward. "Madam, you need help. You must understand that you are in the position that no rational, empathetic human being has ever experienced."

Sitting back, he took a deep breath. "Human beings have killed people by the millions in the past: Hitler and his abomination, Pol Pot and the Cambodian massacres, Ngirumpatse in Africa. But these killers were psychotic, having neither sympathy nor empathy for the human beings they destroyed. In fact, they didn't even look at their victims as people.

"But you're different. You are a compassionate person who was forced to do unspeakable acts on a monumental level. So your recovery is going to be unlike the recovery of any other human being ever."

He shook his head. "And you can't even do it in exclusion since your every move is watched, recorded, reviewed, and critiqued. I can see the news chyron graphic streaming along the bottom of the screen, 'President Harris seeks psychological counseling.' Ignorant Americans will lacerate you, and Republicans will want to invoke the Twenty-Fifth Amendment to have you removed from office."

He leaned forward. "The first thing that you must do is give yourself permission to feel the pain."

At once, her breathing quickened, and, sticking her hand out, she shook her head. "Jesus, I can't do that. It's unbearable."

"You're right. You can't absorb this pain all at once any more than you can learn to swim by jumping into a tidal wave. Let it be a slow process, Madam President. Let your heart ache a little at a time. And when it does, don't push it away. Pay attention to it. Comfort it like you comfort a baby. Nurture yourself. Your heart's trying to heal. Don't let self-criticism get in its way.

"That's how you get access to the absolution you need and crave."

He took a deep breath. "Do you go to church? have trustworthy friends?"

"No to both," she said in a low voice.

"It's much harder without help."

"So," she said, exhaling deeply, "I let myself hurt in little bits for the rest of my life?"

"Well," he said, scratching his head, "healing or not, you will be reacting to these events for the rest of your life. You get to choose how to do it. One way destroys you. The other replenishes."

"When does it end?" she said, looking down.

Kevin stroked his chin, then closed his eyes, saying, "Do you know what the Chosin Reservoir represents?"

"Yes," she said, nodding. "A major battle in the Korean War occurred there where Americans took heavy losses."

"Good historian," he said with a smile, opening his eyes. "When it was time to evacuate, the Americans didn't have the resources to evacuate their dead, and the ground was too cold and hard to bury them. So they lashed the dead bodies to tanks.

"An American lieutenant in charge of the operation never got over that. For years, he dreamed about these dead men, mouths frozen open, arms and legs flapping lifeless in the frigid wind as the tanks lumbered over the frozen ground. But, finally, he absorbed it.

"His wife asked him, 'Did the dreams go away?' He said 'No, I still see the dead soldiers that I commanded. But I've made friends with them now.'"

Something Nari would say, she thought. They sat still and quiet for several minutes.

Then, sitting up, she said, "OK. Thank you, Kevin. This has all been good for me. Let's change tacks for a minute. I know little about you, but what I have heard is impressive. You were part of the CiliCold shop, right?"

"That's right," Kevin said, shifting in his seat. "Jon DeLeon called on me and a few others to help him with what turned out to be fantastic discoveries in the application of mathematics to 3-D protein configuration and then with molecular machines.

"Now," he said with a laugh, hands out, "I'm no biochemist, and I didn't understand many of the details. But I understood enough of them to help steer the company through some difficult times."

"Including financial difficulties?"

He shook his head. "No … not difficulties, just decisions. Jon made enough money from his initial work, and he was frugal most times, so, financially, we were in pretty good shape. In fact, he gave his most successful products away rather than patent them."

She squinted. "I heard about that. How did the company make money if he gave away the product?"

"Worldwide donations in the tens of millions of dollars flooded in that we didn't expect," he said, leaning forward. "People appreciated our work."

She leaned back, clasping her hands behind her neck, looking at him.

Kevin sighed. "Well, the glib answer to the question you didn't ask was we gave it away because the world needed a break. But, really, both Jon and I were uncomfortable with the direction of intellectual knowledge. Wall Street puts financial value on all. We demonstrated that you didn't have to put a price on everything to become prosperous."

He took a deep breath. "To this day, it's still a liberating feeling."

She smiled and, pushing his knee with hers, said, "You socialist, you."

"Yes," he said, laughing. "We were called that on national TV. That was one of the kindest things they said about us. Generosity can threaten selfish people. Anyway, we just moved on." He shrugged.

"Well, I will need a chief of staff for the next six weeks."

"I think that it will be a little longer than that." He smiled.

"Perhaps. Are you interested in the work?"

"If you believe in pri—"

"Excuse me, Madam," Jeff called through the door. "but it's 8:00 p.m."

They turned the TV on.

●

"It's the top of the hour, and we have more poll closings for you. Maine looks like it's going for the Republican. New Hampshire has gone for the Republican.

"Massachusetts, Connecticut, New Jersey, Maryland, and Delaware have gone for the president. DC has gone for the president. So far, this is all predictable. In addition, the president is still holding a sizable lead in Virginia, and her lead is growing in Georgia. Remarkable.

"South Carolina, incredibly, we now call for the president. We remind everyone that the turnout there was record breaking. Florida, which we thought might have been an easy call for the Republican at this point, is now in the president's column.

"And now we have some additional states coming in. Tennessee has gone for the Republican, as has Mississippi, but Alabama is too close to call at this early point in the evening.

"West Virginia has gone for the president. North Carolina, for the president. That's a big win. Also, Ohio is leaning heavily toward the president, but still too close to call. What a surprising night this is turning out to be.

"Wait a moment. Here's a big call. Michigan has gone for the president, as has Illinois. Missouri has gone for the Republican, as has Oklahoma. Texas right now, the big prize for either party, holds a slim but growing lead for the president, but it's still too early to call this.

•

"Kendrick," POTUS said, motioning the assistant chief of staff into the private room with her and Kevin, as Kevin turned the volume down. "This is Kevin Wells. We have been talking about him becoming chief of staff for me. I know that you have no interest in the job."

"My twin daughters would howl if I put more hours in," the assistant chief of staff said with a smile.

"Nari thought so much of your work," she said, smiling. "Would you like to stay on as assistant chief of staff? at least until the inauguration?"

"Of course, ma'am."

"I know that Nari allowed you to manage access to me. Kevin, would it be acceptable to continue this practice until the beginning of the year?"

"Kendrick," Kevin said, standing and turning to face the forty-year-old, "you have served your people well here during an impossible weekend. I would be honored to team up with you."

The three of them talked about the day-to-day operational logistics of their jobs.

"I think of my responsibility as more like an executive officer, Madam," Kevin said. "I have access to the same information you do but will suggest palatable alternatives to your strategy. People will have my cell phone number, not yours. And," he said," I am absolutely transparent to you. What I know, you know."

"I need a trusted team with whom I can share strategies. Let's get Jeff in here."

"What can I do, ma'am?" he said, arriving in a moment.

"Meet my new chief of staff."

"Here come the 9:00 p.m. returns," Kendrick said, turning up the TV's volume.

●

"Ah, nine o'clock closings. As we reported thirty minutes ago, Arkansas is too close to call. New York returns are, I can't believe this, New York State returns, both upstate and for the city, are heavy and overwhelming for the president. The Republicans thought they were making inroads into the Empire state, but not this cycle. We can call New York for the president. Rhode Island is now called for the president as well.

"Louisiana, surprisingly, called for the president. Texas, now leaning heavily for the president. Minnesota and Wisconsin returns show that they are also leaning heavily for the president. North Dakota and South Dakota, still too early to call, but Nebraska, Kansas, Iowa, now for the president. Her Midwest development program is receiving a lot of attention out there.

"Florida, for the president. My goodness.

"Wyoming, for the Republican. Colorado, for the president. New Mexico and now Arizona, clearly for the president. And this just in. Texas has gone for the president. Incredible.

"This is a huge win for the Democrats.

●

"We'd better join the festivities," POTUS said, smiling with her new team.

●

"Midnight. Just to finish things off. Alaska, for the Republican, and Hawaii, for the president. Washington, Oregon, California, all for the president.

"Montana, for the President. Idaho, for the Republican. Nevada, for the president. Utah, for the Republican.

"Just to recap, if these results hold, then the president has earned her first full term in office. Plus, we project there will be eight new Democratic senators and thirty-three new Democratic house members. A Democratic trifecta that we haven't seen since, well, 2008?—No? Thank you—2020.

"Well, there we have it. The president, having held office only two months, the most tumultuous two months in American history for a new president, has earned her right for her first four-year term.

FROM WHERE DOES THEIR HATE COME?

POTUS noticed phone calls, hot and thick with congratulations, were pouring in now.

Kevin picked up a ringing phone, listened, then said, "This one you better take, ma'am."

POTUS put it to her ear.

"You did me a favor."

The raspy voice was unmistakable.

"What was that, sir?"

"You took care of Iran. When I run and win in four years, and make no mistake I will win—you were very lucky tonight, very lucky—then managing the Middle East will be much easier."

Lucky. She was quiet, pursing her lips.

"But for now, I'm going to concede."

"Thank you. And may—"

He hung up.

"Another one for you," JT said, handing her his cell. "Speaker."

"What is this—tag team?" She took the phone. "Madam Speaker, what can I do for you?"

"I just want to inform you that the House is going to begin proceedings to bring impeachment charges against you beginning the first week of December."

"Thank you for the update." She hung up.

•

"Are they serious?" Jeff said, slapping his forehead four hours later after the guests had gone and POTUS described the short call with the Speaker.

"Sure they are," the president said, rubbing her right eye. "They see the handwriting on the wall. They know that we've won a majority in the House and, while not a supermajority, a large majority in the Senate.

"So, no impeachment next year. They must act now while they're still in power in the House. I will not be convicted and, actually, may not even be impeached, but they're going to have hearings, doing their best to damage me so that I emerge a weakened president."

"Jesus," Kendrick said, "where does all their hate come from?"

"America is leaving them behind," Kevin, elbows on the chair, fingers clasped in front of him, said. "That is what they hate. Loss of power. Loss of relevance."

"What are you going to do, Madam?"

The president of the United States, pulling the pain and the losses, the cost in lives, the exhaustion, and the disappointments all to a place deep within, drew her team close, laying her plans.

Printed in the United States
by Baker & Taylor Publisher Services